THE GIRL FROM LAKE MAGGIORE

SIOBHAN DAIKO

Boldwood

First published in Great Britain in 2026 by Boldwood Books Ltd.

Copyright © Siobhan Daiko, 2026

Cover Design by JD Smith Design Ltd

Cover Images: Shutterstock

Maps: Boldwood Books and Shutterstock

The moral right of Siobhan Daiko to be identified as the author of this work has been asserted in accordance with the Copyright, Designs and Patents Act 1988.

Every effort has been made to obtain the necessary permissions with reference to copyright material, both illustrative and quoted. We apologise for any omissions in this respect and will be pleased to make the appropriate acknowledgements in any future edition.

A CIP catalogue record for this book is available from the British Library.

Paperback ISBN 978-1-83633-103-2

Large Print ISBN 978-1-83633-102-5

Hardback ISBN 978-1-83633-101-8

Trade Paperback ISBN 978-1-80656-132-2

Ebook ISBN 978-1-83633-104-9

Kindle ISBN 978-1-83633-105-6

Audio CD ISBN 978-1-83633-096-7

MP3 CD ISBN 978-1-83633-097-4

Digital audio download ISBN 978-1-83633-100-1

This book is printed on certified sustainable paper. Boldwood Books is dedicated to putting sustainability at the heart of our business. For more information please visit https://www.boldwoodbooks.com/about-us/sustainability/

Boldwood Books Ltd, 23 Bowerdean Street, London, SW6 3TN

www.boldwoodbooks.com

Cigogna

La Rocca
Scareno

Cannobio

Pian Cavallone

Cannero
Riviera

Intragna

Esio

Miazzina

Oggebbio

Ungiasca

Mergozzo

Unchio

Ghiffa

Rovegro

Trobasco

Fondotoce

Intra

Verbania

Baveno

Laveno
Mombello

MAGGIORE

Cannobio

'Darkness cannot drive out darkness; only love can do that.'

— MARTIN LUTHER KING, JR

In memory of my parents

PART I

SEPTEMBER 1943

1

Giulia pressed down hard on the brakes of her bike. A woman was running down the middle of the road! Adults and children thronged the *strada* hugging the shore of Lake Maggiore, but they all stopped in their tracks to stare at the woman racing towards them, her face radiating happiness as she shouted, 'Long live the armistice!'

'What armistice?' Giulia's friend, Ester, pedalled up to her and stared open-mouthed at the lady, who was still yelling '*Viva l'armistizia!*' at the top of her lungs.

'Let's head back to the hotel and find out what's going on,' Giulia said, glancing at Ester.

Giulia's father, Aldo Leone, was the owner of the hotel overlooking the lake in Marta, and its thirty rooms had been occupied by Italians fleeing the Allied bombing of their cities, as well as by twelve Sephardic Jews who'd arrived from Greece, including Ester, parents and younger brother and sister. Horror had burnt in the back of Giulia's throat when Ester had told her that, last March, the German authorities had locked the Thessaloniki Jewish population up in two ghettos and had then transported them to a concentration camp in Poland. Luckily, Ester and her family had received the help of the Italian consul general and had managed to escape before making their way up through Yugoslavia to Italy.

Giulia smiled at Ester as they mounted their bikes and set off again in the warmth of the early-September evening. Her heart went out to her friend; it must have been awful for her to have been forced to flee her homeland. Giulia's own experience of the war thus far had been limited, last February, to a night of terror during a massive aerial bombing of Milan, after which her father had ruled that she and her mother would live in Marta full time while he commuted to his office, only visiting them at the weekends. In addition to owning the Lake Maggiore hotel, Papà ran a successful antique furniture business in the city and was used to being obeyed. He indulged Giulia and her mother; they lacked for nothing but, sometimes, Giulia wished he wasn't so authoritarian, that he gave her greater choice about what happened in her life. She sighed to herself; there was little chance of that happening as she was only seventeen, still a schoolgirl, and entirely dependent on him.

Ester and her family had arrived at the hotel at the start of the summer, and Giulia, who'd been feeling lonely, had been delighted to make friends with someone of the same age. The Jewish girl was beautiful, with dark hair and eyes and an oval-shaped face. She was taller than Giulia – which wasn't difficult, given that Giulia was only 156 centimetres tall – but she was also kind and caring. They spent much of their time together, sharing family tales and stories of their childhood, swimming and sunbathing and going for bike rides. Traffic was always minimal on the lakeside roads; only cars with special permits could circulate, so Giulia and Ester would merely encounter bicycles, a few horse-drawn carts and carriages, and the occasional military lorry. Today they'd cycled to Arona, ten kilometres away, where they'd gone to the cinema, passing beautiful neo-classical villas – the holiday homes of wealthy industrialists – on the way there and back.

They'd come to the tree-shaded Marta square now – it was a small resort village – and a fresh breeze blew a loose strand of light brown hair into Giulia's eyes. She tucked it back into her braid and wheeled her bike through the gates of the hotel, gravel crunching under the soles of her shoes. She gazed up at the façade of the edifice, which made her feel even smaller than she already was. Four storeys high in the centre, with three sets of green shutters opening onto wrought-iron balconies, the building was flanked by three-storeyed wings on either side. The hotel had been rebuilt by Giulia's father after he'd bought an old bed-and-breakfast establishment five years ago. She loved the front gardens facing the lake, overlooked by a ground-floor terrace with deck chairs and rattan furniture for their guests to enjoy.

Sudden shouts came from the entrance to the village café on the square and Giulia spun around. Two young men were coming through the doors, shouting, '*E finita la Guerra!*'

Could it be true? Could the war really be over? A bubble of joy formed in Giulia's chest. She could go back to her school in Milan, take the university matriculation exams next summer, and start studying English literature in the School of Letters like she'd long dreamt of doing.

Her nostrils stung from the acrid smell of burning paper. The youths had unrolled a poster with a portrait of *Il Duce* and were setting fire to it while people stood around, applauding. Last summer, after the Anglo-American invasion of Sicily, the Italian king had dismissed Benito Mussolini, the dictator who'd tied Italy to Nazi Germany's coattails, and had given orders for him to be taken into custody. Everyone in Giulia's circle had rejoiced then too, thinking that the war was over. But the king had immediately appointed a new prime minister, Marshal Badoglio, who'd announced that Italy would continue fighting alongside their Axis allies. Giulia chewed at her lip. Perhaps this so-called armistice was just another red herring?

She stared at the young men, who were now dropping the burning portrait into the lake. There was something familiar about one of them. A good-looking youth with dark hair met her gaze, and she recognised Raffaele, the nineteen-year-old eldest son of Maurizio Ferrero, the hotel's manager.

Giulia gritted her teeth. Raffaele was the opposite of his affable father, who ran the hotel like clockwork and made every guest feel important. Signor Ferrero had a room in the staff quarters of the hotel, and his wife and children – all seven of them – stayed in the family home in Baveno. Why was his son in Marta this evening?

Raffaele looked away. Giulia had only met him a few times and, when he'd come to see his father in the hotel last year, shortly after he'd begun a work placement in Verbania as a student chemical technician, he'd made no effort to engage with her, answering curtly with a gruff 'Of course' when she'd asked him if he was looking forward to starting the job. With hindsight, it was a silly question, but she'd only been trying to be friendly.

Giulia gave a shrug and said to Ester, 'Let's leave our bikes in the garage, then head indoors. We need to find out what's going on.'

* * *

'An American radio station has been broadcasting news of an Italian armistice with the Allies, apparently. It's probably just a false alarm, and we mustn't get our hopes up, Giulia.' Her mother, Irma, placed a cigarette holder to her lipstick-red lips before taking a deep draw.

Giulia had found her perched on a stool in the hotel bar, sipping a Campari soda and chatting with Yosef Maduro, a Jewish man from Milan whose wife, Devora, wasn't in the hotel but staying with relatives up in the mountains above the lake. The daughter of schoolteachers, Mamma had grown up in Bolzano in the South Tyrol region of Italy, where German was the main language given that it had been part of the Austrian empire until 1920. After meeting and falling in love with Giulia's father, Irma had fully embraced the bourgeois Milanese lifestyle he'd provided for her: evenings at the theatres, fine dining in swanky restaurants, beautiful tailor-made clothes copied from the latest Parisian fashions, and pampering sessions in beauty parlours. Mamma often said she felt bored on the lake and, if it weren't for the fact that Milan was being mercilessly bombed by the Allies, she would go back there without batting an eyelid.

It was nearly suppertime now; Giulia and her mother ate all their meals in the hotel dining room. Mamma was a terrible cook by her own admission, not that Giulia had ever eaten anything cooked by her. Papà employed a wonderful housekeeper called Maria, who looked after them in their luxurious Milan apartment, and Hotel Marta's chef was just as good. Their guests were wealthy people who could afford the prices Papà charged to feed them with produce his staff bought from black-market traders.

'You might have made more effort with your appearance, Giulia.' Mamma broke into her thoughts, looking her up and down.

'There wasn't time to change. Ester and I only just got back from our bike ride.' Giulia tucked a wayward strand of hair behind her ear. She wished her mother would stop trying to turn her into a carbon copy of herself. Giulia cared not a jot for expensive clothes nor beauty regimes; she was happy with store-bought dresses and only wore lipstick on special occasions.

Mamma got down from her stool and led Giulia into the dining room, Yosef Maduro trotting at their heels. He pulled out a chair for Giulia's mother and went to do the same for Giulia, but she'd beaten him to it and had already started unfurling her napkin. A light music programme was playing on the radio, a background to the hubbub of conversation and the clatter of dishes.

Giulia gazed across the long, narrow room lined with potted palms standing like sentinels, where three waiters dressed in white with black bow ties were flitting between the tables. She caught Ester's eye, gave her a surreptitious wave, then froze. The main presenter of Eiar, the public service broadcasting station, had interrupted a beautiful song about a woodland road to say that Prime Minister Badoglio had arrived in the studio to issue a proclamation. Giulia's skin tingled in anticipation as the raspy voice of the PM came over the airwaves.

'The Italian government, recognising the impossibility of continuing the unequal struggle against an overwhelming enemy force, to avoid further and graver disasters for the nation, has sought an armistice from General Eisenhower, commander-in-chief of the Anglo-American Allied forces. The request has been granted. Consequently, all acts of hostility against the Anglo-American force by Italian forces must cease everywhere. But they may react to possible attacks from any other source.'

Giulia and her mother jumped to their feet, knocking over their water glasses and sending their soup spoons clattering to the floor. The entire dining room had erupted into jubilation, people were kissing and hugging each other, repeating the words 'the war is over' while the sonorous clang of church bells came through the open terrace doors.

Signor Maduro, however, hadn't joined in the celebration. He hadn't even risen from his seat. His face assumed a serious expression as he said, 'Badoglio maintained our forces may react to possible attacks from any other source. That doesn't sound to me like the war is over.'

'Don't be such a spoilsport, Yosef.' Mamma had sat down and was reaching across the table to pat his hand.

Signor Maduro's face slumped, and he nodded.

Giulia smiled to herself, picked up the menu and handed it to her mother. Mamma turned all her admirers into puppies begging for crumbs, and Signor Maduro had certainly fallen under her spell. He didn't stand a chance, of course. Her mother adored her father and would never betray him.

'Oh, dear. It's fish for dinner again,' Mamma said.

'At least the lake provides for us,' Giulia sighed. Meat was one thing that couldn't be bought on the black market, she wanted to remind her mother. But Irma had engaged Signor Maduro in a conversation about pearls – he was in the jewellery business – and Giulia bit her tongue instead.

2

'I heard "*Giovinezza*" on the radio last night,' Signor Maduro announced at breakfast the next morning.

Giulia tensed; the official hymn of the Italian Fascist Party had been off the airways since Mussolini's arrest last July. She remembered it used to be ubiquitous at public gatherings, sporting events, in cinemas, and so on, and there were often unpleasant consequences for those who didn't remove their hats and join in. Blackshirts – Mussolini's armed squads – would rough up anyone who didn't show the proper respect. After so many young Italians had been killed on the battlefields, the chorus, beginning with the words *Youth, youth, spring of beauty*, gave her the creeps.

'Made me sick to the stomach, I can tell you,' Signor Maduro continued. 'In particular, what happened next.'

'Please tell us, Yosef.' Mamma gave him a smile.

'The presenter accused Badoglio of betrayal and announced the formation of a new National Fascist Government that will operate in Mussolini's name. Any Italian caught surrendering to the Allies will be considered a traitor, especially those who fight against the Germans.'

'But surely the *tedeschi* are as fed up with the war as we are, and will head back home to Germany?' Giulia said, crinkling her brow.

'Your guess is as good as mine, my dear,' her mother said.

* * *

After breakfast, Giulia went to find Ester. The Jewish girl was in the reading room with her ten-year-old brother, Michael, and eight-year-old sister, Ruth. Ester got to her feet as soon as she saw Giulia, and they both went out to the garden, where they linked arms and strolled towards the parapet overlooking the edge of the lake.

'Ester, what's your father's opinion of the armistice?' Giulia asked without preamble.

'He's worried about the German reaction and says Italy can't trust the Nazis. We, of all people, know what they're capable of when they receive an order. What they did to our community in Thessaloniki—' Ester shuddered. 'My father believes Hitler won't let the Allies take Italy without a fierce fight. Too much of Italian wealth is shipped to Germany for him to let it go. From what he has heard, the Führer is already garrisoning the country.'

'It's too awful, Ester. What will become of us all?'

'Me and my family are thinking of making our way to Switzerland. It isn't far from here, is it?'

'The border crossing is about forty-five kilometres away, I think. But it would be impossible to find cars to transport you as you'd need a special permit.'

'We're planning on paying some fishermen to take us under cover of darkness in their boats.'

'I wish this hadn't happened. I'll miss you so much.' Giulia reached across the space between them and took Ester's hand.

'I'll miss you too,' Ester said. 'You're the most confident girl I've ever met.'

Giulia gazed at a *burchiello* boat under full sail, tacking its way up the lake towards the island that was home to most Lago Maggiore fishermen. With its flat-bottomed hull, crescent profile, and raised bow and stern, it reminded her of pictures she'd seen of Chinese sampans. Everything seemed so peaceful; it was hard to believe Signor Maduro's news about the Fascists. Giulia hoped against hope that Ester and the other Jews in the hotel would decide not to leave.

'I should go back inside,' Ester said. 'I promised my mother I'd keep an eye on Michael and Ruth.'

'I'll see you later,' Giulia said as they reached the lobby. With a heavy heart, she waved goodbye to her friend and headed upstairs.

* * *

Giulia's father arrived late on Friday night and, on Saturday morning, she watched him unfurl his *Corriere della Sera* newspaper at the breakfast table; he'd had it specially delivered from the city. He began to read, his spectacles halfway down his long, straight nose, and then, without warning, he sat bolt upright, a worried frown creasing his forehead.

'German troops have occupied Parma, Brescia, Bergamo, and several other places.' His voice rasped. 'They've surrounded Milan with their tanks, poised to disarm all Italian troops and occupy the city.'

'Oh, my goodness.' Mamma gave a gasp.

'Will they come here?' Unease swelled in Giulia's stomach.

'I don't know, dear.' Her father patted her hand. 'But we're civilians and have nothing to fear. It's our soldiers I'm worried about and—'

He cast his gaze across the dining room to the tables occupied by their Jewish guests.

'Should we say something?' Giulia's mother's voice trembled.

'No need to worry your sweet head about that, Irma. I'll have a quiet word with them later.'

'I can do it,' Giulia said. 'They're my friends.'

'Absolutely not. I forbid it. It's my place, not yours.'

'But... but—'

'You are not to answer back, daughter,' Papà said in a stern tone.

Giulia nodded and pressed her lips together. There was nothing she could say that would make him change his mind, she knew from experience. When her father forbade her anything, he never backed down. Even so, she couldn't resist rebelling; it was one of her faults. That and her tendency to be bossy. One time, she'd reprimanded one of the hotel maids for not cleaning her room properly. Afterwards, she'd regretted her actions and had apologised. It hadn't been her place to tell the woman off...

'There's encouraging news about the Allied advance,' Papà said. 'The British have occupied Taranto in Puglia and the US Fifth Army is closing in on Naples.'

'It shouldn't be too long before they break through to us, I hope,' Mamma said.

* * *

September Sundays on Lake Maggiore had always been idyllic, even with a war on, Giulia mused as she set off for a bike ride with Ester. But today things were different; there appeared to be fewer people about, and the lake itself looked disconsolate under a steel-grey sky. To make matters worse, today would be her last day with Ester; she and her relatives were leaving tomorrow evening. Maurizio Ferrero, the hotel's manager, had enlisted his son's help to hire some fishermen friends of his who would come and pick up Ester and her family as soon as it was dark.

But now was not the time to think of such things; now she needed to focus on the task at hand. She and Ester were heading for Stresa, about ten kilometres away. There'd been a storm the night before. In the evening, dark clouds had gathered over the mountains and, by the time darkness arrived, fat drops of rain were pitting the surface of the lake. Before too long, a squall sheeted across the water, followed by grumbles of thunder and forks of lightning. The rain had freshened the temperature and there was a nip of autumn in the air now. Even so, pedalling hard, Giulia felt perspiration trickling down the back of her neck, and she was glad when, about half an hour later, they drew up on the lakeside road.

She peered across the water towards the Borromean Islands. They were some of her favourite places and she loved visiting the noble palace and grand gardens of Isola Bella; the lush vegetation, rare plants, exotic flowers, peacocks, and parrots in the wild on Isola Madre; and Fishermen's Island, home to those who would help Ester and her family. The high mountains above Verbania formed a backdrop to the scene and, as ever, Giulia's breath caught at the beauty of the setting.

In the periphery of her vision, she discerned Ester staring at something behind her, and her face had gone as white as freshly fallen snow. The rumble of vehicles approaching made Giulia turn around. Her heart almost beat out of her chest. A column of armoured cars with black crosses on their sides, outlined in white, was coming down the road.

Germans!

'Let's get out of here,' Giulia said, leaping onto her bike.

She checked to make sure Ester was following, and then pedalled as if the hounds of hell were at her heels.

It seemed to take forever to get back to Marta. Her heart thumped an agonising beat against her chest while her breaths came in choking gasps. She wasn't afraid of the Germans on her own account, but she was terrified of them for Ester.

Finally, they arrived at the hotel. After leaving their bicycles in the garage, they ran into the lobby and then through to the lounge, where Giulia's parents were sitting, smoking.

'There are Germans in Stresa,' she blurted as Ester raced upstairs to tell her family the terrible news.

'We know, my dear,' Giulia's father said. 'I received a phone call from a friend in the town hall who told me. They've requisitioned the ground and first floors of the Ducal Palace for one hundred and fifty SS troops.'

Stresa, with its lavish hotels and stunning location, had long been a place for elite tourism. Dickens had once stayed there; Napoleon had enjoyed a sojourn with Josephine, and Hemmingway had been so entranced with Stresa that he'd set part of *A Farewell to Arms* in the town. But recently, it had become the home to numerous Jewish people, not only those escaping the bombing of Milan but also those fleeing Nazi persecution in their home countries. It was awful to think Stresa was now occupied by Nazis.

'My friend also said he'd heard the German commandant say they were about to round up the Jews.' Papà shuddered.

'It's a good thing our Jewish friends are leaving tomorrow,'

Giulia said, jamming her hands into her armpits to hide how much they were shaking.

3

There was another storm during the night and Giulia slept fitfully. She woke late, startled by the roar of vehicle engines, and went to look out of her bedroom window. Several lorries, with black crosses outlined in white on the sides like those she'd seen in Stresa, had pulled up in the parking area adjacent to the hotel. Giulia's blood ran cold. About thirty German soldiers were jumping out of the trucks, armed with rifles and machine guns. Terrified, she threw on some clothes and raced to her parents' room, where she found her mother and father fully clothed, ready to go down to breakfast.

'There are *tedeschi* outside.' Giulia's voice quivered. 'I think they've surrounded the building.'

'Stay calm,' her father said. 'I'll go sort this out.'

He'd barely finished speaking when loud knocks sounded at the door, and a man with dark blond hair barged into the room. Dressed in a grey uniform, he wore a peaked cap with a silver eagle in the centre.

'*Obersturmführer Karl Weber der Panzer-Grenadier Division Waffen-SS Leibstandarte Adolf Hitler.*' He introduced himself, clicking his heels before barking out a succession of words in German.

'He's asking if you're the owner of the hotel, Aldo,' Mamma said. Having grown up in the South Tyrol, she spoke the language fluently.

'Tell him that I am.' Papà spoke his affirmation firmly.

His face hard as stone, the obersturmführer barked something that made Giulia's mother's eyes grow huge.

'He said... he said the hotel is no longer ours.' Mamma's voice quavered.

'Why?' Giulia's father asked.

'Because we're harbouring Jews, the enemies of the Reich.' Giulia's mother rubbed at her arms. 'He has given orders for them to be locked up in that big room on the fourth floor, and he's taking you to his headquarters in Baveno for questioning, Aldo. Giulia and I must stay in this suite until the SS tells us otherwise.'

Dread rolling through her, Giulia stood next to her mother while the obersturmführer marched her father out of the room.

Poor Papà! And what about Ester, her family, and the rest of our Jewish guests? They must be absolutely terrified...

'How can that despicable man believe that Ester and her family are the enemies of Germany?' Giulia crumpled onto a chair. 'What will happen to Papà and them?'

'I don't know, my darling. I don't know.' Mamma's voice choked with tears as she took up her habitual place on her chaise longue.

The hatred Giulia felt towards the German officer was so palpable it made her want to throw up. Her father had never hurt anyone in his life; he'd taken in their Jewish guests out of the kindness of his heart. Papà could be authoritarian, but she loved him for his noble character and generosity. And he worked so hard to give her and Mamma everything they needed...

A sudden idea occurred to Giulia; she remembered her father was on good terms with the German consul general in Milan, Gerhart Bauer, who'd bought several pieces of antique furniture from him and with whom he'd struck up a friendship. Her parents had invited Herr Bauer and his wife to dinner a couple of times, Giulia recalled. Somehow, she needed to get in touch with Herr Bauer and beg him to put in a good word for her father.

With an exhale of breath, she got up from her chair and went to the window. The hotel was still surrounded by armed soldiers. Even if she could climb down from the balcony – they were on the first floor and she might land softly in a flower bed if she jumped – chances were that she'd be shot before she made it to the ground. Her heart heavy, she crumpled back onto the chair.

* * *

The grandfather clock in the hotel lobby chimed past the next three hours. Her mother had stopped crying and, after Giulia had shared her idea about the consul general with her, Mamma started pacing the floor and muttering quietly to herself in German, her first language. Giulia understood little but, from the harsh tone of her words, it sounded as if her mother was swearing.

Her insides churning with worry, she thought about her father, Ester, and the Jewish guests. Giulia's mind raced through endless possibilities: Papà was being tortured, the Jews had been shot while attempting to flee. All of it didn't bear thinking about, but she couldn't help herself. Not even taking deep breaths could calm the turmoil in her stomach.

Mamma had only just sat down when, without warning, Obersturmführer Weber, the German officer who'd taken Giulia's father in for questioning, strode into the room. Smirking, he raked his cold pale blue eyes over Giulia and her mother, then launched into a spiel of German.

The officer's twisted smile gave Giulia the shivers, and she switched her attention to her mother, who was nodding and clasping at her hands. For the first time in her life, Giulia wished she'd learnt to speak German. But when her mother had suggested the idea some years ago, she'd said she preferred learning English. She'd found it easy, having had an English governess when she was little, who'd taught her so well she was practically fluent.

'The obersturmführer has asked me to be his interpreter,' Mamma said in a surprised tone of voice after the SS officer had stopped speaking.

'Did you agree?' Shock wheeled through Giulia.

'How could I refuse? In exchange, you are to be set free from these rooms, but you must stay within the confines of the hotel or risk being shot.' Mamma lowered her voice. 'It's for the best, my darling. This way, I might be able to help your father and our Jewish friends.'

* * *

Blinking to clear the tears from her eyes, Giulia stood by the window and watched her mother climb into the German officer's saloon car. As soon as they'd driven off, she squared her shoulders and made her way out of the suite, down the carpeted corridor to the central staircase. She breathed a quiet sigh of relief that she hadn't encountered any SS soldiers thus far, but her relief was short-lived when she arrived at the lobby. Two sentries stood on either side of the front door, rifles in their hands.

Giulia stopped in her tracks, worried they might not have been told she'd been released. They ignored her, thank God, and she went in search of the hotel manager.

She found him in the kitchen, leaning against the counter with a cup of ersatz coffee in his hand.

'Giulia!' A smile lifted the corners of Signor Ferrero's mouth. 'I'm so glad you've been let out.'

'The obersturmführer forced my mother into being his interpreter in exchange for my freedom. I hope she'll manage to convince him to let my father go.' Giulia glanced at Signor Ferrero. 'Would you have the telephone number of the German consul in Milan, by any chance? I'd like to phone him and ask him to intercede with the SS on my father's behalf. The consul and his wife stayed here last year, I remember.'

'If I found the number, it wouldn't do much good, I'm afraid. The Marta phone lines have been down since early this morning.'

'How annoying!' Giulia swallowed her disappointment and posed the question preying on her mind. 'Are our Jewish guests all right? I mean, I know they're being held prisoner, but how did that happen?'

'You'd better take a seat, my dear.' Signor Ferrero poured her a cup of coffee and asked the cook to heat some soup. 'The SS officer arrived with a list of names and, once he'd identified who the Jews were, he gave orders for them to be locked up in that big en suite room on the fourth floor. Then he instructed me to prepare the prisoners' old rooms with extra beds for thirty of his men.'

Disgusted that the Germans deemed it fit to requisition

rooms in her father's hotel for their men, Giulia asked Signor Ferrero if he'd managed to take their Jewish guests any food.

'There are soldiers everywhere.' Maurizio Ferrero sighed. 'I didn't want to provoke them.'

'I'll go. Is there a spare key to that room? I want to find out how they are.'

'I'll fetch the key for you, but don't you think you're being a little rash?'

'I can pretend the food is for myself if I'm stopped. Would you be able to organise a basket of bread, some cheese and maybe a little fruit?'

'Of course. That's easily arranged.' Signor Ferrero nodded. 'I managed to send a message to my son, Raffaele, by the way, to contact the fishermen who were supposed to take those poor people to Switzerland.'

'Ester told me Raffaele had hired boats for them that were due to take them across to the Swiss side of the lake.' Giulia leant forward. 'Could you ask him if he can still help?' She wouldn't give up on Ester and her family, whatever the cost.

'I'll do my best, my dear, but I fear Raffaele could also be in danger. I've been told that the Nazis are rounding up young men and transporting them to labour camps. My son can't hang around anywhere by the lake. The area is swarming with *tedeschi*, so he needs to head up to the relative safety of the mountains.'

'Oh, I see.' Giulia heard the disappointment in her voice. 'I'll have to think of something else.'

'I'm not saying he won't be able to help, just that it will need to be sooner rather than later.'

4

Giulia had lost her appetite, but she forced down the soup with some bread and cheese, then took the picnic basket Signor Ferrero had arranged for the Jewish prisoners, as well as the key to the room where they were being held, and made her way towards the central staircase. Passing the dining room, she caught sight of SS troops patrolling the terrace and gardens at the front of the hotel, and an unpleasant taste coated her tongue. They were acting as if they owned the place.

Stealthily, she went up the stairs to the fourth floor. Her heart thudded as she reached the top step. A German soldier was sitting at a table outside the prisoners' room, a glass and an open bottle of wine in front of him. Giulia stood still, poised to run. But the guard didn't react. She heaved a sigh of relief. The man gave every impression of having fallen asleep.

Her body quaking, she inserted the key, turned it, and stepped inside.

'Giulia!' Ester rushed towards her. 'What are you doing here? The Germans might shoot you.'

'I've brought you some food,' Giulia said as cheerfully as she could while unpacking the picnic basket. 'Don't worry about me, I'm fine.'

She gazed at the group of twelve. However spacious, the room wasn't big enough for them to be comfortable. They'd made the best of it by taking the mattresses off the beds, which doubled the sleeping space, but they'd have had to share all the same.

Ester's parents – Signor and Signora Cardozo – were sitting with Ester's little brother and sister on one of the mattresses. The Canetti family – a couple in their early fifties, their adult son and his young wife – were positioned on another. The two beds were occupied by a middle-aged couple in their late forties, Signor and Signora Kordovero, on one, and Signor Maduro on the other.

They were a close-knit group who spoke to each other in Ladino – the Spanish dialect spoken by Sephardic Jews – and who supported each other through thick and thin. Signora Canetti was Ester's father's sister and Signor Kordovero her mother's brother. Signor Maduro was a distant cousin, and it was he who'd arranged for them all to stay at Hotel Marta.

'*Ciao*, Giulia,' Signor Cardozo said, smiling. 'Thank you for bringing us some food.'

She'd barely lifted out a loaf of bread when two Nazis came running into the room, shouting unintelligibly and waving their rifles.

'They're saying it is they who decide if and when we Jews can eat,' Signor Maduro said. 'I speak a little German.'

Pushing and shoving at Giulia, the soldiers bustled her out of the room, leaving the picnic basket on the floor. She grudgingly went with them, but they seemed to have forgotten about the food. At least her friends would eat...

* * *

Down in the kitchen, Giulia offered to peel potatoes to keep herself busy. Surely her mother would come back soon. The hours ticked by, though, and it wasn't until the early evening when Signor Ferrero approached with the news she'd been waiting for, and it was even better than she'd dared to hope.

'Your mother has returned,' he said, a smile lighting his eyes. 'And your father is with her. They had some business to transact with the obersturmführer in your father's office, and now they've gone up to your suite.'

Oh, thank God! Giulia leapt up from the stool where she'd been sitting and raced upstairs. Her father opened his arms wide, and she ran right into them.

'Your mother managed to make a phone call to Gerhart Bauer from the SS headquarters. After she'd told him about me being taken in for questioning, he asked to speak to Obersturmführer Weber. Long story short, I've had to pay a million-lire fine to that vile Nazi for giving hospitality to Jews, which is against Mussolini's racial laws, apparently.'

'How awful, Papà. I hope the SS didn't mistreat you—' Giulia stepped back and studied his face.

'They locked me up in a basement room and left me not knowing what the hell was happening. But they didn't hurt me physically.' He smiled at Giulia's mother. 'It was only thanks to my darling Irma that I am here.'

'You're very brave, Mamma. I trust that horrible German wasn't too nasty to you.' Giulia gave her mother a hug.

'He isn't a nice man, my dear. Fiercely antisemitic. Kept on and on about the glory of the Fatherland and the purity of the German race. I had to stop myself from telling him a thing or two. It wouldn't have done any good, though. Not with someone like him—'

'Will he still want you to interpret for him tomorrow?'

'I told the obersturmführer I needed your mother here in the hotel, but he insisted,' Giulia's father said. 'We've decided she'll pretend to be ill when he comes to collect her in the morning. He wouldn't dare drag a sick woman from her bed.'

'I hope not,' Giulia said. 'What did he make you do for him today?'

'He took me to Arona to interpret for him at the villa of a Jewish family. It was heart-wrenching.' Mamma wrung her hands. 'There were lorry-loads of soldiers shouting, "Juden, Juden." Those poor, terrified people were taken completely by surprise. Can you believe the Nazis even arrested the grandparents? They manhandled everyone onto a truck and God only knows what will happen to them.'

'That's why we must help our Jews,' Giulia said firmly. 'They mustn't suffer the same fate.'

'Your mother told me those vile Nazis have imprisoned them on the fourth floor,' Papà said.

'I managed to take them some food. They're terribly scared, of course. We have to facilitate their escape.'

'Escape? But how?' Giulia's father frowned.

'I don't know, but there must be a way.' Giulia went on to tell her parents about her conversation with Maurizio Ferrero. 'Hopefully, his son will lend us a hand.'

'Oh, Giulia.' Her mother shook her head. 'I know you mean well and it devastates me, but it will be far too dangerous.'

'I agree,' Papà said. 'We'd end up being arrested or shot.' He made firm eye contact with Giulia. 'And you're not to go hatching up a harebrained scheme with Maurizio and Raffaele. I'll make sure they know I've forbidden it.'

Giulia stared at her parents, open-mouthed. But they couldn't possibly abandon Ester and her family to their fate. They'd only overreacted to the events of that morning. Tomorrow, they'd change their minds, wouldn't they?

'We are confined to the hotel but not to our suite,' her father said, changing the subject. 'It's vital we don't do anything to provoke the Nazis. Do you hear me, Giulia?'

'Yes, Papà.' She sighed.

* * *

The next day, at lunchtime, Giulia's ears rang with the sound of the Germans at the next table, who were talking loudly in their guttural language as she pulled out a chair to sit beside her father. Clean-shaven, the soldiers billeted in the hotel seemed far too young to be in their grey-green uniforms. Were they disappointed the war hadn't ended like everyone had hoped? They weren't much older than she was...

'I've arranged for a tray to be carried up to your mother.' Giulia's father broke into her thoughts.

Obersturmführer Weber had arrived that morning and, as planned, Papà sent him a note to say that Giulia's mother must have eaten something bad and couldn't stop vomiting. Giulia had stayed out of the way of the SS officer, who'd hung around in the hotel before making the surprise announcement, in highly accented ungrammatical Italian, that the Jewish prisoners could join the rest of the guests in the dining room for lunch.

Clasping her hands together in her lap, Giulia waited impatiently for Ester and her family to appear. Her chest tickling with nerves, she kept her gaze on the door. What if it had been a sick Nazi joke?

The echo of voices speaking Ladino alerted her to her

friends' arrival, and she couldn't help a slow smile spreading across her face. They held their heads up high, but made no eye contact with any of the other guests. Ester walked at the front of the cohort between her little brother and sister, holding them by their hands. Her parents were close behind, followed by the rest of their extended family. All of their faces appeared drawn and weary; they almost certainly weren't getting much sleep.

Giulia wanted to go up and greet them, so she rose to her feet, then abruptly sat back down again.

Good grief! Obersturmführer Weber was striding towards her table.

'*Guten tag,*' the SS officer said.

'*Buongiorno.*' Papà wished him a good day in return.

Weber ignored Giulia and she ignored him back as he pulled out a chair, lowered himself onto it, and then snapped his fingers in the direction of the hotel's youngest waiter, Enrico. Giulia gave the young man an encouraging nod, and he approached with a tureen of fish soup. But poor Enrico's hand was shaking so much he spilt most of the contents of the ladle on the pristine white cloth.

The obersturmführer scraped back his chair and barked orders at his men. Two soldiers took the tray from Enrico. They served Weber, Giulia and her father, before making their way across the room towards the Jews. It was like some kind of bizarre comedy; Ester and her family sat in silence, still as stones, while the SS men ladled the soup into their bowls. Giulia's eyes widened when they went to the kitchen for more soup and proceeded to serve the rest of the hotel guests. The scene had become even more strange, she thought.

She forced down her lunch; the odd turn of events had stolen her appetite. Thankfully Maurizio Ferrero took over service of the main course: grilled perch with fried potatoes and spinach.

The food tasted like blotting-paper in Giulia's mouth, and she washed it down with frequent sips of water. She made no effort to join in the stilted conversation between her father and Weber. His Italian was as terrible as her father's German, but from what she could gather, he was telling Papà that Mussolini had been sprung from the jail where he'd been imprisoned by the Italian government, and would be taken to Germany for a meeting with Hitler.

Things are going from bad to worse.

Frowning, Giulia tried to work out how to speak with Ester before she and her family were locked up in that fourth-floor room again. Earlier, an idea had come to her mind about a potential escape route; she hadn't even told her parents about it yet.

The German officer's gruff voice broke into her thoughts; he was saying something to her father that took him several attempts to communicate. Giulia couldn't believe her ears; Weber had decided that the *Juden* would be allowed to go out for short walks around the village, two at a time, for no longer than half an hour. If they didn't return punctually, he warned, the rest of the prisoners would be shot.

Giulia leant forward in her seat. Had the obersturmführer's words come out wrong? His Italian was so terrible he could have meant the opposite. But, after Weber had left the dining room, Papà went on to say that, yes, the detainees would be permitted a brief interlude outdoors.

'They must take care to be back on time,' he added. 'Best not to give the *tedeschi* any excuse to—'

Papà didn't need to finish the sentence.

* * *

Later that afternoon, Giulia strolled around the piazza, arm in arm with Ester. Her friend's parents had gone beforehand with her siblings, and now it was Ester's turn. Giulia could only be thankful that Mamma had come downstairs once the obersturm-führer had left – presumably to round up more Jews – and she'd persuaded the guards to let Giulia go outside with her friend.

A stiff breeze had sprung up, sending white horse waves galloping across the lake. Tucking Ester's hand into her side, Giulia said, 'I'm determined to help you and your family escape, dearest. All is not lost.'

'But how?' Ester came to an abrupt halt. 'The soldiers will shoot us as soon as we make any attempt.'

'I've been thinking about that, and I've remembered something.' Giulia smiled. 'There's a tunnel leading from the hotel basement to the beach. In times gone by, coal was brought by boat, unloaded onto the shore and transported on carts into the cellars. Papà showed it to me a couple of years ago. The passageway is full of junk, but once cleared, it will be the perfect escape route.'

'But what will we do when we arrive at the beach?' Ester shuffled her feet. 'How will we get to Switzerland? We missed our opportunity with those fishermen.'

'I've asked Signor Ferrero if he can persuade his son Raffaele to help again.' Giulia kept to herself the fact that the hotel manager had been reticent.

'What if Raffaele refuses?' Ester's voice trembled. 'We're all convinced the Germans plan to transport us to a concentration camp, just like they did with the rest of our community in Thessaloniki.'

'Please, don't lose hope.' Giulia brushed a kiss to Ester's cheek. 'I'll do everything I can to help you. And I'm sure Signor Ferrero and Raffaele will do so as well.'

'Have you told your parents what you're planning?'

'I did, and they said it will be too dangerous, but that was before I remembered about the tunnel.' Giulia squared her shoulders. 'Once I remind them about it, I'm sure they'll agree it's a good plan.'

'You're so brave.' Ester hugged her. 'I've never met anyone like you.'

'I'm not brave, I'm determined.' She squeezed Ester's hand. 'I'll work on persuading my parents, and also beg Signor Ferrero to get in touch with Raffaele and ask him to contact those fishermen again.'

'We'll have to escape soon,' Ester said. 'I don't think we've got a lot of time left.'

'Talking about time.' Giulia checked her watch. 'We should go back to the hotel now.'

'Absolutely.' There was a spring in Ester's step. 'I'll tell my family about your plan. I'm sure they'll agree. There's no alternative, is there?'

With an ache in her throat, Giulia gave her friend a big hug.

* * *

Ester and her family were locked back in the en suite room on the fourth floor, and Giulia and her parents ate their supper upstairs. Giulia was just about to share her escape plan with her mother and father when the noise of raucous singing came from the billiard room below.

'It's the soldiers,' Mamma said. 'They sound terribly drunk.'

'Maurizio told me earlier that they'd raided our cellars.' Papà shook his head. 'The *bastardi*—'

Giulia was heading out of the door before she could blink.

'Where do you think you're going, young lady?' her mother called out.

'I'll be back in a couple of minutes, don't worry.' Giulia closed the door behind her.

Her heartbeat racing, she made her way downstairs to the billiard room, hid behind the open door, and peered through the crack. *Oh, dear Lord.* The entire cohort of thirty enlisted men were having a drunken party. One of them was playing the piano while swilling from a bottle of wine. Others were singing and drinking, their faces red and blotchy as they slurred the words to a song. The damp earth aroma of wine permeated the air and the discordant music made Giulia's ears ache.

A soldier had slung two helmets from his shoulders to resemble a woman's breasts, and one of his comrades lay sprawled in his lap, slurping at the helmets like babies at their mothers' teats. Giulia's stomach heaved. Another soldier leaned heavily against the piano, one hand fumbling with a wine bottle as he spilt red liquid down his shirt, his mouth twisting into a lopsided grin.

What Giulia was watching beggared belief; she'd never seen anything like it in her life.

The sound of heavy boots stamping across the marble hallway made her retreat further behind the door. She flinched as Obersturmführer Weber strode past her into the room, followed by his second-in-command. Her heart pounded in sudden fear. What if he discovered her?

The SS officer began shouting at his men. She strained her ears to understand what he was saying, but the only word she understood was 'Stresa'. Maybe he was transferring his men there? *Wouldn't it be wonderful not to have to suffer their hateful presence?*

Weber barked orders and his aide lined the men up in a

motley fashion. They were so drunk they could barely stand. Giulia made herself as small as possible as the officers marched the staggering men out of the billiard room and down the corridor. Holding her breath, Giulia waited and waited, praying Weber wouldn't return. When she was certain the coast was clear, she made her way back upstairs.

* * *

'Thank God you're safe,' Giulia's mother said as Giulia stepped into the suite. 'You shouldn't have run off like that.'

'I'm sorry, I couldn't help myself. I just wanted to see what was happening.'

'It's a good thing you weren't caught,' Papà said. 'Those Nazis are unpredictable. You need to be more wary of them.'

'I know. I realise that now. What I saw made me sick to the stomach.' Giulia went on to describe the scene to her parents.

'Well, I'm just glad you managed to stay hidden.' Mamma glanced at her wristwatch, then yawned. 'I suppose we should get ready for bed.'

Giulia was about to head for her room when the sound of tramping boots echoed from the driveway below. She rushed to the window, and her parents weren't far behind her. Gazing through the glass, she gave a gasp. The company of soldiers – who'd changed into their battle uniforms – were standing in close formation, still unsteady on their feet. Weber and his second-in-command barked orders at them before climbing into a saloon car, and they all set off at an approximate quick march pace, out of the hotel grounds and onto the village square.

'The obersturmführer must be disciplining his men, sobering them up,' Papà said.

'I heard Weber mention the word Stresa. They'll be gone for

at least four hours.' Giulia knew the road and how long it took to get there, having walked it many times. In their condition, the German soldiers might take even longer.

'We can unlock the door to the room where our Jewish guests are being held and let them come downstairs,' Papà said. 'They're probably hungry, so I'll organise some food.'

'There's something I'd like to share with you.' Giulia reached for her parents' hands, looked them in the eye, and proceeded to remind them about the tunnel leading to the beach. 'It would be the perfect escape route,' she said. 'I mentioned it to Ester, and I expect she'll have told her family by now.'

'Giulia,' Papà groaned. 'You shouldn't have got their hopes up. What if Raffaele isn't able to help?'

'Surely he isn't the only person we know who can get in touch with those fishermen.' At least her parents were considering her plan, Giulia thought with relief. 'We can't abandon Ester and the others to the Germans. We just can't.'

* * *

An hour later, after Ester, her close family and relatives had eaten supper in the dining room, Giulia and her parents led them down to the basement. The tunnel was strewn with old coal boxes and other detritus, so they formed a human chain to clear it. It was arduous work, but they pressed on, working in silence, until they'd made a passage down the middle wide enough for one person at a time.

Giulia's father took the lead, and she was glad of it, for it meant he was on board with her plan. But when he came to a halt at the end of the passageway, she heard him let out a groan.

'There's a rusty old iron gate with a padlock,' he muttered. 'I'll need to look for the key before we can open it.'

Giulia checked her watch; time was running out. Her mother echoed her thoughts, saying, 'The Germans will be back soon. Come on, everyone, back upstairs. We'll be in a better position to finalise arrangements tomorrow.'

'Thank you, Mamma,' Giulia said after they'd returned to their suite and had washed the dust from their hands and faces. 'I'm relieved you and Papà have decided to help.'

'Well, it all depends on your father finding that key and also on the fishermen agreeing to take everyone up the lake to Switzerland.'

'Everyone?' Giulia met her mother's worried gaze.

'You do realise we'll need to escape as well. If we don't, the Germans will arrest us for aiding our Jewish guests. We must make absolutely sure we don't implicate Maurizio Ferrero so he can look after things for us while we are away.'

'Your mother is right,' Papà said. 'As soon as everything is finalised, I'll make suitable arrangements with my Swiss contacts. I already have money invested in a bank in Geneva. We could go and live there.'

Leave Italy and all she knew? Giulia's chest scratched with sudden sadness, but she would do all that it took to help her friends.

5

It was a mild evening, and Raffaele had cycled along the lakeside road with his childhood friend, Paolo Demichelis, aiming to get away from their younger siblings and enjoy some peace and quiet on their favourite beach. The curfew was back in force, but they ignored it like many of their compatriots; the Germans stayed in their quarters at that time of the day.

After dismounting from their bikes, Raffaele and Paolo hid them in a thicket of bushes and strolled down to the shore. The lake waters made a sucking sound on the shingle as Raffaele passed Paolo a cigarette and pulled a packet of matches from his pocket. Sitting on their jackets, spread on the pebbles in front of an empty boat shed, they inhaled deeply, each lost in their own thoughts.

'We need to escape up there soon,' Raffaele said, indicating across the lake towards the mountains above the town of Verbania, etched against the twilight sky. He knew the area well; his father came from the village of Ungiasca and he'd enjoyed hiking holidays in the locality since early childhood. 'That *bastardo*, Mussolini, will be back from Germany shortly, asking men like us to follow him again.' Raffaele gritted his teeth. 'Enough is enough!'

'I can't take it any more, either.' Paolo shook his head.

Raffaele didn't need to remind him about the years they'd spent in Fascist youth organisations while growing up. Even thinking about the creed, 'I believe in the genius of Mussolini, in our Holy Father Fascism, in the communion of the martyrs, in the conversion of Italians and in the resurrection of the Empire', made Raffaele's stomach roll with disgust. *Il Duce*, the Caesar people thought would solve all their problems, had led the country into a disastrous war, resulting in the deaths of hundreds of thousands of Italian sons. Raffaele would never forgive Mussolini for colluding with Hitler, but maybe the paramilitary training, the parades and marches and exercises armed with rifles, would stand him in good stead when it came to fighting back. He wasn't under any illusions; he would need to fight the enemy tooth and nail if he were to help liberate Italy from the hated *tedeschi*.

'We'll have to find like-minded patriots.' Paolo's voice interrupted Raffaele's thoughts. 'There'll be anti-fascists like us up there, I imagine.'

'Shush!' Raffaele's skin prickled as the rumble of engines echoed from the road. 'A lorry has pulled up. It could only be Germans. We'd better hide.'

He ran into the boat shed with Paolo at his heels. The window glass was grimy, but they had a clear enough view. Five SS soldiers, under the command of an officer, were herding four people – a middle-aged man and woman and a younger couple – across the beach, forcing them onwards with the butts of their weapons.

'Why have you brought us here?' the older man asked.

Ignoring his question, the officer barked a crisp order to his men. Time slowed down while, to Raffaele's horror, the soldiers opened fire with their automatic guns, mowing down the group within seconds.

Appalled, Raffaele grabbed hold of Paolo, and they sagged against each other, their eyes fixed on the shocking scene as it unfolded. The soldiers were finishing off the prisoners, shooting them in the back of the head at point-blank range. More orders came from their commandant, and the soldiers gathered rocks from the beach. Raffaele recoiled as the soldiers stuffed the rocks and the bodies of their victims into big sacks. It was the most barbaric thing he'd ever seen. Raffaele heaved, and he swallowed bile.

With much huffing and grunting, the SS men were dragging the rock and body-filled sacks across the pebbles and into the lake, where they pushed them out into the deeper water. It couldn't have been more brutal, and Raffaele found it hard to process what he was seeing.

Finally, seemingly satisfied that the evidence of their despicable crime had sunk to the depths, the soldiers regrouped, and their leader ordered them back onto the lorry.

'Good God,' Raffaele said. 'That was awful. I would never have believed it if I hadn't seen it with my own eyes.'

'Who do you think those poor people were?' Paolo asked, clearly shocked.

'I hate to say this, but I think they might have been Jews. Remember, we were going to help the twelve Jews at the hotel where my father works? I hope they haven't come from there.'

'We should try to find out, Raffaele.'

'I agree. Let's head for Marta straight away.'

* * *

About thirty minutes later, Raffaele was leading Paolo through the hotel gates towards the side of the building. They left their bikes propped up by the kitchen door and went inside. Raffaele was hoping his father would be supervising the staff while they served dinner, and he was glad to find that was the case.

'Son, what are you doing here?' His father looked up from where he'd been standing by the counter.

'Can we go to your office, Pa? Paolo and I have something we'd like to discuss.'

'Of course, come with me.'

'Oh, dear Lord,' Raffaele's father said after he'd given him a blow-by-blow account of the terrible events he and Paolo had just witnessed. 'The SS took four of our twelve Jewish guests off for "interrogation" this afternoon.' Pa shook his head. 'In the morning, they let the prisoners out of their rooms, and even gave the children chocolates, but when Obersturmführer Weber turned up for lunch, the atmosphere suddenly changed. We've all been worrying about the Canetti family.'

'Can you describe them?' Raffaele asked.

'A couple in their early fifties, their adult son and his young wife.'

'The description fits the people we saw being murdered.' Paolo sighed.

'Weber brought his men back in time for their meal,' Raffaele's father said. 'He's returned to his quarters in Stresa now, thank God.'

'Is there a way the rest of the Jews can still escape?' Raffaele posed the question.

His father recounted the events of the night before, how the SS officer had ordered his drunken men to go on a forced march to discipline them, and how the hotel's Jewish guests, along with Signor Leone – the owner – his wife, and his daughter had gone to the cellars and cleared rubbish from a tunnel leading to the beach.

'Signor Leone asked me to find the key to the gate at the end of the passageway, and I'm pleased to say I remembered where it was.'

'I could go to the Baveno fish market tomorrow morning,' Raffaele said. 'My fishermen contacts who agreed to help the other night are sure to be there.'

'I'll go with you,' Paolo added.

'Take care, both of you.' Raffaele's father twisted his mouth grimly. 'There might be Germans around.'

'We'll mingle with the fishermen. The SS won't be able to distinguish us.' Raffaele gave what he hoped was an encouraging smile.

'As soon as the dinner service is over, I'll tell Signor Leone you are here, son. He'll want to have a word with you.'

* * *

Raffaele and Paolo shared a plate of leftover pasta while they waited for the hotel owner to appear. It didn't take long for him to do so and, after establishing that Raffaele and his friend knew about the tunnel and were willing to help, Signor Leone thanked them. They then told him about what they'd witnessed at the lake.

'How ghastly,' he said, his eyes widening with obvious distress. 'Totally barbaric. Those poor people—'

'We couldn't believe our eyes, and it made us come here straight away to offer to do what we can,' Raffaele said.

'I'll ask my wife to put her interpreting services at Ober-sturmführer Weber's disposal tomorrow morning, to distract him from taking any more of our Jews in for so-called interrogation.'

Signor Leone furrowed his brow. 'But I won't tell anyone about the murders. It would only upset them. I'll get a message to them about our plan once it's finalised.'

'What exactly will be your plan?' Paolo asked.

The hotel owner made a *hmmm* noise in his throat, and then said, 'We'll have to wait until the soldiers have gone to bed. Then we'll head down to the cellars.'

'How will Paolo and I know when that will be?' Raffaele asked.

'I'll flash a light three times from our window. Will you be able to hide somewhere you can see it?'

'Of course,' Raffaele said. 'But first we need to ask the fishermen if they'll take your Jewish guests up the lake to Swiss waters. It was different before the SS locked them up. It's far riskier now.'

'My wife, daughter and I will be going with them, and I'm prepared to pay whatever the fishermen want.'

'You?' Raffaele eyed Signor Leone. 'Why?'

'Because the Germans will put two and two together after the escape and will know we've colluded with our guests,' the hotel owner said.

'What about my father?' Raffaele took a slight step back. 'Won't he be in danger too?'

'I've thought about that, and I think it's best if I give you a couple of days off, Maurizio. We can tell the staff your wife is ill, and you're needed at home. You should set off straight away. Phone me in the morning after you've spoken to the fishermen.'

'I thought the telephone wasn't working,' Raffaele said.

'The lines have been restored but, from the crackling sound, it's obvious our phone is being tapped.' Signor Leone rubbed his chin. 'We should think of a code you can use.'

'How about "perch was available in the market", if they agree,' Raffaele's father said.

'And if they don't, you could say, "we couldn't get any perch in the market",' Signor Leone said.

Raffaele darted his gaze from his father to the hotel manager and back again. It was like something out of the movies. Except it was real and deadly serious. The events of that evening had made it so.

Signor Leone's plan seemed a good one, but Raffaele wished he wouldn't need to spend time with Giulia. She was a spoilt little rich girl, as far as he was concerned, and her entitled attitude got on his nerves. Hopefully, he wouldn't need to keep company for long with her; once she was on that boat with the others, he and Paolo would make haste for Ungiasca, the mountain village overlooking the lake where his father had been born.

6

The grandfather clock in the lobby was chiming nine as Giulia went downstairs for breakfast. Her parents had risen earlier, and she fully expected them to be at their customary table, lingering over their coffee, but they were nowhere to be seen. Twisting a strand of hair that had come loose from her braid, she headed for the kitchen.

Her father looked up from where he was standing, directing the service.

'Where's Signor Ferrero?' Giulia asked, perplexed. Papà always left the running of the hotel to his manager, and she'd never seen him do anything like this before.

'I've given him the day off, my dear.'

'Oh, I see.' Papà had mentioned the other day that he'd wanted to avoid Maurizio Ferrero being implicated in any escape on their part. She glanced around the room for her mother. 'Where's Mamma?'

'When Obersturmführer Weber arrived to check on his men, your mother met him in reception, said she was feeling much better, and offered to interpret for him again.'

Giulia's chest tightened, and she took a shaky breath. Why would Mamma suddenly make such an offer? It was so strange...

'Have you heard anything from Signor Ferrero about the fishermen?' Giulia lowered her voice. Her father had revealed the plan to her and Mamma after they'd gone up to their rooms last night.

'Yes, I received a coded message that they're willing to help and will wait in their boats offshore until Raffaele and his friend flash them a signal that we're on our way.'

'That's good. Have you told our Jewish guests about all this?'

'I haven't had the chance yet.'

'Let me do it, please, Papà. I can take them some food at the same time.' Giulia paused to collect her thoughts. 'I don't suppose you have any news about the Canetti family?'

When they'd been taken away yesterday afternoon, they'd all expected them to come back before nightfall. But they hadn't. Although Giulia hadn't had much to do with the middle-aged couple, their adult son and his young wife, she knew that Signora Canetti was Ester's aunt. *She must be so worried about her.*

Her father shook his head, and she caught the guarded expression in his eyes. He wasn't telling her everything, she surmised, but she decided not to pursue the matter and to focus on the task at hand.

Before too long, she was carrying a tray of bread rolls and a pitcher of milk up the central staircase, praying fervently that she wouldn't meet any Germans.

At the top of the stairs, her skin prickled, and she came to a halt. Two guards were striding down the corridor, their backs to her as they headed in the opposite direction. Furtively, she placed the tray on the floor outside the prisoners' room, took the spare key from her pocket, and inserted it into the lock.

The door sprang open, and she stepped inside.

'Giulia!' Ester rushed up to her and they hugged.

'I've brought you all something to eat, and also some news.' Giulia set the food down on a table.

'News about my aunt, uncle and cousins?'

The hope on Ester's face broke Giulia's heart; she shook her head as she took her friend's hand.

'Sorry, but the news isn't about them,' she said.

After the rest of the group gathered around her, she told them about the plan for that night, adding that everyone should be ready to leave as soon as it had been confirmed that their guards had gone to bed. They could only bring with them what they could carry.

'How about the sentries at the front door?' Ester's father asked. 'They take it in turns and there's always a couple of them on duty.'

'We'll have to be extremely quiet,' Giulia said.

* * *

Time slowed down while Giulia tried to distract herself by reading, listening to the radio, and practising her callisthenic exercises (she was in the team at her school, and it was one of the few sports Mussolini encouraged for women). She packed a rucksack, filling it with essentials to tide her over until she and her parents arrived in Switzerland, and then waited for her mother to return.

Mamma came back in the middle of the afternoon, saying that the SS were looting artwork from the villas of the Jews they'd rounded up. She'd gone with Weber to explain to the staff in the villas that they were only taking the valuables into storage to protect them from bomb damage, but as they were loaded onto lorries, Giulia's mother had guessed that the paintings, statues and fine furniture would end up in Germany.

'It was dreadful,' she said, wringing her hands. 'And I couldn't do anything but stand by and translate the obersturmführer's vile words.'

Later, Giulia went with her parents down to the dining room for supper. The despicable soldiers at the next table were sloshing red wine all over the pristine white cloth. Anger heated Giulia's face, and she had to use all her self-control not to go over and give them a piece of her mind.

Finally, the meal had finished, and Giulia and her parents returned upstairs. Her heart skittered through a beat when the unmistakable voice of Weber echoed up the stairwell from the lobby. He'd come to check on his men, of course, but Giulia couldn't help worrying that he'd still be in the hotel when she and the others began their escape.

Raucous sounds rose from the billiard room as the soldiers began to sing their drinking songs, followed by the SS officer's loud voice proposing a toast to the Führer.

'*Sieg heil! Sieg heil! Sieg heil!*' the men responded.

'Perhaps it's good they're getting drunk,' Mamma said. 'This way, they'll sleep better when they go to bed.'

Giulia and her parents waited on tenterhooks until the sound of a vehicle made them believe that Weber had left. The minutes had ticked by until, eventually, silence had settled on the hotel like a shroud. The German soldiers had gone to bed.

'You go and let the prisoners out while I flash my torch from our window,' Giulia's father said. 'Your mother and I will take your bag and meet you in the basement.'

Her stomach churning with nerves, Giulia kissed her parents and then left the suite. The corridor was empty, thank God, and so was the staircase. On the fourth floor, Giulia stopped dead in her tracks. Someone was lurking outside the prisoners' room, and she prepared to run. Squinting her eyes, she made out the shadow of a garden tree, flickering through the glass and reflecting on the carpet in the moonlight. She heaved a huge sigh of relief and unlocked the door.

Ester, her parents, and her little brother and sister were sitting on the mattresses, their coats on, and small pieces of luggage at the ready.

Signor and Signora Kordovero looked up at Giulia from one of the beds, and Signor Maduro from the other.

Giulia placed her finger to her lips to indicate no one should speak. She signalled with her hand that they should all follow her.

Sucking in a deep breath to steady her nerves, she led them down the corridor to the central staircase, then slowly and steadily down the stairs.

A musty smell of mouldy walls and vegetation greeted them in the basement, and their faces took on a ghostly tinge in the lamplight. Giulia's father handed her rucksack to her, gave her his torch and a big iron key, and told her to lead the way.

The bare earth in the narrow passageway was damp and slippery under her feet, but she set her jaw and crept forwards with determination. The inky blackness of the tunnel was punctuated only by the distant drip of water. The low ceiling forced her to hunch low, and her breath caught in her throat.

Oh, my God, what was that?

A rustling sound came from the darkness up ahead, followed by a pair of eyes glinting in the faint light. A rat, sleek and dark, darted across her path, brushing against her foot as it scuttled past. Giulia bit back a scream. Without checking if the others were following her, she scurried as fast as she could towards the end of the tunnel.

Her heart drumming a nervous beat, she removed the key from her pocket and unlocked the rusty old gate. Then she turned around, fully expecting to see her parents, Ester, and Ester's family behind her. But no one was there. Where was everyone? Why hadn't they followed her as arranged? She was about to turn around and head back when shouts came from the direction of the cellar. *German shouts!*

Strong arms grabbed her. Pulse racing, she struggled to free herself. One of the SS sentries on guard duty must have come down to the beach.

'Shush, Giulia!' a voice said. An Italian voice. Raffaele's.

'I have to go back. I can't leave my parents to the Germans.' She heard the desperation in her words.

'Wait until the coast is clear. We don't know what's going on inside the hotel. Come with me now to our hiding place. My friend, Paolo Demichelis, is there.'

Raffaele's tone brooked no argument, and Giulia felt in no fit state for a fight. A sick feeling in her stomach, she allowed herself to be led up from the beach to a thicket of oleander bushes bordering the hotel's driveway, where Paolo introduced himself in a whisper and asked if she was okay.

'As well as can be expected,' she said, grateful for his concern.

'Be quiet, you two!' Raffaele shot them both a look.

Her legs trembling, Giulia lowered herself onto the ground between the two young men. What had gone wrong? Who had woken up the Germans? Where were the fishermen? She squinted through the oleander leaves and could just make out the dark shape of boats down on the lake.

The rumble of engines reverberated in the stillness, and Giulia's chest tightened. A saloon car and lorry were pulling up in the driveway.

Oh, dear Lord. Obersturmführer Weber had arrived with his

second-in-command. Giulia watched as the two men jumped out of the vehicle and marched into the hotel.

She felt as if her entire body had frozen as she sat, helplessly waiting. She didn't have to wait long. Within minutes, Ester and her family were being herded into the truck. Then Weber came into view and Giulia's heart almost stopped beating. He and his second-in-command were pushing and shoving her parents into the lorry with the others.

The vehicle departed, with Weber and his aide following in its wake.

No! Giulia screamed the word silently in her head. This couldn't be happening. But it was happening. There was nothing she could do except allow herself to be led to where Raffaele and Paolo had left their bicycles.

'Jump up!' Raffaele pointed at the handlebars of his bike.

'I have my own bicycle,' she said.

'Where is it?'

'In the garage.' She pointed.

'Too dangerous to fetch it,' he said. 'Jump up!'

She did as he'd commanded. What else could she do? If she went back into the hotel, she'd be arrested and put on a lorry like the others. She inhaled a shuddering breath, making a determined effort not to cry.

'Where are we going?' she asked after she'd perched herself on the handlebars and Raffaele had started pedalling.

'My place. My father will know what to do.'

7

'I'll go in to work in the morning as usual,' Signor Ferrero said, his face ashen, when Giulia and Raffaele had recounted the whole sorry debacle. They'd left Paolo on the outskirts of Baveno and then had wheeled Raffaele's bicycle to his family home, where his father was waiting up for him.

'And I'll try to find out the whereabouts of your parents and the others, Giulia,' he added. 'Hopefully, this is just a misunderstanding, and they'll have been released by the time I get to the hotel.'

'Thank you, Signor Ferrero.' Giulia's voice quavered; she was on the brink of tears and took a deep breath to calm herself.

'Try to get some sleep, my dear. I'll fetch a blanket, and you can have the sofa.'

Again, Giulia thanked him. She stole a glance at Raffaele, but he was ignoring her. *What a jerk!* He could have shown some sympathy towards her. After all, she'd been separated from her mother, father, and friends. But no, he was heading upstairs and leaving her alone with his father.

The small house, just two rooms per floor apparently, was

filled to the brim and Giulia was grateful to Signor Ferrero for putting her up. After he'd shown her the way to the privy in the back garden, which boasted a vegetable plot and a chicken run, she returned indoors to find he'd retired for the night. She took her pyjamas from her rucksack and put them on. Then, huddling under the blanket, she tried to get some sleep.

Her brain wouldn't switch off, though; all she could think about was what could have gone so badly wrong. She chewed at her lip while the events played themselves over in her mind. She should have made sure her parents, Ester and the others were right behind her in the tunnel, and she shouldn't have taken fright when she'd come across the rat. Guilt festered like a stone in her throat.

Hopefully, Obersturmführer Weber would take pity on her parents and release them. They weren't Jewish; they'd done nothing but try to leave the hotel with their guests. But the guests weren't exactly guests, were they? They were the prisoners of those despicable Nazis, and the SS officer would accuse Giulia's parents of aiding and abetting them.

Hot, salty tears trickled down Giulia's face, and she curled herself into a ball.

Time passed, and she finally slept, waking to dawn light and the sound of children's laughter. Raffaele's siblings – all six of them – had tumbled into the room, followed by Raffaele himself, and a beautiful, dark-haired woman, who was clearly his mother.

'*Buongiorno*, signorina,' the woman said. 'I hope you managed to get some sleep.'

'I did, eventually, thanks.' Giulia sat up and clutched the blanket around herself. 'Please, call me Giulia.'

'And I am Ludovica, and these are my children.' She introduced the two boys – Luciano, sixteen, and Giuseppe, thirteen –

and four girls, Anna Maria, Gloria, Margherita and Elena, who ranged in age from eleven to four years old.

Raffaele's siblings were all talking at once, and Giulia couldn't imagine what it must be like to live cheek by jowl with so many kids. She smiled at them but couldn't get a word in edgeways as they fired questions at her, to which no one waited for an answer. What was she doing in their house? When did she arrive? What had happened to her parents?

She answered as politely as she could. But it was hard. She had no idea what had happened to her parents and friends other than the fact they'd been taken away by the Germans. Conveying that fact to the Ferrero family brought it all back to her, and her voice cracked with emotion as she spoke.

'Please,' Raffaele said. 'Leave the girl in peace, guys. Go have your breakfast, then get ready for school.'

Within seconds, Giulia had been left to her own devices. She got dressed and went through to the kitchen, which was empty of everyone except Ludovica, who gave her a cup of milky ersatz coffee and a brioche.

Anxiety had taken Giulia's appetite, but she forced herself to nibble the pastry so as not to offend. Had Signor Ferrero discovered what had happened to her parents and the others? Oh, how she hoped they were all right...

'Can I do anything else to help?' she asked, after she'd given Ludovica a hand with the washing-up.

'No, my dear. I'm about to go to the market to see if there are any vegetables available, but you'd best stay here.'

Alone in the house – she had no idea where Raffaele had gone – all Giulia could do was fret. Would Signor Ferrero send a message about her parents? How would it be possible for him to even do so? And where was Raffaele? She kept glancing at her wristwatch while she waited for Ludovica to come home, waited for news, waited for this nightmare to end. She needed to do something, anything, but what? If she left the house, she could bump into Germans who would ask for her ID. They would find out who she was and arrest her, which wouldn't do anyone any good.

After spending the rest of the day on tenterhooks, only distracted by helping Ludovica in the kitchen and listening to her children talk about their day when they came home from school, Giulia found herself alone again, sitting on the sofa, staring at the wall in front of her. There'd been no news either from Signor Ferrero or from Raffaele, and her throat thickened with despair. She kept repeating the adage 'no news is good news', but it was a vain hope. After the Canetti family had been taken for 'interrogation', there'd been no news about them either...

Voices broke into her thoughts; Signor Ferrero was coming into the room with his wife and Raffaele. Giulia jumped up from the sofa and went to him.

'Have the Germans released my parents and the others?' she asked, her eyes begging him to say yes.

'I'm so sorry, Giulia. You'd better sit down. The news is not good, I'm afraid.'

'Are they still in Baveno?' she asked.

'Raffaele and Paolo know someone who's a cleaner at the German HQ, and this person said that the Germans had been holding a man and woman, who match the description of your parents. Just before the cleaner clocked off work, late this morning, your parents were escorted to the train station.'

'The train station?' Giulia shook her head in disbelief. 'Why?'

'I went to find out.' Raffaele took up the tale. 'A porter, who once worked in your hotel, saw them being accompanied by an armed guard onto a train heading for Milan.'

Giulia gasped. She felt the blood drain from her head and a sudden dizziness almost overcame her.

Raffaele's mother put her arm around her, patted her on the shoulder and said, 'You're being very brave.'

'What about my Jewish friends?' Giulia took a breath. 'Do you know what's happened to them?'

A look passed between Raffaele and his father, but they both shook their heads.

'All we know,' Signor Ferrero said, 'is that they weren't dropped off at the SS HQ with your parents.'

'I was certain the Germans had gone to bed last night, but someone must have still been up, and they must have heard us go down in the cellar.' Giulia sighed. 'I thought we were being really quiet.'

'It was bad luck, my dear,' Signor Ferrero said. 'But Weber is furious you got away, and I had to lie to him when he came to the hotel that I had no idea who'd helped you.'

'Is he looking for me?'

'I'm afraid so.'

A cold sweat coated Giulia's body and her mind raced with myriad questions. Was she putting the Ferrero family at risk? Maybe she should leave? But where could she hide from the SS?

'Would you be able to telephone the German consul general in Milan and ask him to help?' she asked.

'I did so this afternoon, but he said the matter is out of his hands. I got the impression, from his tone, that he wished he could have done something but couldn't say so for fear of the phone being tapped.'

'Oh, God, what will happen to me now?' Giulia's voice trembled.

'You can't return to Marta. Neither can you go to your apartment in Milan. It's best you leave with Raffaele and Paolo tomorrow.'

'Where are you going?' Giulia glanced at Raffaele.

'The boys are heading for my cousin's farm in Ungiasca. There are few Fascists in the area and no Germans.' Signor Ferrero answered for his son. 'It would be a good place for you to keep a low profile. In return, you could offer to help with milking the cows, etcetera.'

Giulia frowned. She'd never milked a cow before, but she could learn. Surely, the war would end soon. The Allies were on their way and would send the Nazis packing. Then her parents, Ester, and Ester's family would return and life would go back to how it was before all this heartache happened. Giulia just had to get through it, make the best of things, and be here for them when they returned. If not, she would go and find them herself.

'I'll do whatever I can,' she said. 'You can rely on me.'

'Brava.' Signor Ferrero patted her on the shoulder. 'Now, I must be heading back to Marta before I'm missed.'

'Thank you for all that you have done for me,' she said.

Raffaele's father seemed at a loss for words. He gave her a sad smile and wished her goodbye.

'You can take my bicycle,' Ludovica chipped in. 'I don't use it much.'

'*Grazie.*' Giulia thanked her. 'Please, have mine instead. That's if you can retrieve it from the hotel. I don't want to put you out.'

Later, after supper, when she was getting ready for bed, she heard Raffaele and his mother's voices echoing from the kitchen. Curious, she went to the door and listened.

'I don't see why Paolo and I have to take Giulia with us,' Raffaele was saying. 'She's a spoilt brat and will never adapt to life on the farm. She'll be more of a hindrance than a help.'

'I think you're wrong, son. I spent most of the day with Giulia and there's more to her than meets the eye.'

Giulia's spine stiffened with indignation. She hated Raffaele for being so judgemental and arrogant. How dare he categorise her? She'd show him that his mother was right; there was definitely more to her than met the eye.

The door suddenly opened, and Raffaele came through, nearly knocking Giulia off her feet as he barged past. He shot her a withering look, and she glared back at him.

He really was an odious so-and-so.

PART II

OCTOBER 1943–
FEBRUARY 1944

8

Giulia concentrated hard as she sat on a stool, squeezing milk from the teats of a cow. When she'd first arrived at Signor Ferrero's cousins, the Bertrandi family's farm, a month ago, she'd thought she'd never get the hang of milking. Her arm and hand muscles were weak and would hurt for hours afterwards. Emptying a cow's udder would take about thirty minutes, and she had two to do before breakfast. She was onto her second one now, and she was so tired she couldn't wait to finish.

As she milked, Giulia dwelt on her life since leaving Marta. After depositing her with the Bertrandis, Raffaele and Paolo had gone to stay in a stone hut known as a *baita*, built on the Alpe Aurelio mountain pasture high above the village, where Signor Bertrandi herded his animals every summer to escape the heat. Giulia had been glad not to suffer Raffaele's arrogant presence a minute longer than necessary – his comment to Ludovica still rankled – and Giulia was even more happy he'd been conspicuous by his absence from that moment onwards.

What she hadn't been happy about, though, was the fact that she'd had no news about her parents and Ester. She missed them dreadfully. Where were they? How were they? Her heart had been aching so much she was surprised it still functioned. She felt isolated and abandoned and completely helpless. If she weren't wanted by the Germans, she'd have left for Milan immediately and gone to her father's office, where his deputy, Signor Perego, would be holding the fort. Then she would have begged him to give her money for living expenses while she did everything she could to find her loved ones and bring them home.

Giulia released a heavy sigh. Life was hard on the farm, much harder than she'd thought it would be. She rose at daylight in the room she shared with Silvana Bertrandi, who was her age, and Silvana's sister, Concetta, two years younger, to milk the cows and then help make butter and cheese to be sold on the black market.

Every morning, she and the two sisters would light their candles and stumble downstairs, carrying their chamber pots with the contents slopping around. After they'd emptied them, they went to the yard behind the house, where they pumped a jet of water into a large stone trough. Giulia would often put her head under the stream of water to help wake up with a jolt. Then she'd brush her teeth, and the water was so icy it made them sting.

While Giulia and the girls were milking, Signor Bertrandi would muck out the pigsties and cowsheds, and his wife would be in the kitchen, getting the cast-iron stove going, its silver-painted stovepipe rising like a chimney stack and vanishing into the wall just under the ceiling.

After breakfast – warm milk stirred into barley coffee into which the family dunked chunks of stale bread – Signor Bertrandi would go outside to tend to his animals (besides the cows, there were chickens, ducks, geese and rabbits) and Giulia would help the girls with butter and cheese production. It was tiring work but, at midday, the family stopped for lunch – generally a thick vegetable soup with beans and pasta, bread with cheese, and wine. Everyone was too tired to do anything but eat, and as soon as the meal was over, and Giulia had helped the sisters clear away the dishes and wash up, everyone except Signora Bertrandi, who would spend the time knitting, fell asleep over the table for an hour.

In the afternoons, Giulia and the two sisters carried on churning butter and cheddaring, salting and shaping the cheeses they'd made that morning before preparing the evening meal. It was such a different life to what Giulia was used to, but she never complained, far from it; she wouldn't give Raffaele the satisfaction. Instead, she'd bend over backwards to be accommodating, clinging to the hope that the war would shortly end, that this was only a temporary situation, and she would be reunited with her parents and friends soon. If not, she would have to take matters into her own hands and go and find them herself.

Before going to bed, she and the Bertrandis would listen to the BBC's *Radio Londra*, on shortwave, although it was forbidden, to avoid being bombarded with Nazi-fascist propaganda on the regular stations. A month ago, Mussolini had established the Italian Social Republic, a puppet regime whose strings were pulled by Hitler. There'd been good news amongst the bad, however; after a popular uprising in the city, Allied troops had entered Naples and now controlled most of the southern part of Italy. Everyone hoped they would break through to Rome soon, then make haste to liberate the north. Giulia prayed fervently for that to be so.

At least the SS were no longer detaining Jews in the area; the *Leibstandarte SS Adolf Hitler* had been sent to fight the partisans in Yugoslavia, and Giulia hoped they'd soon be given a taste of their own vile medicine. A German presence remained, however, with the *Feldgendarmerie* commanding local Fascist militiamen, who were capturing Italians who'd deserted from the armed forces, as well as rounding up youths like Raffaele and Paolo to be sent to work camps. Giulia's chest tightened with apprehension. Signor Bertrandi had informed her that she was still wanted by the *tedeschi*, given that she was the only person they could identify as being involved in the Marta escape attempt. Neither Raffaele nor Paolo's names had been revealed; they'd flown completely under the enemy's radar. The only reason they'd gone into hiding, as far as Giulia was aware, was because they feared being used as slave labour by the Germans like so many young men their age.

The cow's udder felt soft and empty now, so Giulia dipped the teats in an iodine-based solution to disinfect them. From the corner of her eye, she saw that Silvana and Concetta had also finished milking, so she got up off her stool and fell into step beside them as they headed towards the farmhouse for breakfast.

Strangely, Signor Bertrandi wasn't there, and Giulia didn't see him until just before lunch. He gave no explanation about where he'd been, and she thought it impolite to ask.

But when the meal was over and she made a move to go and help with the washing-up, he indicated with his hand that she should remain seated.

She did as requested and gave him a sidelong look.

'I went to see the *ragazzi* this morning,' he said. He always referred to Raffaele and Paolo as 'the guys'.

'Oh?' She tilted her head towards him.

'I went to tell them you can't stay here any more, my dear.'

For a split second, words failed her, and then she asked, 'Is it because I haven't been pulling my weight?'

'Not at all, you've worked hard, but there's been talk in

Ungiasca about you and I don't want to put my family at risk.' He gave her an apologetic smile.

'But where will I go?' She couldn't keep the dismay from her voice.

'You can hide out at the *baita*,' he said. 'No one will know you are there.'

'But what will I do all day?'

'The *ragazzi* will appreciate having someone to cook and clean for them, I'm sure.'

Giulia wanted to argue that she wasn't a maid, only she didn't have a leg to stand on. She felt as if she was a piece of baggage being passed from pillar to post, but all she could do was force a smile and ask, 'When do I leave?'

'The guys will come and fetch you after supper, so you should have your bag packed before then. I'm sorry it's come to this, but I'm sure you'll understand.'

Giulia nodded; what else could she do? Signor Bertrandi was already nodding off for his post-lunch nap, and his daughters had returned to the table to do likewise.

Agitation jittered in her belly. Clearly, she was still a wanted person and, of course, she didn't want the Bertrandis to suffer for harbouring a fugitive. She got to her feet and made her way upstairs to repack the bag she'd brought with her from Marta.

* * *

Later, after supper, Giulia watched as the Bertrandi sisters went to stand before a small mirror on the wall by the stairs. With pins in their mouths they combed their hair, barging one another out of the way to have a better view before pinning their long, dark tresses into rolls at the nape of their necks. Giulia had no chance of pushing between them, but she wore her own hair in braids to keep it tidy, and, in any case, she saw no need to make herself presentable for arrogant Raffaele.

A knock sounded at the door, and Signor Bertrandi went to open it. He led the two young men to the table and offered them a glass of wine.

Giulia hovered next to a piece of furniture known as a *madia*, in which the flour used to make the pasta was kept. She gave an inward sigh; she'd accepted her fate with resignation as there was nothing else she could do. *For the time being.*

But Raffaele seemed to have other plans.

'Wouldn't it be better for Giulia to help the nuns at the TB sanatorium in Miazzina?' he said. 'It's where we go to get rations after being contacted by a committee set up in Verbania to support the *resistenza*. Her reputation might be tarnished if word got out that she was living with a couple of men.'

'You could ask the nuns, but do that in your own time, my boy. I'd like you to take Giulia to the *baita* tonight, as arranged.'

Chewing at her lip, Giulia kept silent about the TB sanatorium. She'd do everything she could to avoid being sent there. The thought of it gave her the heebie-jeebies.

The fact that the *ragazzi* were being supported by a committee set up to aid the Resistance had sparked an idea, though. She must have some skills that could be used against the enemy. What these abilities were, she had yet to discover but discover them she would. It would be something useful she could do until such time as it was safe for her to head for Milan to contact her father's deputy and find out where the Germans had taken her parents and Ester.

9

The following morning, Giulia found herself waking up in a hayloft above the barn next to the hut. The straw bedding was damp and smelt of mould, but she'd slept deeply after the one-hour hike up the steep mountainside. Thankfully, there'd been a full moon lighting the path, otherwise she'd have been at risk of tumbling down into the valley.

She stretched her tired muscles, then climbed down the ladder, balancing her chamber pot under one arm. After emptying it, she went to a stone trough, with a pipe of freezing water – presumably fed from a mountain spring – where she washed her face.

Directly below, the river Toce wound its way towards its mouth in Verbania, where it emptied itself into the deep blue waters of the lake. On the other side of the *lago*, in Lombardy province, the scenic town of Laveno hugged the shoreline, its pretty terracotta-tiled buildings shaded from the morning sun by the steep Sasso del Ferro crag behind. *Breathtaking*. Giulia released a sigh. If only she could share this beautiful panorama with her loved ones. How she prayed they were safe.

With a heavy heart, she turned and headed for the stone-built *baita* across the yard. The squat, grey, shed-like building appeared to have been flattened by its undulating slate slab roof. She pushed open the wobbly wooden door and went inside.

The *ragazzi* were in the kitchen area of the one room, their blankets spread on the flagstone floor.

'*Ciao*, Giulia. Would you like a cup of coffee?' Paolo poked at the kindling in a wood-burning stove, which was similar to the one at the Bertrandis', with a pipe rising like a chimney stack.

'*Sì, grazie.*' She thanked him and pulled out a rickety chair at the big oak table. 'What do the two of you do with yourselves all day?'

'We keep surprisingly busy,' Raffaele said curtly. 'Between gathering wood and chopping it, going to Miazzina for supplies, and practising target shooting, time passes quickly enough.'

'I'd like to help as much as I can.' Giulia took a sip of coffee. 'Until you get rid of me, that is.'

Raffaele glanced away from her, but she detected no shame in his face. Did he really dislike her? Or was he simply worried about her reputation, like he'd said last night?

'How about you and I go foraging in the woods, Giulia?' A smile tugged at Paolo's lips, and he pushed his dark blond hair back from his forehead. 'There're mushrooms all over the place, and I've been making some great risottos with them.'

'Sounds like a good plan. I'd love to do that.'

After breakfast – which consisted of stale bread dunked into coffee like she'd had at the Bertrandis' – Giulia set off with Paolo, basket in hand. Luckily, Silvana had lent her a pair of mountain boots, or she'd have found the going difficult. The earth was squidgy underfoot with fallen leaves, but the golden and russet colours in the canopy of chestnut trees were magical.

'It's lovely here,' Giulia said. 'But how do you know which mushrooms are poisonous and which aren't?'

'I used to go mushrooming with my big sister, Teresa, and her husband, Massimo, before the war, so I learnt all about which ones are safe.' A shadow crossed Paolo's face as he shifted the weight of the rifle he'd slung over his shoulder. 'Massimo was killed in Russia last February and now Teresa has become an anti-Fascist activist in the factory where she works.'

'I'm sorry to hear that,' Giulia said. 'I mean about her husband.'

'What Mussolini did to our country was criminal.' Paolo bent to pick a mushroom and placed it in Giulia's basket. 'He deserves to be shot.'

'I wonder if that'll ever happen.'

'Maybe. That'll depend on how this godforsaken war ends.'

'Let's hope it will be soon.' Giulia breathed a sigh. 'I want my old life back again.'

'Me too. I miss my fiancée and my family.'

'Does Raffaele have a *fidanzata*?' The question left Giulia's lips before she'd even thought about it. She felt her cheeks grow hot and hoped Paolo hadn't thought she was interested in his friend.

Paolo laughed and said that Raffaele liked to play the field.

Of course he does. He's arrogant enough to expect women to fall for him left, right and centre. Giulia kept her thoughts to herself, though, and she and Paolo lapsed into silence as they foraged until the basket was full.

* * *

Paolo turned out to be an excellent cook, and the mushroom risotto he made for lunch was delicious. Giulia washed the

dishes while the *ragazzi* snoozed. She left the plates to dry in the
rack above the sink before returning to the table. But she
couldn't settle. Where would she be this time tomorrow? Would
she be scrubbing floors in the sanatorium? The thought made
her feel slightly nauseous.

What she really wanted to do was to return to Marta. When
she'd asked Raffaele last night before bed if that could be
arranged, he'd been curt and had said that the *Feldgendarmerie*
were looking for her. If she returned to the hotel, she might put
his father and the staff in danger.

A sudden loud knock banged at the door of the hut, and
Giulia almost jumped out of her skin. Surely the Germans hadn't
found out she was here...

Raffaele and Paolo leapt to their feet, grabbing the rifles that
were never far from their reach. They went to the front window
and peered outside.

'It's my sister, Teresa,' Paolo said, a smile spreading across his
face.

A tall woman of Amazonian stature with bobbed auburn
hair, whom Giulia guessed to be in her early twenties, came into
the hut, a rucksack slung over her shoulder. She kissed both
ragazzi on their cheeks and shook hands with Giulia when
introduced.

'It's good to see you, sis,' Paolo said, pulling out a chair for her
at the kitchen table. 'But why are you here and how did you
find me?'

'I'm in trouble with the Fascists.' Teresa shook her head. 'A
spy in the factory caught me sabotaging some goods due to be
sent to Germany. I managed to get away before I was arrested. I
contacted the secret committee in Verbania that supports the
Resistance – one of my anti-Fascist friends had told me about it –
and, remembering you'd gone to Raffaele's cousin's place, I made

my way there. Signor Bertrandi showed me the path to this *baita*.'

'So, you're hiding from the enemy like us?' Raffaele poured her a glass of water from the jug that was always kept filled from the outside pump.

'Indeed. I also have a message for you from the committee.' Teresa took a sip of water. 'A group of six escaped Allied prisoners of war is being brought to Fondotoce by train, and they want you to escort them to a place above Cannobio, from where some smugglers will take them across the border into Switzerland.'

'Finally, a job we can sink our teeth into.' Paolo rubbed his hands together.

'They'll arrive tomorrow morning,' Teresa said. 'And the committee needs you to let them stay here until a messenger turns up when it's time to convey them across the mountains.'

'Tomorrow was when we were planning on taking Giulia to the sanatorium.' Raffaele frowned.

'Why would you do that?' Teresa asked.

'It's not right for a girl to be living with a couple of men.'

'Now I'm here, I can be her chaperone.' Teresa winked.

'I think it would be safer for you in the sanatorium, too, Teresa,' Raffaele said. 'You can help out on the wards.'

'I'm not a skivvy.' Teresa shook her head. 'I'm here to contribute to the cause, and I'm sure Giulia feels the same.'

Giulia smiled and nodded; she liked the direction the conversation was going. Her idea about being able to join the Resistance might come to fruition after all. Only as a temporary measure, of course. Her primary goal was still to find her way to Milan; she might even be able to contact the German consul general and ask him to help find her loved ones.

'The committee didn't know about Giulia,' Teresa said. 'But

they told me that women are already playing a big role in the Resistance. The Nazi-fascists are such misogynists they don't believe females have the wherewithal to be rebels. Consequently, we can move about unnoticed, carrying messages and conduct even more dangerous tasks with impunity.'

'I had an English governess when I was little,' Giulia said, her chest tingling with excitement. 'I speak the language quite well and could interpret for you, Raffaele, when the Allied POWs arrive.'

'Why doesn't that surprise me?' He gave her a disparaging look. 'Girls like you lack for nothing.'

'There's no need to be so judgemental.' Giulia folded her arms. 'I didn't ask to be born into a wealthy family.'

'Giulia is doing the best that she can, Raffaele.' Paolo patted his arm.

She winced with embarrassment, but she refused to succumb to mortification and pulled herself up to her somewhat insignificant height instead.

'I won't let you down,' she said.

'Good wine comes in small bottles.' Teresa met her eye. 'I bet you're full of surprises.'

'I wouldn't go as far as to say that.' Giulia fanned the heat from her face.

'The committee said we must choose battle names and hide our identity documents until the conflict is over.' Teresa changed the subject.

'Why?' Giulia asked.

'It's obvious.' Raffaele smirked. 'If we're caught and they find out who we really are, our families could suffer.'

Pain pierced Giulia's chest. Raffaele had rubbed salt into her wound. Swallowing hard, she turned away so he wouldn't notice the tears prickling her eyes.

'I've always liked the name Luna.' Teresa glanced at Giulia. 'What name will you pick?'

'Hmmm.' She took a breath. 'I remember my governess reading me *Peter Pan* when I was little, and she would call me Tinkerbell because I'm so short.'

'Tinkerbell is too English,' Raffaele said gruffly.

'Then I could be Piccola, instead. Nothing to do with Peter Pan, but I'm small so why not be called "Little One"?' Giulia shot Raffaele a defiant look. 'What would be your battle name?'

'Maybe Lele?' He grinned. 'It's a bit close to Raffaele, but I couldn't answer to anything else.'

'And I could be Biondo because of the colour of my hair,' Paolo said.

'All sorted then.' A smile curved Teresa's lips.

'Not so fast.' Raffaele held up his hands. 'You and Giulia will have to prove yourselves equal to the job before I allow you to stay.'

'You need have no worries on my score.' Teresa shot him a fierce look.

'Mine neither.' Giulia set her jaw, but doubt washed through her. Would she be up to the task? She would, she decided. Whatever it cost, she would prove to Raffaele she was a force to be reckoned with. Hadn't Ester said she was the most confident girl she'd ever met?

Oh, Ester...

* * *

Melodic male voices and the sound of splashing echoed from out in the yard early the following morning. Giulia rolled over on the straw where she'd been sleeping next to Teresa and gave her a nudge.

'The *ragazzi* are up,' she said with a yawn.

'I suppose we should wait until they've finished washing.' Teresa giggled. 'We don't want to see anything we shouldn't be seeing.'

Snuggling into her blanket, Giulia pushed the thought of what she shouldn't be seeing from her mind. Her experience of the opposite sex had been limited to a few stolen kisses at high school dances. She'd never brought a boy home to meet her parents; something told her that Papà would have grilled the young man as if he were applying for a job, and Giulia hadn't met anyone she was interested in enough to put through that.

Her thoughts turned inevitably to her parents. She missed them so much; it was like an ache deep in her soul. How long would she have to remain in isolation up here in the mountains? She needed to get to Milan as soon as she could.

Distractedly, she scratched at an itch on her thigh and longed for a nice, warm bath. Such luxury was well in the past, as was running water, both hot and cold. At the Bertrandi farm, bathing was only done on Sunday mornings before attending mass, when a tin tub was brought out of storage and placed in front of the hearth. The rest of the time, like now at the *baita*, she'd had to content herself with sponge baths. Last night, she and Teresa had carried basins of water to the barn, where they'd shivered while getting themselves clean for bed.

Within minutes more voices joined those of the *ragazzi* outside, and it was clear that the escaped POWs had arrived.

'Should we go down and help with breakfast?' Giulia asked.

'I suppose so. But the men must do their share, or they won't think of us as equals.'

'You're very strong, Teresa. I hope I can be as strong as you.'

'You'd better start calling me Luna, Piccola. We're about to meet a group of strangers, so now is the right time. And, as for strength, you'll be surprised how much you have when you're called upon to use it.'

'Everything is so different to what I'm used to. Raffaele, or should I say Lele, thinks I'm a spoilt brat – I overheard him saying so to his mother – and I'm determined to prove him wrong. It's hard, though.'

'Lele has a chip on his shoulder. I've known him since he and Paolo became friends when they were at elementary school together. The oppression that boys suffered under Mussolini, the indoctrination and forced adherence to the Fascist youth organisations, it affected Paolo. Made him cling to his family, his sweetheart, and buddies. Lele seems to have developed a resentful outlook, and it might take time for him to get over it.'

Giulia sighed, remembering how she'd make excuses to get out of the Saturday meetings of the *Giovani Italiane*, Mussolini's organisation for girls. She'd hated the courses on childcare, flower arranging, and crafts. In contrast with the boys' military drills, the girls had 'doll drills', where they paraded with their dolls, careful to hold them as if they were real babies. Boys had to promise to give their lives in battle to Italy, but girls were made to promise to endure the dangers of childbirth and serve their families. Giulia had wanted more from life; she'd wanted a university education followed by a job. What that job would be, she didn't know; she simply sought the opportunity to choose and not have her future foisted on her by a dictator.

'Let's go meet the Allied prisoners, Luna,' she said. 'If I can help by interpreting, maybe I'll show Lele I have just as much right to be here as he does.'

'I like your attitude, Piccola. *Andiamo!*'

* * *

The six escaped prisoners turned out to be two New Zealanders, a South African, one Australian and two Englishman. They told Giulia, while having breakfast, that they'd been held in a camp to the north of Modena, and that they'd been assisted since escaping by a group from Milan.

Three chaperons had taken them to Modena train station early in the morning two days ago, escorting them from the farmhouse where they'd been hiding. The guides had given them each an overcoat, a hat, a pair of shoes and a scarf, which they were expected to hand back before crossing the border. They were also given food for the journey, a railway ticket, and an Italian newspaper to pretend to read on the way.

Subdivided so as not to appear obvious, they'd embarked with one of the chaperons in a crowded carriage in the middle of the train, while the other two guides got on the first and last coaches, respectively. When Fascist militiamen began checking the passengers – which experience had shown always started from one end of the train or the other – the chaperons at the two ends of the train warned the POWs in the middle, so they could get off at the next stop and get on again in the carriages which had already been checked.

'We spent the night in Milan station, in an empty train due to depart some hours later,' Piet, the South African, said as he dunked stale bread into his coffee. 'A few minutes before it left, we were transferred to another train, and then to a third. After curfew had ended, the guides led us to a safe house, where we rested and were fed, then given more rail tickets and taken to the train which brought us to the lake today.'

'The chaperons escorted us as far as Ungiasca and showed us the way up here,' one of the Englishmen added.

Piet spoke a little Italian, but the other five didn't, and Giulia interpreted their story to her companions with ease. Both Teresa and Paolo praised her efforts, but Raffaele merely scowled and then said he would go to Miazzina for supplies as they barely had enough to eat themselves, let alone for six prisoners of war.

Giulia ignored him; she had too much to think about. The story of the POWs' escape had sparked her interest. They'd travelled from Milan without being discovered. Maybe she, too, could do that? But how? She would need help, but who could she ask? Remembering the old adage *'volere è potere'*, she resolved not to succumb to defeat. 'Where there's a will, there's a way' had been the motto she'd lived by since early childhood. She wouldn't give up on it now.

* * *

For the next week, Giulia and the others followed the same routine: the escapees hid in the hut during the day while Raffaele and Paolo went for supplies and Giulia and Teresa foraged. Finally, a messenger arrived with a military tent, and said everything had been arranged for the men to be taken across the border, and they were to set off the following morning and hike over the mountains, sleeping in the tent en route to where the smugglers would lead them to the Swiss frontier.

On the POWs' last night, after Paolo had made his signature mushroom risotto for supper, Giulia was in the kitchen, perched on a rickety wooden chair between Teresa and Piet, the South African. Burning wood crackled in the stove, and Giulia leant towards the radiating heat to warm her body. Teresa had been passed a bottle of grappa by Raffaele, from which she swigged before handing it to Giulia. She took a small sip and passed it to Piet. The South African tipped his head back and swallowed a mouthful. His eyes watered and he coughed.

'What's this made of? Tastes like firewater and has a kick like a mule.'

'Distilled skins, pulp, seeds, and stems left over from wine-making after pressing the grapes,' Giulia said. 'It's excellent for digestion.'

'What are you discussing?' Raffaele asked, shuffling his chair towards them.

Giulia started to fill him in, only for him to cut her off and say, 'It's time for bed. We have an early start tomorrow.'

Not a word of thanks, and his terse tone made her nostrils flare, but Giulia kept her cool. One day, she would have words with Raffaele. *When the time was right.* She rose to her feet, and Teresa did likewise. They wished everyone *buonanotte*, bid farewell to the POWs, who were leaving with the *ragazzi* before daylight, and went through the door, across the yard, and up the wooden ladder to the hayloft.

* * *

The following morning, Giulia woke to silence. She took her time getting up, waiting until hunger pangs forced her to stir.

Down in the kitchen, she found Teresa brewing a pot of barley coffee.

'Are you up for some target practice?' Teresa asked as she poured them both a mug.

'Target practice? What do you mean?'

'We need to be able to shoot if we want to stay with the *ragazzi*. Things are quiet at the moment, but with more and more rebels arriving on the mountainside, the Nazi-fascists won't put up with it for long, and I imagine they'll try to get rid of us all. So, Piccola, if you want to fight back, which I expect you do after what happened to your parents and

Jewish friends, then you'll have to learn how to use a weapon.'

'I wish I knew where the Germans took them.' Giulia sipped her coffee. 'There has been no news—'

'I know the feeling. My husband was killed in Russia, but I lived in limbo for months until I got the news. It's what made me want to join the Resistance. You have good reason to do the same, Piccola. We mustn't let Raffaele shunt us off to that sanatorium.'

'I'm sorry about your husband. I hate the Nazis so much for their antisemitism. And the Fascists for colluding with them. I can only pray that my loved ones are okay, and we'll be reunited sooner rather than later.'

'That's why we must fight back,' Teresa said. 'To end the war as soon as possible. Let's finish our breakfast and take a couple of rifles from the stash at the back of the room. My father taught me how to shoot when I was younger. He was a keen huntsman until he got too old for it. Paolo and I learnt a lot from him.'

'Is it very difficult?' Giulia asked.

'It can be hard at first, but once you've mastered the fundamentals, you'll be fine.'

Would she get the hang of it? Giulia fidgeted with one of her braids of hair. More to the point, would she ever be able to shoot at a person with the intention of killing them? She would have to, she decided, if she was to help bring the war to an end. She would do all that she could to make that happen, even if it meant the risk of dying herself.

* * *

Out in the yard, Teresa set an empty tin can on top of a barrel and showed Giulia how to stand with her feet apart, approximately at shoulder-width, square to the target. Once Giulia had confirmed she was right-handed, Teresa demonstrated how to hold the fore stock with her left hand, elbow pointing down, before going on to coach her on what to do.

After listening carefully, Giulia took aim and squeezed the trigger. The bullet missed the can, and she moaned in disappointment.

'Keep practising, Piccola,' Teresa said. 'Practice makes perfect.'

It took ten tries, but eventually Giulia succeeded in shooting the can off the barrel.

'Great shot!' Teresa patted her on the back. 'You're a natural. It took me weeks of practice before I could achieve half of what you've done in just one morning.'

'I can't quite believe it,' Giulia said, pride swelling her chest as they headed back indoors. 'This is something I never expected I'd be doing in my life.'

'War does that. It makes people do things they wouldn't have otherwise contemplated. Both good and bad. We can only pray that peace will come soon. But for that to happen, the *nazifascisti* must be defeated and we all need to play a role.'

'I realise that. My parents and friends must have been terrified when they were taken away from the hotel. How could the Nazis have done that to them?'

'I don't know, Piccola. It's terrible.'

Giulia sucked in a breath as sorrow wrenched at her heart, and a lone tear trickled down her cheek.

10

'I've been teaching Giulia how to shoot,' Teresa said when Raffaele and Paolo returned the next day. 'She's learnt incredibly fast and is an excellent shooter.'

'What?' Raffaele felt his muscles tighten in anger. 'Who gave you permission to do that?'

'Sorry?' Teresa's face had turned red. 'Nobody told me we had a leader—'

'I thought it was understood. Lele is in charge here,' Paolo said. 'Someone has to be, and he's the best person for the job.'

'If you and Giulia are to be part of this group, you must realise we are a military formation with a structure of command.' Raffaele made firm eye contact with Teresa. 'It's how things work. Accept it or leave. Your decision.'

He caught the girls giving each other a look.

'I want to stay,' Giulia said.

'So do I,' Teresa added.

'Then you'll do as you're told. Only what you are told. No more taking your own initiative, okay?'

Both women nodded, and Raffaele couldn't resist smiling.

'So, you've been engaging in target practice, have you?'

'I managed to shoot a can off a barrel,' Giulia said in a proud tone of voice.

'Really? That's not bad for a beginner.'

He caught the flush blooming on her cheeks. It made her seem younger than she was, and he chided himself for not insisting that she seek refuge in the sanatorium. She would be putting her life in danger, staying with him and the others. But who was he to deny her the chance to fight back? After all, it was what he, Paolo, and Teresa were doing, and she clearly wanted to do the same.

'When we handed the POWs over to the smugglers above Cannobio, they mentioned there's an officer from Treviso who's set up a base with some soldiers from his unit at the Alpe Steppio summer pastures,' Raffaele said, changing the topic. 'They're heavily engaged in escorting Allied prisoners of war across the mountain to the smugglers.'

'So, we're not the only rebels in the area?' Teresa grinned. 'When do we get to meet them?'

'Soon. But first Biondo and I will do a reconnoitre and find out if they're *bona fide*.'

'Can't we come too?' Giulia asked.

'Definitely not,' Raffaele snapped. 'Don't question my decisions, Piccola. You must learn to be a good soldier and follow orders.'

He caught the brief stare, filled with challenge, and the fleeting curl of her lip before she nodded.

'I'll do that,' she said.

'Good girl. Now, let's all head for bed. Biondo and I have had a long day and we're tired.'

* * *

A week later, Raffaele left with Paolo for Alpe Steppio, and as they hiked the steep mule paths between the thick conifers, he remembered his father's words, '*Mountains are the strength of a man who surpasses himself by confronting his own limits, both physical and mental. You cannot lie to mountains; you cannot look for excuses or postpone decisions: giving the best of yourself is a must.*'

Never were truer words spoken. Mountaineering had been his passion since he was in his early teens, and he loved it for the challenge it represented, the reward of overcoming obstacles, the sense of accomplishment, the beauty of the natural world, and the thrill of adventure. It was also a way to push his personal limits, connect with nature, and experience a unique sense of freedom. Up here was where he felt happiest. Even now, living rough with no guarantee of survival and the uncertainty of what was to come, he couldn't help feeling the thrill of his surroundings and the desire to exert himself.

The track, supported at times by dry stone walls, entered a beech forest, offering a beautiful view of the Nivia valley and Steppio, their destination, on the opposite side of the gorge. The route continued halfway up the gradient, with a succession of short climbs and descents and the need to cross a couple of fords through streams of gushing water surrounded by the woodland.

Finally, they arrived at a group of low rock-built buildings with their ubiquitous slate roofs, set in the middle of a strip of meadow lit by sunlight filtering through the trees.

'Halt, who goes there?' a gruff voice growled.

Raffaele and Paolo identified themselves with their battle names and asked to be taken to the commander. But a man was already approaching who, from his demeanour, was plainly in charge.

'I'm Aquila.' The officer bore a striking resemblance to his eagle battle name, with his beaky nose, tawny hair and pin-sharp eyes.

He led them to a hut, where Raffaele counted fifteen men, whom Aquila proceeded to introduce before saying they had ten army rifles between them, as well as a few pistols. Their aim was to steal more from the Fascists as soon as possible.

'We have six rifles of our own, plus half a kilo of gelignite, Italian hand grenades and several pistols at our *baita*,' Raffaele boasted. 'They were collected after the armistice and transported in suitcases from Milano to Verbania, from where messengers brought them to us.'

'Ah, yes, the famous committee in Verbania.' Aquila smiled. 'They send us escaped Allied POWs to escort to smugglers who guide them across the border into Switzerland.'

'That's how we learnt about you,' Paolo said. 'The committee had us carry out the same task last week. It wasn't much fun.'

'How many are in your group?' Aquila asked.

'Just four.' Raffaele glanced at Aquila. 'Biondo and me, Biondo's sister Luna, and a girl who goes by the name of Piccola. The committee said they'll be sending us some recruits to swell our ranks soon.'

'How about you bring the next lot of POWs to us, and we'll handle the transfer?' Aquila pierced him with his pin-sharp gaze. 'There are more of us, so we can divide up the duty.'

'I like the sound of that,' Raffaele said. '*Grazie.*'

Aquila invited him and Paolo to eat with his men, plates of watery stew with polenta, and, after agreeing to keep in touch, they took their leave and set off back to their base.

Walking down the steep mountain path, Raffaele's thoughts turned to Giulia. For the past week, he'd found himself avoiding her. There was something unsettling about the girl; she was turning out to be not what he'd expected. Maybe she wasn't as entitled as he'd thought she was? Unexpectedly, she'd fitted into his small band as if she belonged, ever helpful and never with a word of complaint. Her prowess at shooting had taken him completely by surprise and she'd turned out to be a competent seamstress, able to patch up the rips in their clothes and even sew sacks together to fill with straw and make improvised mattresses. He'd also noted that her skills extended to more physical arts – he'd often find her doing handstands and cart-wheels across the yard.

While both Paolo and Teresa appeared to like her, Raffaele was still reserving judgement. Why had he been avoiding her? He didn't know the answer to that question; he just felt less unsettled when he wasn't around her.

Before too long, he was heading up the steep path to their *baita*, trudging in Paolo's footsteps as a chilly wind blew down from the mountain.

The echo of unfamiliar voices made Paolo come to an abrupt halt. He crouched down and Raffaele did likewise, his heart hammering. Had the Nazi-fascists discovered their hideout?

He and Paolo crept forward.

Three strange men were in the yard, chopping wood. They weren't wearing uniforms, so they couldn't be militia, and militia wouldn't be chopping wood, anyway. Still, it was better to be safe than sorry, so he raised his rifle, took a step, and barked, 'Who are you?'

'It's all right, Lele,' Teresa said, coming out of the hut. 'These are new recruits sent by the committee. Meet Lungo, Rock, and Duke.'

The three men saluted.

'I'm Lungo,' a skinny young man, with bushy dark eyebrows, said.

'Rock at your service.' The second youth waved, a smile gleaming in his pale blue eyes.

'And I'm Duke,' the last man said. The tallest of the cohort, he towered over his companions and appeared slightly reticent, as if he didn't know what to say or do.

Giulia was approaching from the barn, lugging a straw mattress she must have just made. Lungo went to help her, and it was on the tip of Raffaele's tongue to reprimand him and say the girl could fend for herself. He did no such thing, though; it might paint him in a bad light. Instead, he asked Teresa how they were coping with supplies.

'We went to Miazzina this morning and got some wheat. Piccola and I have made fresh tagliatelle. I hope you're hungry as I've made a meat ragout.'

'We're starving, Luna,' Paolo answered for him. 'Lunch at Alpe Steppio was terrible. I can't wait to fill my stomach.'

While they ate, their new recruits told them their story. They were originally from Verbania but had deserted from the army after the armistice, and they'd all had some military training. Raffaele expressed his relief that they weren't without experience, then gave details about the situation at Alpe Steppio, adding that Aquila and his men's aim for the immediate future was to appropriate as many firearms as they could.

'We should do the same,' Paolo said, wiping sauce from his mouth with the back of his hand. 'Our rifles are outdated and we need automatic weapons.'

'I've been thinking about that and have already come up with a plan.' Raffaele smiled. He'd tell them about it in due course. It would need the girls to be on board, especially Teresa, but knowing her he was sure she'd agree. 'In the meantime, how about some grappa before we hit the sack?'

'You've taken the words from my lips,' Paolo chuckled.

11

It had been Giulia's idea to decorate the cypress growing in front of the *baita*. If anyone had told her that, one day, she'd be hanging hand grenades instead of baubles from a so-called Christmas tree, she would have said they were crazy. But here she was, out in the yard on a cold December afternoon, stamping her feet to try to keep warm, the sweet resinous scent of pine in her nostrils.

Remembering last Christmas with her parents in Milan, Giulia felt sadness weigh down on her. There'd been a lull in the Allied bombing of the city, and Papà had treated her and Mamma like he always did: gifts galore and the finest food that could be bought on the black market. No wonder Raffaele considered her entitled. She'd taken her lifestyle for granted, that was certain. When this terrible war was over, she would relish each and every moment of the days ahead.

Worry wrinkled her brow. What if Mamma and Papà never returned from where they'd been taken? What if she was all alone in the world? No, that couldn't be. She wouldn't let it happen. As soon as the opportunity arose, she'd leave and go to find them.

The echo of footsteps startled her, and she turned around. Raffaele and Paolo were approaching, laden with supplies.

'We've managed to get a demijohn of red wine to have with our Christmas lunch,' Paolo said, grinning.

'And I've bagged us a pheasant.' Raffaele lifted the bird by its legs. 'It was being attacked by a crow, and I shot it.'

'That'll make a nice change from our monotonous diet,' Giulia said.

'You're lucky to have food on your plate when so many of your fellow Italians are going hungry,' Raffaele snapped.

God, he was insufferable.

'Give it to me,' she huffed. 'I'll pluck it, then look for somewhere to store it.'

She took the bird from Raffaele and went into the kitchen area of the *baita*. After the arrival of Lungo, Rock, and Duke, the men had swapped sleeping quarters with her and Teresa, as the hut was too small for the five of them. Giulia had missed the barn at first, the mouldy smell of the hay, the cooing of wood pigeons in the rafters. But she'd soon got used to bedding down on the straw mattress she'd made, and it was much warmer in the hut, with the wood-burning stove retaining heat for most of the night.

Teresa looked up from where she was sitting, cleaning a rifle.

'What have you got there, Piccola?'

Giulia explained where the bird had come from and how she was about to strip it of its feathers.

'But maybe wait a few days before plucking it,' Teresa said. 'Pheasant is difficult to pluck unless it's been aged.'

'Thanks for letting me know. Where should we store it?'

'Hmm. Let me think.' Teresa tapped her chin. 'It's cold enough in the shed for it not to go off.'

Giulia took the bird back outside. As she crossed the yard, she spotted the new recruits returning from wood-collecting duties. They were weighed down with fallen branches to chop for the fire, and bags of chestnuts, which had become a staple part of their diet since the end of the mushroom season.

After greeting the men, she took the pheasant to the shack next to the barn, where she found a piece of wire and proceeded to try to suspend it. But she was too short to reach the ceiling hook. She dragged an old box across the floor to stand on.

'What are you doing?' Raffaele's voice almost made her jump out of her skin.

After she'd explained, he offered to help.

'I'm taller than you.' He smirked. 'Let me do it.'

She was about to protest that she could manage, but he held out his hand to take the bird from her and it would be rude not to accept his assistance, so she stepped forward to give it to him.

His fingers brushed hers, and a jolt passed between them.

Where had that come from? Giulia couldn't fathom, but one thing was sure: she felt an instant need to remove herself from Raffaele's presence. They'd never been alone together before, and he was making her feel a little strange. Her chest had fluttered at his touch, which was extremely odd.

'I'd better go,' she said.

'Aren't you going to thank me for helping?' He lifted an eyebrow.

'*Grazie*. But I was about to climb on that box.' She pointed. 'And hang the pheasant on my own.'

'Maybe I should have left you to it, then.' A mocking laugh bubbled out of his throat.

'No, you've got me wrong. Sorry. I appreciate you helping me,

Lele.' She glanced at him, mortified he'd taken her explanation the wrong way.

'Apology accepted, Piccola.' A smile beamed in his eyes. Beautiful deep blue eyes, as blue as the waters of the lake.

She tore her gaze from his and made her escape; she shouldn't have noticed his eyes. Raffaele Ferrero was arrogant and judgemental, and she didn't like him. The less time she spent in his presence, the better...

12

Christmas lunch with her new friends was a bittersweet occasion for Giulia. She missed her parents so much that she had to sniff back her tears. Paolo cooked the pheasant after she'd plucked it, simmering it in some of the red wine from the demijohn. It was delicious, although scarcely enough to feed the seven of them. Fortunately, they could fill up on potatoes and chestnuts.

Afterwards, everyone except Raffaele – who said the wine had gone to his head, and he needed to take a nap in the barn – played *scopa*. It was a fast-paced card game that involved capturing cards from the table by matching table cards with the cards in your hand.

By the end of the game, Raffaele had returned.

'I'd like us to go down to Intra tomorrow evening, to relieve *Feldgendarmerie* soldiers and Fascist militiamen of their arms,' he said without preamble. 'I've thought of a plan. It will be a practice run for future actions where we'll work together.' He proceeded to outline the scheme to Giulia and her companions. They would hide while Teresa approached a suitable enemy soldier to ask for a light. While he was distracted, the others would relieve him of his weapon. Everyone liked the strategy, and excitement fizzed in Giulia's chest, tinged with a touch of regret that Raffaele said she was too young and inexperienced to play an important role. But, at least, she would be included in the action – her first as a partisan – and for that she was grateful.

* * *

The following day was Boxing Day, the feast of Saint Stephen, and thankfully it was still dry. If it had snowed, the going would have been too difficult for what Raffaele said he had in mind.

Giulia and her comrades ate a big breakfast of fried eggs, mopped up with stale bread and washed down with barley coffee, before setting off for the two-hour hike. They departed mid-afternoon and, as usual for that time of the year, it had started to get dark.

Armed with pistols, they walked down the winding road to Intra. Below, the lake shimmered as a glorious sunset pinked its water. Feeling the sharp sting of homesickness for Marta and the life she'd left behind, Giulia headed with the others along a narrow alley that led to the waterfront.

A lone German was standing under a streetlamp.

Giulia's heart thudded. Although she'd been told the *SS-Feld-gendarmerie* military police wore the same grey-green uniform as their army counterparts, it was a shock to see someone dressed like those who'd taken away her parents and Jewish friends. The man was lighting up a cigarette and there was no one else around.

Raffaele made a signal with his hand that everyone except Teresa should hide in doorways. Teresa, who'd put on a dress and makeup, took the Nazionale cigarette Paolo had given her from her pocket and strolled up to the German, swinging her hips.

'Can I have a light?' She held out her cigarette. If the soldier spoke no Italian, it was clear from her gesture what she was asking.

'*Natürlich.*' Of course.

He struck a match, and Teresa cupped his hand while she brought the tip of her cigarette to the flame. The glow of the match lit up the stubble on his face.

'*Grazie.*' Teresa lowered her gaze, clearly not wanting to be recognised if ever she saw him again.

Furtively, Raffaele crept up behind the German and pushed his weapon into the man's side.

'Hands up!' he growled.

The German yelped, complying in an instant.

Raffaele kept his weapon where it was, then removed the pistol from the German's holster with his other hand.

Teresa threw down her cigarette, unbuckled the man's trousers, and pulled them all the way down his surprisingly smooth legs. When the trousers got stuck on his boots, she undid the laces and made him step out of them.

'Keep still,' Raffaele ordered.

It was the signal for Giulia and the others to make an appearance, help strip the Nazi of the rest of his uniform and tie him to the lamppost.

Giulia had been tasked with putting the garments they stole into her haversack, and she carried out her duty with ease.

As the evening progressed, and they encountered another German as well as two Italian militiamen, their haul increased until, in addition to the pistol, they'd appropriated hand grenades, rifles and more clothes.

'Best head back to base,' Raffaele said eventually. 'Well done, guys. You did great, brilliantly worked as a team.'

The hike back up the mountain to Alpe Aurelio seemed to take forever, and Giulia's legs ached with the effort. They marched in single file, Paolo leading and Raffaele bringing up the rear just behind Giulia. Everyone had complimented Teresa on keeping her cool and acting her part well. Envy burned in Giulia's chest at this; she wished Raffaele wouldn't treat her like a little girl. But who was she kidding? She was the youngest of the group – by far – as well as being the smallest, and her baby-faced looks would have prevented her from sidling up to the enemy to ask for a light. Besides, she didn't smoke and would have coughed until tears ran down her face.

Her foot knocked against a loose stone, and she stumbled. But before she fell to the ground, strong arms grabbed her.

'I've got you,' Raffaele said, setting her back on her feet. 'Are you okay to carry on?'

For the second time in a week, mortification tingled in her chest. God forbid Raffaele would think she wasn't up to the task.

'I'm perfectly fine,' she said, squirming from his hold. 'It's so dark. I just tripped on a stone.'

'If you say so.' He obviously didn't believe her.

'No. Honestly. I can do this. I'm tougher than you think.'

He chuckled. Had he been teasing her? Surely not.

They lapsed into silence the rest of the way, and she was glad about that. Raffaele's baritone voice had made her skin tingle and had given her a funny feeling in her chest.

Back at the *baita*, a warm feeling spread through her as she sat at the wooden table with her comrades. It was good to be with these people; she felt accepted by them despite her background. Everyone except Raffaele, of course. He would look at her as if she was something nasty he'd trodden on that clung to his shoe. Except, maybe not so much of late. Could he be changing his opinion of her? How she hoped that might be so. It would make life easier not to feel so uncomfortable in his presence.

Duke, who'd brought his accordion with him, proceeded to play mountain songs, and Giulia and the rest of the group sang along with him.

> Up there in the mountains,
> among woods and golden valleys,
> among the rugged rocks echoes
> there is a song of love.

While she sang, she caught Raffaele watching her and a flush warmed her cheek as she glanced away.

* * *

Everyone woke up late on New Year's Day; they'd celebrated the arrival of 1944 the night before with another demijohn of red wine, as well as multiple shots of grappa and hearty singing.

Teresa went to brew coffee, and Giulia joined her.

'Want a cup, Piccola?'

'*Grazie.*' Giulia proceeded to slice stale bread and place it in a basket. The men would be here any minute, hungry as wolves.

Sure enough, she'd barely formulated the thought when the door banged open, and they all appeared.

Breakfast was generally eaten in silence, unlike their other meals, which echoed with chat and laughter, and this morning was no different. Each of them appeared lost in their own thoughts, and Giulia couldn't help thinking about the progress of the Allied advance. Or lack of progress, it appeared, from what Raffaele had said after he'd gone for their New Year's Eve supplies from the sanatorium. The staff there were deeply anti-Fascist and listened to a secret shortwave radio tuned in to *Radio Londra*.

He'd mentioned that he wanted to pay a visit to his family soon, and she'd felt a stab of envy. Paolo and Teresa had already gone to Baveno three days ago, under the cover of darkness and a full moon. Duke, Rock and Lungo's families lived in Verbania, and they'd met up with them in Miazzina shortly before Christmas.

Without warning, a loud knock sounded at the *baita*'s door, and they all leapt to their feet.

'Shush!' Raffaele placed a finger to his lips and, crouching low, made his way to the front window to peer outside. 'Who's there?' he barked.

'We've come from Commander Aquila at Alpe Steppio,' a voice said.

'How do I know you are who you say you are?' Raffaele asked.

'We have a message from him.'

Raffaele opened the door and ushered two youths into the room. After taking the note from them, he offered them a coffee and told them to take a seat.

Raffaele read the note, then put it in the stove to burn.

'Aquila says there are huts available at the Alpe Pechi mountain pasture, just below Steppio, where we can live more comfortably than here. What do you think, guys?'

'Maybe we can check it out?' Lungo tilted his head.

'Agreed. We could go there tomorrow, then put it to the vote—'

'All of us?' Giulia held her breath, eager to be included in the mission.

'I don't see why not. It would be our new home, so we should all have the chance to decide,' Raffaele said.

Releasing the breath she'd been holding, Giulia placed a hand over her mouth to cover a smile.

13

Raffaele was sitting on a bench in the sunshine, cleaning his gun and remembering how he'd laughed when his group had decided to give the name 'Peking' to their new base, Pechi. Not to be outdone, he'd immediately proposed that Steppio became 'Shanghai', and the proposal had met with everyone's approval. The vote to move to the cluster of *baite* above the village of Intragna had been unanimous, for the greater space and security it offered, and now, a week later, they'd settled comfortably into the four stone huts occupying a verdant meadow surrounded by thick forest. The girls had one of the buildings to themselves, the second housed their kitchen, dining and recreation area, and he and his men slept in the other two. Because of their proximity to 'Shanghai', rations were shared between the two camps, and life had been uneventful until yesterday.

Glancing up from his rifle, Raffaele spotted Rock approaching. He'd sent Rock down to the nearby village of Intragna to buy wheat with the money they received for supplies from the Verbania agency, which had come under the umbrella of the

National Liberation Committee for Northern Italy, an organisation acting as a clandestine shadow government in the German-occupied north.

Rock reported he'd seen two *carabinieri* policemen roaming around the village. Raffaele's heart leapt; he'd been chaffing to do something practical. So, he suggested they relieve the men of their weapons. Dressed in their usual assortment of odd clothing – studded military boots they'd stolen from Germans, and waterproof wax jackets – he and Rock marched boldly into the centre of the village, their pistols tucked into their belts, hidden under their jackets. It wasn't difficult to find the *carabinieri*; they were standing in front of the town hall in the main square, and they barely acknowledged Raffaele's and Rock's presence, clearly believing them to be a couple of woodsmen.

It would have been foolhardy to relieve the policemen of their arms in the middle of Intragna, but Raffaele had already thought of a plan.

'There are some guys I know to be draft dodgers who are living rough in the woods just outside the village,' he said, going up to the tallest of policemen. 'Would you like to arrest them?'

'With pleasure,' the man responded.

'Follow us.' Raffaele spun on his heel.

No sooner had he and Rock led the men out of Intragna than they drew their weapons.

'Hands up!' they barked.

The *carabinieri* were so taken by surprise that they complied without hesitation. Within seconds, Raffaele and Rock relieved the men of their Beretta pistols, and all that remained to be done was to tie the men to trees to prevent them giving chase.

The strenuous hike back up to Peking hardly dented the sense of euphoria racing through Raffaele. He thrived on action;

it distracted him from worrying thoughts. A couple of days ago, he'd gone to visit his family in Baveno, and had found them struggling to feed themselves. For years, they'd relied on whatever his father could add to their rations with extras from the hotel. But now the hotel was closed, Pa was no longer receiving a salary, although he kept an eye on things for Signor Leone. Giulia's father had promised to send money from Switzerland to keep things going, but that had been before he and his wife were captured.

Resentment constricted in Raffaele's throat at his father's loyalty to Giulia's father. Fair enough, the hotel owner had been generous in allowing Pa to take food home, but he'd expected him to work all the hours God sent in return. Pa could get a job elsewhere, one that actually paid him, but he'd been adamant that Signor Leone would reimburse him once the war was over, and they could manage in the meantime on his savings.

The sun was setting by the time Raffaele and Rock arrived back at the camp. They stepped into the main *baita* to find the entire band sitting at the wooden table, plates of potato soup in front of them.

'A messenger came from Shanghai while you were away,' Paolo announced without preamble. 'Aquila and his men went down to Intra last night to relieve a squad of about a dozen militiamen of their weapons. After they'd shouted, "Hands up!", instead of complying, the Fascists opened fire, wounding three of them in the process – one in the chest and two with flesh injuries.'

'Good God!' Raffaele exclaimed, shocked.

'The messenger said Aquila wants all of us to attend a meeting tomorrow evening to discuss tactics, and I agreed to the request on your behalf.'

'You did well, Biondo.'

Things were hotting up. Until then, none of them had exchanged fire with anyone. But what did Raffaele expect? This was war, and war meant people got hurt.

He glanced up from cleaning his gun now as Giulia came into his periphery.

'I wonder what tactics Aquila will propose at the meeting,' she said, lowering herself onto the bench next to him.

He breathed in the earthy scent of the vegetable oil soap she used and turned to look at her. She appeared so much younger than seventeen: plump cheeks, creamy skin, full lips, and chestnut hair braided into long plaits. But her childish appearance belied a maturity beyond her years, he was starting to realise. Maybe she was a spoilt little rich kid, but what girl from her background would muck in like she'd done with barely a complaint?

'I expect Aquila will want us to join up with him,' Raffaele said in answer to Giulia's question.

'Would you like that?' She met his gaze, tilting her head to the side. Surprise fluttered in his belly as he found himself in danger of losing himself in her beautiful amber-coloured eyes.

'That'll depend,' he said, forcing himself to look away. 'We'd better go round up the others and get a move on.'

* * *

The *baita* that posed as the Shanghai meeting room boasted a wooden floor and a stove that emanated more smoke than heat. Raffaele led his band into the low building, where everyone was sitting on straw bales, and they listened to Aquila illustrate the errors committed during the action two nights ago; his men had been too complacent and should have been quicker off the mark.

'The enemy opened fire first. From now onwards, it's open

warfare,' the eagle-eyed man added. 'I've decided my formation will be known as the "*Cesare Battisti*" henceforth, to differentiate us from the other partisan bands in the area.'

Trust Aquila to name his group after one of the most important figures in the unification of Italy and a political hero, Raffaele thought, sweeping his eye around the *baita,* where Eagle's twenty men – recently augmented by new recruits – and his own group comprising Giulia and five others were gazing at Aquila with evident affection. It was clear they believed in him and that the first blood to be shed hadn't put them off. Eagle was a strong commander, although only in his mid-twenties, and his military experience showed. Raffaele's ribs squeezed tight with envy, which he quickly suppressed. He had nothing to be jealous about; the loyalty of his own band couldn't be questioned.

Duke had brought his accordion, and he taught them all a song he'd composed: *Partisans are coming down from the mountains and heading into the heart of the city...* They sang along with fervour, not because they were homesick for their loved ones, nor because they wanted to pass the time, but because they were inspired by the desire to fight against the people who'd hurt their companions, a desire not caused by hate, but by a firm sense of justice, Raffaele thought.

He caught sight of Giulia, singing her heart out with the rest of them. Her resilience impressed him, but how she would cope now that matters were intensifying remained to be seen.

'Can I have a quick word?' Aquila asked, coming up to him.

'Of course.'

'How would you feel about merging your group with mine?' Eagle came right out with the expected suggestion. 'There's greater strength in numbers—'

'Let me think about it,' Raffaele said, although he'd do no such thing. His band was his, and his alone. They were too close to Shanghai, risked being absorbed into the *Cesare Battisti* for their proximity. It would be better if they found a new base sooner rather than later. He relished his independence and liked being in charge. For the time being. If things became really difficult, he might reconsider. Whatever happened, he'd do the best thing for his comrades, he resolved.

14

In early February, Raffaele found himself in the sanatorium with Paolo, collecting supplies. They were about to head back to Peking when one of the nuns who worked as a nurse in the facility told them there was a band of partisans at Ompio mountain pasture, overlooking the village of Rovegro, and that they were supposedly in possession of machine guns.

'Can you head over there and find out more?' Raffaele asked Paolo as they set off down the road. 'I'll carry your haversack with mine and return to camp.'

Heavily burdened with sacks of potatoes and bags of flour, Raffaele took four hours – twice as long to get back to Peking as he normally would have done – and he was glad they were enjoying a spell of fine weather and that the ubiquitous winter snow had held off.

He stepped out from under the treeline into the clearing that housed their stone huts, then stopped in his tracks. Two strange men were sitting in the sunshine with Teresa and Giulia. He went up to them and discovered they were new recruits, sent by the Verbania committee. One of them had pepper-and-salt hair and appeared to be in his forties and the other was so young he could be a boy. Raffaele could scarcely contain his surprise that the older man only had one hand, and he politely averted his gaze from the stump.

'My name is Giorgio,' the man said. 'Call me *Il Monco*.'

It seemed a bit harsh to refer to him as 'the Maimed One', but if that was the name he'd chosen, then so be it. Strange for the committee to have sent such seemingly poor recruits, and Raffaele couldn't help questioning their reasoning. The younger man was awkward-looking and gangly. Raffaele almost laughed out loud when he learnt the boy had chosen the battle name 'Tarzan'. The most unlikely looking king of the jungle he'd ever seen.

'Where's Biondo?' Teresa's question broke into Raffaele's thoughts, and he filled her in on the latest developments.

'It would have taken him about an hour to get to Ompio from Miazzina, and I guess he'll be there for about an hour or so. By my calculation, he should be back here in about another hour in time for supper.'

This proved to be the case as Paolo, unencumbered with supplies like Raffaele had been, made quick work of the hike and turned up when Raffaele had expected.

'There are about fifteen men at the camp and they call themselves the Valdossola Battalion,' Paolo said, pulling out a chair at the kitchen table. 'Under the command of a certain Major Sabadini and a Major Moretti. I think the group could be even bigger, as some of them were away on a mission.'

'Interesting.' Raffaele rubbed a hand through his hair. 'Did you find out where they came from and why they were there?'

'The major told me he formed his band in the Ossola Valley after the armistice, about fifteen kilometres northwest of Verbania and, after they'd disarmed the local *carabinieri* and

Captain Moretti had turned up with his own men, they decided to join forces and move to Rovegro.'

'Did they show you their armoury?'

'They did. Two 12.7 machine guns without tripods, probably once used on aeroplanes, four Beretta submachine guns, as well as rifles. I found them staying in a villa, and they gave me some lunch. Steak!' Paolo was obviously impressed. 'They knew all about us from the Verbania committee and asked me to extend an invitation to Aquila to visit them.'

Slightly put out that he, too, hadn't been invited to pay a call on the major, Raffaele tucked into the plate of bean soup Giulia had ladled for him. He caught her glancing at him, but she'd averted her eyes before he could read her expression.

Later, when they'd all finished eating and had cleared up, they went to sit on straw pallets in their recreation area, to sing along while Duke played his accordion.

Raffaele's gaze lingered on Giulia sitting next to Tarzan. She lifted her face and gazed at him, a sweet smile curving her lips. Unexpectedly, he found himself smiling back at her and a bewildering feeling of euphoria spread through him.

* * *

It was early morning a week later, and sleet sheeted across the grassy area between the huts, causing Raffaele to skid on ice as he made his way to the outside privy. Without warning, from a distance, crashing and whooshing sounds echoed in the freezing air. Raffaele startled. The noise was coming from Alpe Pala mountain pasture above Miazzina, if he wasn't mistaken. He wrinkled his brow. A detachment of Shanghai partisans had established a camp there. What the hell was going on?

He proposed to Teresa, Giulia, Paolo and Lungo that they set off on patrol. He'd selected the girls to go with him as they were damn good shots, better than Duke and Rock, and Giorgio *Il Monco* and Tarzan had yet to prove themselves.

The Mitra submachine gun Aquila had lent him felt heavy and cumbersome, slung in a lanyard over Raffaele's shoulder, and the cartridges he carried in a belt across his chest irritated him so much he almost regretted ever having asked for the weapon. He fell into step beside Giulia.

'Everything okay, Piccola?' he asked.

'Yes, Lele. I'm excited you've asked me to come along. Just hope I don't let you down.'

'I'm sure you won't,' he said, and left it at that.

Three hours later – it had stopped sleeting, thank God – he led Giulia and the rest of his squad up the mountain behind Miazzina to Alpe Pala, cautioning everyone to keep quiet and tread carefully. But the closer they got, the more it became obvious that no harm had occurred there. The *baita* was undamaged, and a lookout told them that it was the Valdossola Battalion, Major Sabadini's band, that had been attacked.

More crashing and whooshing sounds boomed from the other side of the valley, followed by the loud bang of hand grenades detonating and the thunder of the 12.7 machine guns. Raffaele's heart sank as columns of black smoke rose in the distance. He hoped against hope that the enemy wasn't burning dairy farmers' *baite* in retribution.

'Let's go,' he said to Giulia and the others. 'If we head for Unchio, we might be able to ambush the Fascists when they return to Verbania.' He and his companions carried four rifles and a submachine gun between them; hopefully that would be enough to inflict some serious damage on the enemy.

After spending a couple of hours lurking in the woods above the main road, to no avail, Raffaele decided to lead Giulia and the rest of the squad down to the Rovegro road. The sun soon disappeared below the horizon, casting long shadows and pinking the sky. A rumbling noise resounded and Raffaele's pulse raced as a column of trucks headed towards them; it could only be the Nazi-fascists.

'Follow me,' he shouted. 'Make for the bridge!'

They raced through the village, Giulia keeping pace with him, and the few people they encountered shrank back. Raffaele's chest tinged with anticipation when they reached their destination. A *polizei* vehicle was approaching, and he gave the order to crouch down by the side of the road at the exit of the bridge.

'Wait until the last vehicle approaches,' he commanded in a low voice. 'We can't take on the whole column.'

Darkness had descended like a velvet curtain, and the trucks had all switched on their lights. Raffaele undid the buckle on his ammunition belt, while indicating to Giulia and the others that they should release the safety catches on their weapons and get into position.

A feeling of calmness took hold of him; he was about to kill or be killed. Teresa's face to his left and Giulia's to his right also appeared calm. It was the first time the majority of them would be shooting at the enemy; but not Lungo, who'd been stationed in Albania a year ago.

Thirteen trucks passed over the bridge and, at the approach of the last one, Raffaele wondered if he should shoot his gun in a fan-like motion or not. It was too late for such debate, however; the final truck had rounded the curve.

Taking aim, Raffaele tightened his finger on the trigger of his weapon and unleashed a flurry of fire. The windscreen glass smashed into smithereens, and he squeezed his trigger again.

Nothing. The damned gun had jammed. *Merda!* He shook it furiously, but it remained blocked.

The truck had come to a halt, and Teresa and Paolo were throwing hand grenades, while Lungo and Giulia were shooting. One grenade exploded on the bonnet of the vehicle and another on the roof.

'Go, go, go,' Raffaele heard the enemy soldiers shouting, plainly about to retaliate.

'Time to retreat,' he barked the command.

But Giulia carried on firing, visibly aiming to empty her cartridge. Sudden fear for her rippled through him. *What on earth?*

'Piccola, come!' he yelled, turning to make sure she'd complied.

She'd returned her weapon to its lanyard, thank God, but bullets whistled past their heads, flinging stones into the air as they landed.

'Onwards!' Raffaele shouted, every muscle in his body poised for flight. And they ran, oh how they ran, the crack, whine and hiss of the bullets being fired from behind them growing fainter as they put in more distance.

Finally, they slipped between the houses at the side of the road and raced into the woods.

Raffaele let out a huge breath. They'd made it. *Phew!*

He turned his gaze to Giulia, who was walking next to him. She'd been brave beyond measure, but also hot-headed and fool-hardy; he would need to reprimand her when they got back to their base.

* * *

Two days later, Raffaele rolled over on his straw mattress as dawn light came through the dusty window of the *baita*. With a jolt, he remembered it was his twentieth birthday, but he was in no mood to celebrate.

Yesterday, he and his group had spent the day resting and cleaning their weapons. In the evening, a messenger had arrived to inform them that the Fascists had gone back to Alpe Ompio that morning with massive numbers of German troops, around one thousand in total. Major Sabadini had retreated with his men to a position higher up in the mountains after four of his battalion had been taken prisoner, one of their machine guns captured, and forty-eight stone huts burnt down. It was a regrettable situation, and Raffaele wondered if his, Giulia's and the rest of his group's attack on the column had been worth it. Had they even killed or wounded any of the enemy? He wished there was some way of finding out...

Wrinkling his brow, he thought about the progress of the Allied advance. The last time he'd spoken to staff at the sanatorium, they'd informed him the British and Americans were fighting the Germans south of Rome, but they'd encountered stiff resistance on a beachhead called Anzio. Raffaele sighed to himself, praying that the British and Americans would break through soon. If not, in all likelihood, civil war would erupt between the Italian Fascists and the partisans, with the former in a position of power given that they were supported by the Nazis. It was like David taking on Goliath, but at least the Resistance had right on their side. Good would win over evil, God willing. The *partigiani* were like grains of sand, but they would form a desert and stop the Germans and Italian fascists in their tracks, eventually. In the meantime, they just had to stay positive, be resilient and fight on.

'Happy birthday!' Paolo's voice broke into Raffaele's musing. 'Get up, breakfast is waiting for you!'

Raffaele levered himself off the bed, only now realising he'd been alone in the *baita*. His roommates must have thought a birthday treat would have been to allow him to sleep late. He flung on his clothes and followed Paolo to the kitchen.

Everyone greeted him with claps on the back, except for the girls, who kissed him on both cheeks.

'We've pooled our cigarette rations for you,' Teresa said, a big smile on her face.

'*Grazie*, but I can't accept. We all need our smokes to calm our nerves.' He hoped he hadn't sounded ungracious.

Breakfast over, the need to get some fresh air overcame him, and he went outside. Snow clouds were gathering over the mountains; he huddled into his coat and stepped onto the grass as his thoughts returned to the action they'd taken against the Fascists. He'd yet to reprimand Giulia for carrying on shooting when he'd given the command to retreat. She might have been killed, and it struck him that he would have been devastated; she'd become an integral part of his band. About to return to the kitchen hut, he spotted her heading for the girls' accommodation. There was no time like the present to rebuke her.

'I know what you're about to say,' she said when he approached. 'And let me apologise before you say it. I disobeyed your order. I'm sorry. It's just that I was so caught up in the moment and I wanted to prove myself worthy of being a combatant.'

'In the army, you might well have been discharged.' He heard the formality in his tone, but it was needed under the circumstances. 'We're a military formation, don't forget. You were far too impetuous. When I tell you to do something, you must do it or you could end up compromising not only your own safety, but more importantly, the welfare of your comrades.'

A flush of evident embarrassment bloomed on her lovely cheeks, and she lowered her gaze before repeating how sorry she was.

'Don't do it again, Piccola.' A gust of icy wind lifted the hair that curled around her face, making her amber eyes water. 'Go inside or you'll freeze out here.'

'Is that an order?' She dimpled a smile that unaccountably tugged at his insides.

'It is,' he said, keeping his voice stern.

'Then I'll obey.' She looked him in the eye. 'I would really like to visit Milan soon so I can find out if Mamma and Papà are still being held there by the Germans.'

'It would be extremely dangerous, Piccola. Far better you stay under my protection.'

'I just want to know what has happened to them.' He heard the sadness in her voice. 'Happy birthday, by the way. It's a shame you can't spend it with your family—'

'Indeed. But we must all make sacrifices.' He'd have given anything to be with his parents and siblings, truth be told. Giulia must be distraught. 'If I could find out about your parents for you, I would.' He sighed. 'We can only pray for the Nazis to be defeated soon, so that all who are separated from their loved ones can be reunited.'

Aghast, he watched a lone tear trickle down her face, and he felt the inexplicable urge to enfold her in his arms and comfort her. He resisted the urge – it would have been a big mistake – and gazed at her back as she turned away and headed for her *baita*.

15

Giulia couldn't sleep. All she could think about was Raffaele's refusal to allow her to go to Milan. If she took matters into her own hands and set off on her own, she would no longer be under his command. Surely, it wouldn't be difficult to travel to the city by train. After all, the British POWs had done it. When Fascist militiamen began checking the passengers – which the Allied soldiers had maintained always started from one end of the train or the other – she could get off at the next stop and get on again in the carriages which had already been checked. The fact she'd be travelling without a guide to warn her was slightly worrying, but she'd manage somehow.

Giulia's scrambled thoughts were like a tangled ball of yarn, looping backwards and forwards until dawn light filtered through the windows of the *baita*. She rolled herself off her mattress and tiptoed across the floor to where she'd stashed her rucksack. There was no need to pack as that was where she always kept her few clothes and personal effects. All she needed was to take some bread to munch as she made her way down the mountain to Fondotoce.

She glanced at Teresa, fast asleep on the straw mattress, and gave a sigh. Luna had become a good friend, and she would miss her. Likewise, Paolo, Lungo, *Il Monco* and Tarzan. As for Raffaele, he'd probably be glad she was no longer underfoot. She'd been mortified by his response yesterday when she'd apologised for disobeying his order; she hadn't considered she was part of a military formation, and she hadn't realised that she could have compromised the safety of her comrades. It was far better she act on her own in future and be the only person to suffer the consequences of her actions.

After a final glance around the *baita*, she pushed open the door and stepped into the yard. Peking was a quite a pleasant place, she thought to herself as she gazed at the base to commit it to memory. Most days, it was sunny, and she loved the beautiful green meadow that surrounded the stone huts. It was much better than Shanghai, which was always windy, and where the paths between one *baita* and the next were covered in mud...

The skin on the back of her neck suddenly prickled, and she came to an abrupt halt. Raffaele was at the water trough, washing his face.

'Where the hell are you off to?' he barked.

'I've decided to go to Milan and find out about my parents.' She folded her arms and shot him a determined look.

'The Germans would make mincemeat out of you in seconds.' Raffaele shortened the distance between them and planted his legs wide. 'Don't forget you're still wanted by the SS.'

'Oh, I was hoping they'd forgotten all about me.'

'No chance of that. You defied them by helping your Jewish friends and made it worse by getting away.'

'I'm only a girl, for goodness' sake. They must have far bigger fish to fry. I doubt they'd waste their efforts on me, Lele.'

'You have no idea what they are capable of—'

'What do you mean?'

There was something in Raffaele's grim expression that set Giulia's heart pounding. Had he received news about her parents? Her mouth went dry.

'There's no easy way to say this.'

'Please, tell me. I can take it.' She gritted her teeth.

'If you are sure.'

'Absolutely.' Giulia held her breath. From the look on his face, she was about to hear something terrible. But hear it she must, for she not knowing would be much, much worse.

'After we'd come up to the mountains, all along the lakeside, people starting spotting dead bodies floating on the surface of the lake. Some had even floated ashore and were recognised as Lago Maggiore's Jewish residents. Those *bastardi* SS soldiers appear to have shot them, then tried to get rid of the evidence in the *lago*. But... but they didn't weigh the bodies down properly.' Raffaele stuttered the words. 'Afterwards... afterwards, the Nazis used flamethrowers to burn the corpses and then their remains sank.'

'Oh, dear God, how awful!' Giulia recoiled in horror. Hot tears ran down her face, and she brushed them away with the back of her hand. 'Didn't they transport anyone to a camp like they said they would?'

'Not one Jew, apparently. They just sent local Italian soldiers who'd deserted from the army and young men to slave labour lagers.'

'My poor friend, Ester, and her family.' Giulia hiccoughed a sob. 'She was such a wonderful person, bright and spirited with a brilliant future ahead of her. I can't believe I'm talking about her in the past tense.'

'There's something else. I didn't tell you before as I didn't want to upset you, but before we left Baveno, Biondo and I witnessed a middle-aged man and woman and a younger couple being shot on a beach and their bodies thrown into the lake. My father and yours both thought they were the four Jewish people the SS took from your hotel to supposedly interrogate them. Remember they never returned?'

'Is that why you decided to help with the second escape plan?' she asked, the whole sorry debacle coming back to her.

'Biondo and I couldn't sit back and do nothing.'

'It's all too awful.' Giulia's voice trembled. 'If only we'd been successful—'

'Indeed.' Raffaele glanced at her.

'What about my parents?' Doubt suddenly assailed Giulia. 'I hope you've told me the truth about them. If they, too, were murdered and their bodies dumped in the lake, I hope you haven't kept it from me.'

'I swear to you someone saw them being put on a train.' He fixed her in his gaze. 'You have to believe me.'

'How can you be sure it was them?' She frowned.

'Because the person who saw them once worked in your hotel, remember? They recognised them immediately.'

'Poor Mamma and Papà.' Giulia knuckled away more tears from her cheeks. 'What has happened to them? How will they cope?'

'In times of war, we all have to make the best of it. I'm sure they are fine.'

'You can't be sure. You're just saying that.' She sighed. 'If the Germans murdered my Jewish friends, there's nothing to stop them from doing the same to my parents.'

'I hope it hasn't come to that, Piccola. But, in future, please don't take matters into your own hands. You mustn't be so impulsive. Whether you like it or not, you are part of my team and you must play by the rules. In these terrible times, there's strength in numbers. If this were to happen again, I'd have no recourse but to discharge you from the group. You wouldn't last five minutes on your own.'

His voice was stern, but she caught a gleam of concern in his eyes. Maybe Raffaele was right? She shouldn't be so impetuous; she'd be eighteen soon and should behave more like an adult.

'I'll do my best,' she said.

'Brava. Now go indoors. It's freezing out here. No need to tell the others about our conversation. We wouldn't want to give them cause for concern.'

Cause for concern? Of course, Raffaele was putting the safety of the group before everything else. It brought home to her that she was living in an entirely different world to the one she'd been used to.

She set her jaw as she returned to her and Teresa's *baita*. She still needed to find out about her parents, but she would bide her time. The chance would come, sooner or later, and she would seize it without hesitation. She owed it to Mamma and Papà to do everything she could for them; they deserved nothing but her absolute devotion.

PART III

MARCH–SEPTEMBER 1944

16

I wish Raffaele hadn't decided to move us all up to this hotel, Giulia thought as she gazed down towards the valley while on lookout duty. Built on a sunny south-facing slope, over 1,500 metres above sea level, and with few trees to block the stunning view of the lake below, the square two-storey building of Albergo Pian Cavallone was only accessible on foot, and its elevated position meant they could easily see if anyone was approaching.

When explaining his reasons for them transferring their base up here, Raffaele had said there was a muleteers' path leading directly to Miazzina, and it would be easier to fetch supplies. Giulia remembered her father once telling her about the mountain hotel, a *rifugio*, where hikers would find a bed for the night before the war. Surely it would be more spacious, and it made sense for the ease with which they would get to the sanatorium. But a finger of worry had stroked her insides. The *albergo* was extremely isolated, which would separate her even more from her missing loved ones.

When, a month ago, soon after new recruits had arrived to swell their numbers, Raffaele had taken the decision to transfer his group of fifty partisans from their old base, everyone had thought it was a good idea. There'd been a massive change in the weather. No longer could they sit outside in the sunshine at Peking. It often snowed and the wind never let up; it blew from all directions, whipping up the smoke in their wood-burning stoves. In the evenings, when they played cards, the fumes were so bad that tears streamed down their faces, making them cough and curse.

Consequently, they'd hiked up here to occupy the empty *albergo* and, within days, they'd emptied the rainwater cistern. The few litres obtained by melting ice on the stove would only be used for cooking, so they couldn't wash. The wood they burnt was obtained by cutting trees further down the slope. Because the green wood smoked more and was less efficient than seasoned wood, half of the partisans were occupied in that never-ending task each day, while the others took lessons in weapons handling from the more experienced, or did callisthenic exercises in the dining room or the yard to pass the time, with Giulia teaching them push-ups, handstands and squats. In the evenings, by candlelight, they played interminable card games, sang patriotic songs and even embarked on political discussions. Giulia was surprised to discover that some of the new recruits were Communists. Unsure of her own political leanings, she kept quiet during the often highly heated debates.

Every day, fatigue patrols set off to collect rations from Miazzina, and Raffaele placed one person on watch in daylight hours, and two at night.

That morning, Giulia had risen early. Her feet felt as if they'd turned into ice cubes as she'd put on her boots and, despite sleeping in a sweater, she was chilled to the bone. She and Teresa had been allocated a room to themselves, but she missed the warmth of their cosy, albeit smoke-filled *baita* in windy Peking.

Teresa was still snoring and, after shrugging on her outdoor coat, Giulia had crept out of the freezing room to make her way down the wooden staircase to the kitchen. The cooking range, set against the far wall, was still warm from burning the last of their wood supply the night before, and she'd wanted to hug it, she was so cold.

'*Buongiorno!*' Giorgio, *Il Monco*, had come up from behind. He'd taken on the role of the camp's cook, and they all took it in turns to help him.

She'd wished him good morning and had accepted the cup of barley coffee he'd offered her, along with a couple of pieces of stale bread for dunking.

As she ate, she'd thought about how, not long after the arrival of even more new recruits at Pian Cavallone, soft white flakes of snow had started to drift down and settle on their base. Before too long, a blizzard was blowing, and a blanket of white had covered the landscape like a veil. Raffaele had immediately given orders for food portions to be halved and, by the third day of the storm, the snow had reached at least a metre and a half in height, submerging the low walls and boulders around the hotel. But, despite the cut in rations, Raffaele had been forced to convene a meeting to announce there was practically nothing left to eat and their supply of wood had been exhausted.

She'd spent long hours with her comrades in the dining room, where the snow had reached the top of the ledges of the windows and an arctic wind howled outside. They did sit-ups and other callisthenic exercises to keep warm and ate the last of the stale bread and cheese in the larder. On the third night, Teresa suggested she and Giulia snuggle together to keep warm, and she got into bed with her to share their body warmth. Hunger had made her tired, and she'd fallen into a deep, dreamless sleep.

The next morning, she'd gone to the window. A blanket of white enveloped the world outside, the snow gleaming in the morning sunshine, an eery silence of stillness completing the picture. Her heart had leapt with the realisation that the blizzard appeared to have blown itself out.

She went downstairs and found Raffaele putting together a fatigue party to go for supplies: Tarzan, Paolo, Duke, Rock as well as himself. When Giulia had volunteered to join the group, Raffaele said that the snow drifts were so high she'd have been swallowed up by them, and it was safer for her to stay behind.

She checked her watch now; the fatigue party had been gone for over twenty-four hours. What if something terrible had happened to them? They could have frozen to death...

Movement at the base of the slope on which the hotel had been built caught her eye. Could it be Raffaele, Tarzan, Paolo, Duke, and Rock? Blurred white shapes were struggling through the snow drifts.

'Oi,' Raffaele's voice echoed. 'We need help.'

Giulia raced inside, where she found Giorgio, Lungo and Teresa at the kitchen table.

'They're back, at last,' Giulia blurted. 'Raffaele called for help, so they must be exhausted.'

Her companions had already jumped to their feet and were shrugging on their coats. Within minutes, Giulia was making her way through the banks of snow. Her feet sank in the drifts, and she found herself having to drag them free, step after tiring step.

On reaching Raffaele and the rest of the party, she held back while Teresa embraced her brother, and the men all patted each other on the back.

'I'm dead beat,' Raffaele said, handing his heavy rucksack to Giorgio.

Giulia went up to Raffaele and touched her hand to his arm.

'Come indoors and I'll make you a hot drink,' she said.

'Brilliant idea, Piccola.' His mouth twitched. 'Is there no end to your talents?'

* * *

The next afternoon, Giulia sat peeling potatoes in the kitchen, enjoying the warmth from the kitchen stove. Yesterday, Raffaele had given the order to chop up any tables and chairs they didn't need and keep them as wood for the kitchen range, so they could melt snow in big pots and use it for cooking. She caught sight of him coming into the room and gave him a big smile.

'Would you like a hand?' he asked, approaching.

She thanked him and passed him a potato and spare paring knife.

'A little bird told me it's your birthday on Sunday,' he said.

'Which little bird?' she asked, surprised.

'Remember when we buried our identity documents at Alpe Aurelio? Before we did so, Luna memorised everyone's date of birth.'

Trust Teresa to spill the beans, but Giulia couldn't be angry with her. In fact, she couldn't help feeling pleased that her eighteenth wouldn't slip by unnoticed.

'Would you like to go down to Miazzina to celebrate? I discovered that the village fills up with hundreds of partisans every Sunday. The Fascists only garrison the lakeside towns and stay away from Miazzina due to the large number of *partigiani*.'

'What about the Germans?' Giulia asked.

'On the weekends they remain in their Stresa and Baveno headquarters. People from Intra and other nearby towns arrive in the village to support the partisans. They have no fear of the risk of betrayal that could lead to them being arrested for aiding and abetting bandits.'

'Will your parents be there?' Giulia asked.

'I've asked the innkeeper to send a message to them, so I hope they will.'

'That'll be nice for you.' She heard the sadness in her tone.

'I wish there was some way I could find out what's happened to your mother and father, Piccola. I'm sorry it's impossible for you to go and find them. But hopefully, the war won't last many more months—'

'The Allies will be in Rome soon, won't they?' She'd injected a note of optimism into her voice.

'Any day now, by all accounts.'

'But the Germans will fight to hold on to the north of Italy. And, even if they're defeated here, they'll still have much of the rest of Europe. It could be months before the conflict ends.'

Raffaele put down his knife and reached for her hand.

'You're being very brave, and I'm sorry it took me so long to see that,' he said, squeezing her fingers.

'Yes, well. You weren't exactly my favourite person in the world, either.'

He laughed and she laughed with him.

'I can't wait to start harassing the Nazi-fascists again,' he said. 'Not sure if living up here in isolation has been such a good idea.'

'We're not the only ones. Aquila's *Cesare Battisti* has remained at Shanghai, and the Valdossola are lower down still, and neither band had carried out any guerrilla actions either, as far as I'm aware. The weather has been terrible.'

'You're right, Piccola. As soon as a proper thaw sets in, we'll all get back into action.'

She passed him another potato, and their hands touched. As she lifted her gaze to his, a tingly feeling spread through her. His blue eyes locked with hers, warm and glowing. A sudden knot formed in her stomach, making her feel vulnerable and exposed. She gave herself a little shake and got on with peeling the vegetables.

* * *

On the morning of her birthday, Giulia went down to the dining room to be regaled with the sound of '*Buon compleanno*' being repeated by her comrades as they wished her happy birthday.

She thanked them and received an assortment of gifts: a penknife from Paolo, a new comb from Teresa, a pair of woollen socks from Giorgio (clearly one of his spare pairs as they were much too big for her). Glancing at Raffaele, she wondered if he had anything for her, too.

Her heart beat a strange rhythm as he reached behind his back.

'These are for you,' he said, pulling out a posy of wild cyclamen and handing it to her. 'I got up early and went to pick them.'

'They're beautiful,' she said, raising the flowers to her nose and breathing in the sweet, floral scent. '*Grazie.*'

'You're welcome.' A smile lifted the corner of his mouth. 'Now let's go and have breakfast.'

Sitting at the refectory table in the dining room, she found herself pushed up against Raffaele on a long bench, squeezed between Teresa and Paolo. The heat of Raffaele's body radiated through her. She wanted to fan herself with her hand, but she wrapped her fingers around a cup of barley coffee and took a deep breath instead. Raffaele smelt of fresh soap. Thank God the thaw had lasted, and they now had enough water for washing. Before the snowmelt, they could only avail themselves of the liquid that dripped from the roof when the sun came out. They would collect it in pails, which they set aside for cleaning their teeth, faces, necks and feet, as well as for the men to shave with. It had been wonderful to wash properly again, and the smell of unwashed bodies no longer permeated the air.

Lifting her hand to twirl one of her plaits, Giulia stopped herself just in time. She'd been thinking about cutting her hair for weeks, and yesterday she'd asked Teresa to cut off her braids, saying they'd become hard to manage. Teresa kept her own hair short, trimming it herself from time to time. It was easy for her to wash and dry, and Giulia hadn't hesitated in saying she was adamant that was what she wanted too.

After Teresa had finished styling her hair, Giulia had stared at her reflection, almost not recognising the young woman staring back at her. Gone were the chubby cheeks of her childhood, and her eyes appeared huge in her slimmed-down face. Teresa had cut her hair to chin-length, and relieved of the weight of its old length, it fell from a centre-part in soft chestnut waves to cover her ears.

The best thing about it had been Raffaele's reaction. He'd joined in with the others in saying how much the new style suited her, and the fact that he'd done so had gladdened Giulia's heart. Not so long ago, he would have remained silent or said something disparaging. Why did she care so deeply about his opinion of her? *Search me*, she thought, giving him a sidelong glance.

17

Raffaele fell into step beside Giulia on the way to Miazzina. He couldn't take his eyes off her; she looked so beautiful with her bobbed hair framing her lovely face. Had he done the right thing by suggesting an outing in public to celebrate her birthday? *It will be fine*, he told himself. *The Nazi-fascists never come to the village on a Sunday, and the locals who do so are either friends or family of the partisans.*

He held on to that conviction all the way down the steep mountain and soon he was leading her and the rest of the Pian Cavallone band into the café in the centre of the village, which was frequented by the *partigiani*. They went to find seats at tables where the *Cesare Battisti ragazzi* were already socialising with local people, who were buying everyone drinks and plying them with food.

Raffaele stopped in his tracks; he'd spotted Aquila propping up the bar, so he looped Giulia's arm through his and walked them both up to him.

'Lele and Piccola, good to see you, my friends,' Eagle said, a

Nazionale cigarette burning in the ashtray in front of him. 'How are things?'

Unlooping Giulia's arm from his, Raffaele told Aquila they'd narrowly avoided starvation during the blizzard. Aquila said his formation had been in the same boat.

'Now the weather has improved,' Aquila added, 'we can't wait to get back into action.'

'Us too,' Raffaele said, and Giulia nodded in agreement beside him. 'We've been far too isolated up at Pian Cavallone.'

'The Committee of National Liberation for Northern Italy in Milan is looking for flying squads to carry out sabotage actions down on the plain, in particular blowing up train tracks.' Aquila fixed Raffaele with his eagle-eyed stare. 'Would you be interested?'

'Hmmm.' Raffaele thought for a moment. 'We'd need explosives, tinned food, money, fake documents, up-to-date maps and a vehicle in which to travel.' He ticked the items off on his fingers. 'If the Committee can provide all that, I'd be more than interested.'

'I'll set up a meeting for you.' Aquila took a drag of his cigarette. 'A courier will be in touch.'

Raffaele felt a tug at his sleeve. Giulia indicated towards a group of people coming through the door. 'Your parents and the Bertrandis have arrived, Lele.'

'Off you go, guys.' Aquila smiled. 'I'll catch up with you later.'

Looping Giulia's arm through his again, Raffaele steered her towards where his family had found the only unoccupied table.

'How are things at home?' he asked his parents after he'd pulled out chairs for Giulia and himself.

'Not so bad.' Pa was plainly putting on a brave face. 'We're planning to grow some vegetables now that spring is on the way, and soon the chickens will be laying again.'

'Have you heard anything about what's happened to Giulia's parents?' Raffaele asked on her behalf.

'Not a word, unfortunately. We're completely cut off from Milan these days.'

'I wish I could go there and contact my father's deputy, Signor Perego,' Giulia said with a sigh.

Raffaele smiled at her, feeling proud she hadn't revealed what Aquila had proposed. It dawned on Raffaele that he might be able to kill two birds with one stone: meet with the Liberation Committee and try to find out more about Giulia's parents. She'd probably want to go to Milan with him, but that would be far too dangerous. He became aware of the strength of his own heartbeat as he felt an overwhelming desire to protect her. Best to change the topic of conversation. He asked about his siblings and listened to his mother recount how well they were doing at school.

Pa and his cousin, Signor Bertrandi, went to the bar to buy drinks, and Giulia asked Signora Bertrandi if she'd heard anything more about the Germans searching for her.

'Not since before the snowstorm, my dear.' The signora patted Giulia's hand. 'Be careful. They have spies all over the place—'

'Raffaele is keeping me safe,' she said, her eyes on his face.

Accordion music almost drowned out her words. Duke was playing a catchy tune, and before too long, practically the entire café had risen to their feet.

After his parents and the Bertrandis had got up to enjoy a waltz, Raffaele smiled at Giulia. He would ask her for a dance too. No harm in that. But, before he could do so, Paolo came up and whisked her onto the floor. Raffaele's stomach clenched with envy. If Paolo didn't already have a *fidanzata* in Baveno, Raffaele would have felt more than envious; he'd have found himself feeling downright jealous.

He approached an attractive young woman at the next table. Her name was Elena, and soon she began asking him so many questions about his activities that Raffaele started to feel uncomfortable. A tap on his shoulder caused him to release the girl from his arms. Aquila had come up, and he put his hand on Raffaele's back and led him to the bar.

'The innkeeper told me your dance partner forms part of a group of girls who fraternise with the partisans on Sundays. He said we should be careful not to share information with them, as they could be Fascist spies.'

'I told her nothing,' Raffaele said, watching Elena saunter across the room and approach one of the Pian Cavallone men. He was about to go and warn the man to be discreet. But, from the corner of his eye, he saw that Giulia had returned to the table by herself, so he made his excuses to Aquila and went to join her.

'Did you enjoy your dance?' he asked.

'Not really. Biondo kept stepping on my toes.' She pulled a face. 'Did you enjoy yours?'

He said that he hadn't and then told her about Aquila's suspicions towards the girl.

'That's awful,' she said. 'I'm so sorry.'

'And I'm sorry about Biondo stepping on your toes.'

A downright lie. Although Paolo was 'taken', he hadn't seen his girlfriend in months. And Giulia was no longer the kid she used to be. She'd grown into a beautiful young woman, and Raffaele didn't want her to be dancing with anyone but him.

In need of distraction, he went to the bar to get them both a drink. By the time he'd returned to the table, the dancing had ended, and the entire café had joined the partisans in singing the anthem 'The Wind Whistles', followed by a rousing rendition of 'Bella, Ciao'.

Raffaele went up to Duke and whispered to him to play the 'Happy Birthday' song.

'*Buon compleanno*, Piccola,' everyone sang.

Raffaele glanced at her, and the sadness in her expression tore at his heart. She must be missing her parents so much. He should pull out all the stops to help her find them.

* * *

Raffaele was on lookout duty with Giulia a week later. He was due to leave in two days' time with Paolo, Giorgio, Teresa and Tarzan, who'd agreed to be part of the mission after Raffaele had received a couriered message from Milan three days ago. They were to meet a *gappista*, as the urban guerrillas were known. Giulia had kept silent about not having been included in the mission, and Raffaele steeled himself as he waited for her to bring up the subject.

'Erm, can I ask you something?' She twisted her fingers together in her lap.

'Sure, go ahead.' He leant towards her.

'Please take me with you, Lele. I know Milan like the back of my hand, so I could be useful.'

'You're safer here, Piccola. The city is crawling with Germans. They'll have found out that's where you usually live and are sure to be keeping an eye out for you.'

'Then I won't go to my old home. I just want to see Papà's deputy. He might know something about my parents, and, at the same time, I could ask him to make sure payments of your father's salary are resumed.'

She'd played her trump card, and she knew it. But Raffaele

wasn't going to back down so easily. Taking her on the mission to Milan might put the entire squad in danger.

He placed his hands on either side of her face and looked her in the eye.

'I'll think about it, all right? But you must promise me that if I decide against it, you'll accept my decision and not try to make me change my mind.'

She opened and closed her mouth, then nodded.

'Yes, Raffaele,' she said. 'I promise.'

'Good girl.' He planted a brotherly kiss on her forehead.

Giulia tilted her face up and, before he knew it, he was kissing her properly. His mouth claimed hers, and he lost all sense of time and place. The world around him shrank until it was just him and Giulia and nothing else mattered. He deepened the kiss and, as her arms stretched around his neck, he forgot about his responsibilities. They were two young people on the brink of something wonderful. Then, with a start, he found himself being jolted back to reality.

He pulled away, taking her hands from his neck.

'Piccola, I don't know what I was thinking. I'm sorry.'

He mustn't let his feelings interfere with his responsibilities. There was a war on, and he should focus on helping to win it. That must be his top priority. He was a partisan leader and had to put his squad first.

Confusion played across her lovely face, and she gazed at him with her beautiful amber eyes. Eyes that begged for more. Eyes in which he was in constant danger of losing himself. He wanted to take her in his arms and kiss her until she was breathless.

But he didn't, of course. Instead, he glanced at his watch and said it was time to go back inside. He needed to prepare for the mission to Milan. Luckily one of the partisans at Pian Cavallone was a photographer and he'd brought his camera with him. He'd set up a dark room where he developed his pictures. Raffaele would go to ask him to take photos of him and his comrades for their forged documents.

* * *

On the night before Raffaele and his squad were due to set off, Giorgio came to see him.

'I hope you don't mind, Lele,' the older man said. 'But I'd like to withdraw from the mission. I'd prefer to wait for more information but won't try to dissuade you if that's what you really want.'

Relief coursed through Raffaele; he'd been worried about leaving the Pian Cavallone formation without an experienced leader.

'In that case, my friend, I'd like you to take over command.'

'I accept, of course,' Giorgio said without apparent hesitation.

'Make sure there are always sentries posted. I'm glad you're staying behind, to be honest. Nazi-fascists might come up here looking for Piccola.'

'Good thing you're taking her with you to Milan, then. And don't worry about us, we'll send any unwanted visitors packing.'

Raffaele sighed. A message had come from Aquila yesterday to say that a mole working for the Fascists in Intra had learnt that a spy had informed on Giulia. One of those godforsaken girls in the café last Sunday had told the *fascisti* that a young woman fitting Giulia's description was hiding out with the partisans. Raffaele had immediately decided to include her in the mission to Milan and keep her under his protection.

He sighed again. Perhaps he was being selfish leaving Giorgio and the rest of his men to face the Nazi-fascists without him. But

Giorgio would take care of them, and they'd have the upper hand if any undesirables came up the mountain.

Guilt panged in Raffaele's chest when he went to bed later. After they'd been equipped by the Liberation Committee in Milan with everything he'd ask for, he'd be leading Giulia and the rest of the team into the unknown. Why do that? Truth be told it was for his own personal satisfaction. Being stuck up on a mountain, with neither Fascists to fight nor the weapons with which to do so, had been frustrating him for weeks. He'd turned into an egoist, and now he found himself resenting Giorgio, who clearly didn't have a selfish bone in his body.

Raffaele's thoughts turned to Giulia. She'd been subdued since their kiss. Had she been longing for him to kiss her again as much as he'd been aching to do so? He couldn't stop thinking about how sweet her lips were, but at the same time how innocent. Had he made the right decision to take her with him? Whatever happened, he would do all that he could to keep her safe.

18

Milan looks more like a battlefield than the city I remember, Giulia thought as she walked with Raffaele, Tarzan, Teresa and Paolo down a blistered, charred street flanked with rubble. Not one building had been left standing, and the piles of debris everywhere broke her heart.

They were being escorted by one of the *gappisti* urban guerrillas to a safe apartment, where they'd be staying until their forged documents were ready. Early-morning light filtered between the bombed-out buildings, and Giulia's breath caught at the sight of a crater barring their way. Cautiously, she and the others edged around it. Filthy water lingered in the bottom of the hole, giving off a putrid stench.

Her feet dragging with tiredness, Giulia concentrated on remaining focused. After they'd left Pian Cavallone two nights ago – when she, Raffaele and the rest of his squad had crept out of the hotel without a word of 'goodbye' to anyone – they'd hiked many kilometres to cover as much ground as possible during the hours of darkness. Thankfully, at dawn, they'd been able to find an abandoned barn in which to set up camp and had pitched the military tent provided by the Verbania committee. Hunkering down with three men wasn't as awkward as she'd imagined it would be. They'd rolled themselves up in their blankets in a row, with Giulia at one end, Teresa behind her, Paolo next to his sister, followed by Raffaele and Tarzan. If Mamma and Papà could have seen her, they'd have been flabbergasted.

A thick lump formed in Giulia's throat. Were her mother and father still being held by the Germans in the city? She prayed earnestly there'd be a chance to visit Papà's deputy. And, if and when she did so, that he'd have news...

Without warning, the *gappista*, a burly young Milanese who went by the battle name Wolf, indicated with his hand they should all crouch down behind the ruins of a house. Giulia's heart skittered; a German patrol was heading their way. Peering around the blackened stones, she stared at a group of six men marching down the street.

The sound of children's laughter tinkled. Four or five youngsters, covered with filth, had come to play in the bomb site. Would the Nazis tell them off? But no, the troops marched past, clearly intent on a more pressing objective, and soon the young man in charge of Giulia and her companions stood up and led them away.

Before too long, they'd left the waste land behind and had entered a neighbourhood that appeared to have lost fewer buildings. The scene reminded Giulia of a mouth with missing teeth: some broken, some gone, and some still standing between the gaps.

They arrived at two intact blocks of apartments side by side and went into the one on the right. It was as if they'd entered a human beehive buzzing with life. There were *bambini* playing everywhere and people sat in their open doorways, smoking and chatting to each other. Climbing up to the first floor with

Raffaele and the others, Giulia couldn't help but feel her spirits lift.

'We're here.' Wolf extracted a key from his pocket and unlocked a door at the end of the corridor. A hallway opened onto two bedrooms, a bathroom and a living-dining room, furnished in a basic style, with a kitchen at the end.

'There's sufficient food to last you a week,' Wolf said. 'That'll be more than enough time to forge your documents.' He glanced at Raffaele. 'Did you bring photographs?'

Raffaele reached into his knapsack and handed the *gappista* an envelope.

'In the meantime, don't leave the apartment.' Wolf shot a stern glance at them all. 'If the *tedeschi* catch you without papers, they'll shoot you in a flash.'

* * *

The week passed slowly, and Giulia and her friends kept themselves occupied by sleeping a lot. When they'd had enough rest they played cards, practised callisthenics, and sat in pairs to talk. Giulia spent a lot of time with Paolo, trying to cheer him up. He'd been upset that his mother, father, and girlfriend hadn't come to the café in Miazzina. His parents had probably been worried about leaving his younger siblings to fend for themselves, but Paolo said that his *fidanzata* had been cold towards him when he'd gone home to visit his family after Christmas and he feared she no longer loved him.

Giulia enjoyed chatting with Paolo: he was kind and uncomplicated. And he distracted her from thinking about Raffaele. Since he'd kissed her up at Pian Cavallone, she'd tried to keep her distance from him. She'd been hurt that he'd pushed her away. Maybe she wasn't as good a kisser as the other girls he'd kissed? Or did he still consider her a spoilt brat? Whatever the case, she hadn't been able to stop thinking about the feel of his lips on hers, the way he'd taken possession of her mouth so passionately he'd made her heart race and her skin burn. She'd surrendered herself to the moment so completely that she'd melted into him, wanting the kiss to go on forever. When he'd removed her arms from around his neck, it had been as if he'd slapped her, and the pain of his rejection still festered like an open wound.

Another distraction had been the time she'd spent with Tarzan. He was Milanese like she was, and they would reminisce together about how beautiful the city had been before the Allied bombings.

Today, Giulia and Teresa had been left behind in the apartment while Raffaele, Tarzan and Paolo had gone with Wolf to meet with representatives of the Liberation Committee. The *ragazzi* had taken their forged documents with them, but Giulia and Teresa still had theirs. Although Giulia knew Raffaele would be annoyed with her and accuse her of being impetuous, she also knew that if she didn't take this chance, she might never get another opportunity to go and see her father's deputy.

She told Teresa her plan, adding, 'I'd like you to come with me, but fully understand if you'd prefer not to.'

'I can't let you go on your own, Piccola,' Teresa said. 'And I wouldn't be able to stop you if I tried. I just hope you know what you're doing.'

'It'll be fine, you'll see. We've both packed dresses in our knapsacks. If we put them on, we'll look like typical Milanese women out shopping. Especially as we have forged ration cards along with our IDs.'

'I've been bored out of my mind waiting in this flat.' Teresa pursed her lips. 'How far away is your father's office?'

'Not far. About half an hour's walk. We should be back before the guys return.'

'We can leave them a note to say where we've gone, so they won't worry.' Teresa smiled. 'Raffaele didn't tell us we weren't supposed to leave the apartment. Technically, we won't be disobeying any orders.'

Giulia pulled in and then slowly released a deep breath.

'Raffaele couldn't care less about me,' she said.

'I think you're wrong, Piccola.' Teresa shook her head. 'I've seen the way he looks at you. I believe he cares about you a lot.'

'He's such an egoist. I doubt he realises how much I miss my parents and how awful it is for me not to know what's happened to them.'

'Maybe he does realise? Maybe he wants to protect you and spare you from disappointment. I mean, you might not like what your father's deputy tells you—'

'I'd rather know than not know. Living in the limbo of ignorance has been hell.'

'I understand.' Teresa touched her hand to Giulia's arm. 'We'd better get a move on if we're to be back before the guys.'

* * *

Half an hour later, after Giulia and Teresa had left the apartment and were walking arm in arm across the city centre, they arrived at a sandbagged and heavily fortified checkpoint in San Babila square. Although the *gappista* who'd brought them to the flat had told Giulia and the others about how the Nazis had set up barriers dividing Milan into sectors, it was still a shock to find her way barred. She knew this square; she would cross it every day as she walked to school. Sadness scratched in her throat as she gazed at the beautiful old buildings that had been damaged by the Allied air raids.

Giulia tried to keep calm while she and Teresa skirted around the sixteenth-century basilica presiding over the *piazza*, but nervous butterflies fluttered in her chest.

'*Unserer Papiere*,' a fresh-faced guard demanded at the barrier.

Giulia's hand trembled as she opened her bag to extract her documents. Who was Emilia Lamberti, the woman whose photo had been replaced by hers? They were the same age, roughly, and the same height.

Her chest tightened with nerves. The German seemed to be taking far more time than was necessary to inspect her identity card. She feigned nonchalance and had to stop herself from letting out a huge breath of relief when he waved her and Teresa through.

They strolled in silence through what appeared to be one of the least damaged areas they'd seen thus far in Milan. The shops, restaurants, and bars were open and filled with Nazi officers and their women. The streets were as familiar to Giulia as her family home, and it pained her that they were packed with German vehicles: Mercedes and Volkswagens instead of Fiat and Lancia cars.

The pink-hued white marble of the cathedral shone in the sunshine to her left. Giulia squeezed Teresa's arm and whispered they'd almost arrived.

They crossed Corso Vittorio Emmanuele II, famous for its swanky shops selling luxury goods, and proceeded to Via Pietro Verri, the heart of the fashion district. It was there that Papà had established his antique furniture business before Giulia was born. Specialising in pieces from the Italian Renaissance, which he would sell for millions of lire, Giulia's father had a knack for sourcing items from old villas which their owners put up for sale to cover upkeep expenses.

Giulia gave a start. A Daimler-Benz like the one belonging to the German consul general had rolled to a stop right in front of her father's store. However, it wasn't her father's friend emerging from the vehicle, but a Nazi officer wearing a trench coat over his shoulders. He muttered something to the driver before entering the shop.

'We can't go in now,' Giulia said to Teresa. 'Let's find somewhere to hide and wait until that man comes out again.'

They concealed themselves in the doorway of a boutique that was thankfully closed and waited for what seemed like an age. Checking her watch, Giulia became aware that their return to the safe apartment would be delayed. Chances were, the *ragazzi* would get back well before they did. *Can't be helped*, she thought.

Finally, Signor Perego and a shop assistant emerged, carrying an antique desk which they loaded into the trunk of the car. In the meantime, the German had slid into the back seat. Relief washed through Giulia as she watched the Daimler-Benz set off back down the road.

'The coast is clear,' she said, taking Teresa's hand. 'Come with me.'

Pushing open the door to the shop, Giulia felt her spirits lift. Nothing appeared to have changed. She gazed at the ubiquitous walnut credenzas, chairs with velvet upholstery and bone, horn, and boxwood inlays, and sumptuous *cassoni* marriage chests. Her nose wrinkled as she breathed in the familiar scent of beeswax furniture polish. She glanced around for Papà's deputy and smiled when she recognised the middle-aged man standing behind the counter.

'Giulia! What a surprise! Why are you here? The Germans

have been looking for you—' Signor Perego's voice had gone up an octave.

'I'm trying to find out what's happened to my parents. The SS took them away last September.' She indicated towards Teresa. 'This is my friend, Luna, by the way.'

'*Piacere*.' Papà's deputy shook Teresa's hand. 'Come through to the back office, both of you. It isn't safe out here.'

Giulia's eyes prickled as she stepped into the room. So many memories of the times she'd spent with her beloved father. Memories so vivid she could almost smell the tobacco he smoked and his sandalwood cologne.

After arranging with his assistant to mind the shop front, Signor Perego offered Giulia and Teresa refreshments.

'Thank you, but we can only stay a short while,' Giulia said before asking without preamble, 'Do you have any news about my mother and father?'

Signor Perego's mouth twisted grimly, and he appeared to hesitate before speaking, as if weighing his words.

'It's a long story,' he said, hanging his head. 'You and Luna had better sit down.' He pulled out chairs for them and himself.

'So, did you hear from my mamma and papà?' Giulia asked, her heart in her mouth.

'They were taken to San Vittore prison and your father managed to smuggle a note out to me not long after they'd arrived.'

Giulia sagged back in her chair. She'd been driven past the impenetrably high, dingy white walls of the jail on numerous occasions. Inside, the prisoners were incarcerated in cells housed in a starfish-shaped building. Her mouth turned dry at the thought of her parents languishing inside.

'What did the note say?' she asked.

'Your papà wanted me to contact the German consul general

on his behalf. I tried to see him, but when I arrived at the Consulate, I learnt that he and his wife had just left Milan.'

'Oh, no.' Giulia's heart sank. 'Were you able to go to the prison and visit my parents, by any chance?'

'Before I could do so, the Gestapo turned up and took me in for questioning. They did everything they could to get me to inform on your whereabouts, Giulia.'

She gaped at her father's deputy, aghast. The poor man, and all because of her. A lump formed in her throat, and she had to swallow it before she could speak.

'I hope they didn't hurt you, Signor Perego.'

'I'm afraid they did. They whipped me. But as I knew nothing, I revealed nothing. Eventually, they gave up. Unfortunately, I found out later that they also questioned Maria, your family's housekeeper. Those *bastardi* beat the poor woman senseless.'

'They're so cruel.' Giulia fumbled for words. 'How could they have done that to you both? I'm so sorry—'

'I won't tell you about the horrors they've inflicted on Milan. I wish I didn't have to do business with them, but I have no choice. Either I sell them our stock at cut-price rates, or they'd find some excuse to appropriate it by nefarious means.'

'I understand,' she said with a sigh. 'My father would do the same, I'm sure. Are he and my mother still in San Vittore?'

'When the Gestapo released me, I contacted the Liberation Committee to find out if the *gappisti* could mount a rescue operation. But it was too late.' Signor Perego looked Giulia in the eye, and dread filled her as she waited for what he would say next. 'Your parents had already been transported to a labour camp in Poland, my dear. There was nothing I nor anyone else could do.'

'Oh, my God.' It would be impossible for her to travel to Poland. She placed her head in her hands and sobbed.

'It's okay to cry, Piccola.' Teresa had put her arm around her.

'Sometimes crying can help. At least that's been my own experience.'

Giulia remembered Teresa had lost her husband in the Russian campaign. But she refused to believe Mamma and Papà might have suffered a similar fate. They were both fit and healthy and could work hard. The war would end sooner rather than later. Especially now that the Allies were about to take Rome. Giulia inhaled a deep breath and pulled a handkerchief from her pocket.

'We'd best head back to Raffaele and the others,' she said, drying her eyes.

'I won't ask where you've been or what you are doing, Giulia.' Signor Perego fixed her with a wary look. 'That way I can be totally honest if the Gestapo question me again.'

'*Grazie.*' She thanked Signor Perego. 'I pray they'll leave you in peace now.' She proceeded to tell him about the horrific fate of Ester and her loved ones.

'That's why your parents were arrested, isn't it? The Gestapo told me your mamma and papà were helping them. When I asked if the Jews had been imprisoned in San Vittore, the Nazis who were interrogating me laughed and said they had no idea where they were.'

Fear for her parents made Giulia feel nauseous. But she wouldn't lose hope. Until she knew otherwise, she would believe in a good outcome. Mamma and Papà would come home eventually, and life would return to normal.

'I've just remembered something else.' Giulia leant forward in her chair. 'Maurizio Ferrero, the hotel manager, is working without pay, keeping an eye on things for my father. Is there any way you can take steps for payment of his salary to be resumed and for him to receive back pay? He has a wife and young family—'

'That won't be a problem,' Signor Perego said. 'I'll cable him to collect funds from the post office. I've also arranged for Maria to continue to be paid.'

'*Grazie.*' Giulia forced a wan smile. 'Luna and I will leave now. We don't want to put you in danger.'

'Come through to the back door.' Signor Perego rose to his feet. 'It would be safer if you and your friend took a short cut through the side streets. I presume you have false papers?'

After Giulia had confirmed that was the case, he led her and Teresa outside.

'We can only pray for the war to end soon,' Giulia said. 'And then all will be well.' She refused to believe anything else, for to think otherwise could only lead to despair.

Her father's deputy waved her and Teresa off and, as they made their way towards the San Babila checkpoint, she couldn't help feeling tempted to visit Maria at her family's apartment in Corso del Littorio. It was still in the fashion district, but closer to the La Scala opera house, the Galleria shopping mall, and the Piazza Duomo, the cathedral square.

Although she wanted to apologise to the housekeeper for what she'd suffered on her behalf, the sensible voice in Giulia's head told her it would be foolish. If anyone saw her, they could report the incident to the Germans and that might make things even worse for poor Maria.

Her thoughts turning to Raffaele, Giulia's steps lightened. She was looking forward to seeing him. Had Teresa been right when she'd said she thought Raffaele cared about her? Giulia touched a finger to her lips, remembering their kiss. Raffaele certainly was an expert kisser; he probably had a lot of experience, unlike her. The boys who'd kissed her at high school dances had been sloppy in comparison.

At the barrier, the guards scarcely glanced at her and Teresa's papers before waving them through. They'd barely taken a few steps before a shout made Giulia spin around.

A man was running towards them, pursued by three German soldiers with their weapons raised.

Terrified, Giulia grabbed hold of Teresa's arm, and they stopped dead in their tracks.

The man and the guards sped past them and halted at the far side of the square.

Giulia's heart was racing so fast she felt dizzy. What on earth was happening? She stood and watched the soldiers search the man. They made him face the wall of a building and spread his legs. He was crying and pleading with them, but she couldn't make out his words. One of the soldiers shouted something in German, and the other two shuffled a few steps back.

The guard who'd barked the orders raised his pistol and shot the man in the back of the head. Giulia watched in horror as he crumpled to the ground in a pool of blood.

'Let's get out of here,' she said to Teresa, preparing to run.

'Walk slowly, Piccola. We don't want to raise any suspicions.'

All the way back to the apartment, Giulia couldn't stop thinking about the poor man and his shocking death. The sooner she and the others left Milan, the better. This was no longer the city she knew and loved. It had become a dangerous place where people like Signor Perego and Maria could be tortured by the Nazis, and men like the one killed in the square could be shot for God knew what.

19

Raffaele was pacing the floor of the apartment while Paolo and Tarzan sat stone-faced on the sofa. They'd returned half an hour ago after an unproductive meeting with a man from the Liberation Committee. When Raffaele had described his plans about how he and his group would blow up the train tracks between Milan and Lake Maggiore, he was told there were no longer enough explosives, nor was there a spare vehicle available for them, and that he and his squad should head back to Pian Cavallone. His body had grown heavy with disappointment and, to make matters worse, on returning to the flat he'd discovered Giulia's note. How could she have been so irresponsible? He'd thought she'd overcome her impetuosity. If she and Teresa were caught, they'd be tortured until they revealed information, and he couldn't bear the thought of her going through that.

He was just about to leave the apartment to search for them when the door crashed open and they rushed inside.

'So sorry we're late back,' Giulia said, her face flushed. 'We had to wait for a German officer to leave my father's shop before we could go inside.'

Raffaele stiffened his jaw, relief that she and Teresa were safe combining with anger at Giulia's casual attitude towards her and the squad's wellbeing.

'You could have been arrested,' he said. 'Didn't you realise you could have put us all in danger? Not to mention your personal safety.'

'But... but we had our forged documents. No one would know who I was. We were extremely careful going into Papà's shop.'

'I hope it was worth the risk,' he said in a terse tone.

'I found out... I found out that my parents have been sent to a labour camp in Poland.' Her voice quavered and her mouth turned downwards.

'Go easy on Piccola, please, Lele.' Teresa touched her hand to his arm. 'She's had a terrible shock. But she also managed to ask her father's deputy to organise that your pa's salary be reinstated. He will send him a cable to pick up funds from the post office.'

'Thank you for that, Piccola,' Raffaele said. 'I'm grateful for what you did. I would have gone to visit your father's deputy in your place, by the way. I'm sorry about your parents. It was always my intention to discover what I could before we left Milan.'

'Why didn't you tell me?' Giulia lifted her gaze, and he saw the unshed tears glistening in her eyes. Tears that tugged at his heartstrings and made him ache to hold her.

'I hadn't got round to it yet,' he said before going on to tell Giulia and Teresa about the unproductive meeting, adding that it would have been impossible to carry out sabotage actions without enough explosives. 'I don't know why they made us come all the way to Milan.'

'Maybe the situation has only just changed.' Tarzan got up from the sofa. 'I mean, when the meeting was arranged, they probably thought we could go ahead.'

Raffaele raised an eyebrow. Tarzan and the *gappista* had walked to the meeting together, chatting like long-lost friends. Was there something they hadn't told him?

'I'll go make us some lunch,' Paolo said, breaking into Raffaele's thoughts. 'We can discuss what to do next while we eat.'

* * *

It was decided they would set off at nightfall. There was no point hanging around. But, after Giulia and Teresa had gone to their room for a nap, Tarzan came up to Raffaele.

'I'd like to stay in Milan and join the urban guerrillas, if that's okay. I've been missing my family, and this would be a way of getting to see them from time to time.'

'I noticed you and that *gappista* appear to have become as thick as thieves.'

'He didn't tell me anything about himself, but I'm sure I've seen him before. I think we went to the same school. When I asked him if I could join his cell... the urban guerrillas operate in small groups, apparently... he said he'd be happy to have me. I'll learn more once I'm formally a member.'

'If you're sure that's what you want.' Raffaele shot him a look. 'What's the plan?'

'I'll stay behind after you've left, then Wolf will come and collect me.'

'Piccola will be sad not to have you around any more.' Raffaele had noticed them giggling together like schoolkids. The green-eyed monster had stirred up jealousy within him, which he'd made a huge effort to quell. That was the problem with him developing feelings for her; it made him distrust every man in her presence, including Paolo, his best friend, who seemed to have been spending an excessive amount of time in her presence lately.

'She only has eyes for you, Lele.' Tarzan smirked. 'Haven't you noticed?'

'Can't say that I have.' He pretended indifference. Was it true? And, if it were, what could he possibly do about it?

Tarzan went to pack his rucksack and Raffaele did the same. He found Paolo sitting in a miserable heap on the big double bed the three of them shared.

'What's wrong?' Raffaele asked.

'I think I've been jilted,' he said.

For a moment, Raffaele thought he meant by Giulia. But that was ridiculous; they were hardly a couple. He hoped. Paolo could only be referring to Cristina, his *fidanzata*.

'What makes you say that?'

'When I went home before Christmas, she was cold towards me, and she didn't come to the café. The more I think about it, the more I'm convinced she has gone off me.'

Raffaele lowered himself onto the bed next to his best friend and put his arm around his shoulder.

'Don't lose heart, *amico mio*. She could simply have been too afraid to travel from Baveno. Why haven't you mentioned this before?'

'I didn't want to bother you. You've enough on your plate, Lele.'

'I'm never too busy for you. Feel free to bother me any time you like.'

'*Grazie*.' Paolo sighed. 'Frankly, I'm looking forward to getting back to the lake. I know it's only been a short while, but I've been missing it.'

'That and the mountains,' Raffaele agreed. 'We'll be home before we know it.'

'Pian Cavallone?' Paolo cocked his head to one side.

'I'd prefer us to carry on being a flying squad.' Raffaele kept to himself the fact that the enemy had found out Giulia was hiding out with the partisans. She'd be safer moving around with him and their friends than living in a permanent base. 'We can operate better that way.'

'If you say so, Lele.' Paolo shrugged. 'With luck, it won't be for long. The Allies will arrive soon, won't they?'

* * *

Back at Lake Maggiore, after a repeat of the journey they'd made to Milan, but in the opposite direction, Raffaele and his squad pitched their military tent in woodland about three-quarters of an hour's hike above Intra. Leaving the girls behind in the relative safety of their camp, Raffaele and Paolo went down to the lakeside to inform the Liberation Committee of their return. There, they learnt they were to come under the command of the Valdossola Battalion and would be tasked with operating independently in and around the Miazzina area, getting supplies, and harassing the enemy. They also discovered that Aquila, too, had attached his band to the Valdossola. Sabadini's battalion had grown to around 150, by all accounts, and he'd staggered them in various camps throughout the Val Grande valley. Apparently, Eagle had been persuaded to ally himself with the Valdossola because Major Sabadini had contacts with the Allied consular representatives in Switzerland, who'd recently organised two airdrops of one hundred semi-automatic weapons, as well as ammunition, explosives, foodstuffs and clothing. If it was the right thing for Aquila, it was good enough for Raffaele.

Subsequently, he went to meet with Sabadini, and obtained two Stens, numerous hand grenades, incendiary bombs and new khaki clothing for himself, Giulia, Teresa and Paolo. Between the four of them, they had three semi-automatic guns now, as well as several pistols. They kept their weapons close, going to bed at night not knowing how or by whom they would be woken.

Were their picturesque surroundings lulling him into a false sense of security? Raffaele asked himself as he fell asleep to the sound of nightingales singing in the chestnut trees and, on waking, gloried in the beautiful view of the lake shimmering in spring sunshine far below.

Torn between the desire to hide Giulia from the Nazi-fascists and the need to get back into action against the enemy, Raffaele found his resentment of Paolo's easy friendship with her was making him grumpy. He was short with her and the others. But perhaps it wasn't jealousy. How could he be jealous of his best friend? Absolute chaos reigned inside the camp: shoes mixed up with blankets, dirty clothes next to their bread rations, boxes of butter invaded by ants. Maybe they simply needed better accommodation where they wouldn't be living cheek by jowl? He resolved to go and visit his cousins in Ungiasca as soon as possible. They might know of an abandoned house where he and his squad could set up a new base. Only temporary, of course. To keep Giulia safe, they'd need to move around.

On a crisp May evening, Raffaele was building up a campfire in front of the tent – he and his comrades would sit out there in the evenings after supper to enjoy some fresh air before bedtime – when the sound of familiar voices made him glance up. Giorgio, Rock, Lungo and Duke were approaching. They must have found out about Raffaele's failed mission to Milan from the Liberation Committee, who would also have told them about the squad's location.

'How are things?' he asked, indicating that they should sit in front of the fire.

'Not good.' Giorgio gave a sigh. 'Yesterday, Pian Cavallone came under attack.'

'What? How?' Raffaele heard the shock in his tone.

'A group of *fascisti* came up the slope under cover of thick mist. They demanded that we hand Piccola over to them, calling her Giulia Leone. I pretended not to know who they were talking about, but I put two and two together, of course, remembering you'd warned me that it might happen, Lele.'

'Please, tell me more.' Apprehension twisted in Raffaele's gut.

'They refused to leave until we handed her over. Wouldn't accept our denial that she wasn't with us. We couldn't fire on them as our only heavy weapon was one machine gun, which had jammed. So, I ordered my men to retreat up to the mountain behind.'

'Those *bastardi* burnt the hotel down to the ground.' Rock took up the tale.

'Good God.' A painful lump formed in Raffaele's throat. *Goodbye, Albergo Pian Cavallone.*

'We loved that place,' Lungo said. 'It sheltered us from the cold and the storms. Toughened us up and taught us the meaning of life.'

'Now it's nothing but a pile of bricks and rubble baked by fire and blackened by smoke,' Duke added, releasing a heavy sigh. 'I'm just glad I managed to retrieve my accordion in time.'

It was then that Raffaele noticed Duke, Lungo and Rock's kit bags, which they'd placed on the ground between their rifles. From the corner of his eye, he also saw that Giulia, Teresa, and Paolo had emerged from the tent. Had they heard Giorgio mention the attack on the hotel?

'I'm so sorry you've suffered because of me.' Giulia lowered herself in front of the fire, and Paolo sat next to her, with Teresa on the other side. There was a haunted look in Giulia's eyes, and Raffaele found himself wanting to reach out and comfort her.

'Everyone suffers in times of war,' he said instead. 'You weren't to blame, Piccola. Just the circumstances.' He turned to Giorgio and asked, to change the subject, 'Where are you headed with all that kit?'

'The *ragazzi* were hoping to join your squad, Lele. They've brought their own weapons.'

'We'd be happy to have you, wouldn't we, guys?' He swept his gaze from Giulia to Paolo and Teresa. He liked Rock, Lungo, and Duke, and having them around might dilute the amount of time Giulia spent huddled with Paolo.

Teresa said she'd be delighted, and Giulia and Paolo concurred.

'How about you, *Monco*?' Raffaele asked Giorgio. 'You didn't mention yourself.'

'I've been put in overall charge of your squad and mine,' the older man said. 'We now form part of a band called "Young Italy". Sabadini gave us a Breda 37 machine gun. And our numbers have grown to eighty overall, since the arrival of the latest recruits.'

'Congratulations on the Breda.' Raffaele wasn't at all resentful that Giorgio was now in command. Everyone liked *Il Monco*; he would tell interesting stories about his tour of duty in north Africa before it had fallen to the Allies. What Raffaele respected most about him was that he never complained and he was able to do with one hand what many people struggled to do with two.

'I like the new name,' Raffaele said. 'But where are you based now that Pian Cavallone is no more?'

'I like our name too, although I'm not so young any more.'

Giorgio grinned ruefully. 'We've set up camp at an alpe above Miazzina.'

'How about Aquila?' Giulia asked.

'He and his band have left Shanghai and are living in a hikers' refuge on a hillcrest overlooking the Cannobina valley,' Duke said.

'How many partisans are there in this area nowadays?' The question came from Teresa.

'Last count was about 400 in total. There're 240 under Sabadini, and Aquila's battalion is similar in size to ours.' Giorgio looked down at his hands. 'Because our numbers have grown so much, there've been rumours of an imminent round-up of all the partisans by the Germans, unfortunately.'

'Who told you that?' Paolo wrinkled his brow.

'Sabadini. Oh, and another thing. He has appointed an Alpini lieutenant, battle name Carlo, to be in command of us all.'

Giorgio gave the impression of having chosen his words carefully, probably expecting Raffaele to react negatively. Which he did.

'I'm not happy to be part of the Valdossola, to be honest, and have strangers in charge,' he said. 'I mean, we were doing fine on our own.'

'A unified command will be vital if the enemy does decide on a *rastrellamento*.' Giorgio ran a hand through his pepper-and-salt hair. 'There are difficult times up ahead, I fear.'

'We'll stand firm against the Germans.' Raffaele hoped he sounded confident. 'We have right on our side.'

'I pray you aren't wrong, my boy.' Giorgio got to his feet. 'In the meantime, I'll wish you goodnight and head back to my men. Keep the faith! As you said, we have the moral high ground. Evil will be defeated.'

Giulia and Teresa kissed *Il Monco* on both cheeks before he left, and Raffaele and the rest of the men shook his hand.

They sat back down around the campfire, and Duke began to play his accordion. Soon, they were singing the partisans' anthem, 'The Wind Blows'.

> If cruel death takes us,
> harsh revenge will come from the partisan.
> Already certain is the unforgiving fate of the vile
>   treasonous Fascist.
> The wind ceases and the storm grows calm.
> The proud partisan returns home.
> Blowing in the wind is his red flag.
> Victorious, at last we are free.

20

Fireflies lit up the night with their enchanting glow as Giulia gazed from her and Teresa's bedroom window in the safe house Signor Bertrandi had found for them on the outskirts of Ungiasca. They'd been staying there for a month now, and had given it the name 'Tipperary', after Giulia had introduced Raffaele and the others to the marching song. She'd taught it to them when they'd been making their laborious way back to their base after relieving a Fascist militiaman of his Sten submachine gun on the outskirts of Intra. It was one of many actions they'd been carrying out to accumulate weapons, and Giulia had relished fighting back against the enemy. After finding out what had happened to her parents, she wanted revenge. Helping the Resistance kept her going. Surely her efforts, however small, would reduce the time it took for the war to end.

Just last week, she, Raffaele and the others had hiked across the hills and valleys to Premeno to steal guns from a Fascist garrison. At 850 metres above sea level, the lovely village had been a popular tourist destination before the war, because of its stunning views of the lake. The seven of them had gone against ten *repubblichini*, the derisive term given by anti-fascists to Mussolini's militia. Giulia had been thankful the mission had been successful, but it hadn't come without a fierce fire fight. A sick feeling had spread through her as she'd stared at the corpses of the men they'd killed. One Republican Guardsman lay crumpled onto his side, his head blown to bits by the bullets from Raffaele's submachine gun. Another had lain sprawled flat on his back, his lifeless blue eyes staring into oblivion, a hate-filled, derisory grin on his face. It was the first time Giulia had seen dead bodies at close range, and it had made her throw up. She'd fully expected a reprimand from Raffaele, but he'd comforted her and told her it was a completely normal reaction, and she shouldn't feel ashamed.

Giulia sighed to herself. Raffaele was such a conundrum. One minute he was stern with her, the next as sweet as honey. She couldn't figure him out. Paolo said that Raffaele liked her, but Raffaele had never given any indication. That kiss must have been a spur-of-the-moment thing. Why couldn't she forget it?

Sudden tiredness overwhelmed her. Teresa had already gone to bed and she went to join her.

Giulia was dreaming about being at the summer festival in Arona and watching the fireworks when she woke with a start. Those weren't fireworks she could hear; they were bombs. Fear trembling in her chest, she threw on her clothes, hurried down the stone staircase and out into the front yard.

Raffaele was there, staring up at the sky. Three German Stukas were flying low, whirling in a westerly direction, then swooping down towards the Val Grande river basin. Massive explosions boomed as crimson flashes winked from the wings of the planes.

'The Valdossola Battalion must be under attack,' Raffaele said.

'Oh, my God. I hope they'll be all right.' Giulia felt the hairs lift with terror on her arms and neck.

'Could be the *nazifascisti* have started a round-up. We'll have to wait for orders,' Raffaele said. 'A messenger will arrive soon, I'm sure.'

'I'm scared,' Giulia said.

'Don't be, Piccola. I'll keep you safe.'

She wanted to go to him and bury her face in his chest. But before she could do so, their comrades began erupting from the house.

'What's going on?' Teresa asked.

'I think the *rastrellamento* has started.' Raffaele straightened his shoulders. 'We should go inside and wait for orders.'

They spent the rest of the day in preparation, cleaning their weapons and packing their kit bags. The ricochet of explosions echoed from a distance and, from time to time, the thunderous rumble of enemy aircraft roared overhead.

Finally, late in the afternoon, a courier came from Sabadini to say that Raffaele's squad should make their way up to Pian Cavallone the following morning to meet up with Giorgio and his men in the ruins of the hotel. If they came under attack, they were to resist until they ran out of ammunition, then fall back to Aquila's position farther along the ridge.

After a supper for which she had no appetite, Giulia and the others went up to bed. She tossed and turned for hours before eventually falling asleep.

'Wake up, Piccola.' Teresa was shaking her as dawn light filtered through the window shutters. 'It's time.'

Giulia put on her khakis and went down to the kitchen, where the rest of the band was silently dunking stale bread into their morning coffees.

Without warning, the rumbling noise of motor traffic came from the Ungiasca road behind the house.

Giulia broke out in a cold sweat.

'Wait here,' Raffaele commanded. 'I'll go take a look.'

The loud crack of gunfire rent the air, and Giulia gave a gasp. She gazed at Teresa and Teresa stared back at her, worry for Raffaele's safety in her eyes.

It seemed hours before he returned, but it was most likely only a few minutes.

'There's a German patrol on the road, and they're shooting at something in the trees. I couldn't see anything.' Raffaele took a quick breath. 'We must leave immediately. Lighten your loads. Take nothing but soap, toothpaste, toothbrushes, towels and cigarettes as we'll need to move quickly.'

Giulia and her friends did as commanded and, after they'd repacked their rucksacks, they stepped out of the house. Giulia's heart dropped to her boots; persistent fine rain had started to fall, and it would make the going much more difficult.

They went through the woods, bypassing Miazzina, and Raffaele took the lead, following the muleteers' path.

Suddenly, he raised his hand, then indicated they should crouch down.

The growl of a vehicle engine reverberated from a distance, followed by bursts of gunfire and the characteristic loud bang of exploding hand grenades.

Giulia trembled. They were on the crest of the hill now, fully visible from the villages below.

'Run for the woods,' Raffaele shouted. 'We need to get under cover.'

Deafening explosions ripped through the air, and they made it to the treeline just in time.

Holding her breath, Giulia watched Raffaele raise his binoculars.

'The Nazis are firing on Pian Cavallone with a machine gun,' he muttered. 'We can't head up there. The *bastardi* have cut us off.'

All Giulia could think about was Giorgio and his men. A sick feeling squeezed her stomach.

The shelling went on for ages, and then, praise God, an answering shell, which must have been fired from Young Italy's Breda 37, whistled overhead. The partisans were fighting back.

Clinging to each other on the steep, wooded section of the mountainside with nothing to eat or drink, Giulia, Raffaele and their friends observed the battle until darkness fell, with neither side victorious.

'Try to get some sleep, guys,' Raffaele said, eventually. 'Wedge your feet against a tree so you don't slip down the slope.'

Soaked through by the persistent rain, Giulia began shivering. Her teeth chattered and her entire body shook. Biting back a sob, she was certain that, if she closed her eyes, she would tumble right down to the valley.

'I've got you.' Raffaele put his arm around her. 'We're safe here.'

She turned to face him. It was so dark, she could barely make out his features. But he was holding her close and she breathed in his masculine scent. Finally, she could bury her face in his chest, and she did so now.

'Oh, God, Piccola.' He lowered his voice to a whisper. 'I've been wanting to hold you for so long. Wanted to comfort you for what you've been going through.'

'Why didn't you?' She lifted her face.

'Because... because,' he groaned, 'I didn't think it appropriate.'

She stiffened. He would always put his duty before her, and it was right that he should do so.

'I understand, Lele,' she said.

'You're so brave. I'm sorry. Sorry for the mess you now find yourself in.'

'If I'd stayed in Marta, the Germans would have arrested me, so don't be sorry.' She snuggled back into his chest.

Was that a kiss she felt him brush to the top of her head? She closed her eyes, enjoying the sensation; she felt safe with Raffaele. Protected. Was that so wrong? She wasn't a weak damsel in distress; she was a *partigiana combattente* seeking vengeance. But she was also very tired and soon she fell into a deep sleep.

* * *

Raffaele was lying behind her, one arm around her waist while she faced away from him, when Giulia blinked her eyes open the next day. She squirmed, waking him in the process as she turned to face him.

'I'm sorry I was such a baby last night,' she whispered. 'It wasn't the Germans I was scared of.'

'Don't worry, Piccola. I get it. None of us wanted to slide down this mountain while asleep.'

Her stomach rumbled, and she glanced away from him in embarrassment.

'I'm hungry too,' he said. 'As soon as the coast is clear, we'll go get some food in the village below.'

He'd barely finished speaking when a sound that reminded Giulia of an express train roared overhead, followed by the crash of an explosion. Her heart in her mouth, she peered through the trees and gave a gasp. Coils of black smoke were rising from Pian

Cavallone.

'*Merda*,' Raffaele swore. 'The Germans must have brought a mortar into Intra and are shelling our position from down there.'

'I had no idea big guns had such a huge range.'

'Those cannons, 149s, can reach up to 9,000 metres, I believe.'

'Lele's right.' Lungo's voice came from the other side of Raffaele. 'They're extremely powerful.'

'We can't go down to the village now,' Raffaele said. 'It's too dangerous. We'll have to wait until it gets dark.'

'If you're thirsty, you can suck water from a tree leaf.' Lungo proceeded to reach up and pull one from a chestnut tree.

Lungo's matter-of-fact tone and calm demeanour reassured Giulia, and she inched her way between the trees to where Teresa, Paolo, and the others had spent the night. After showing them how to take a drink, she told them about Raffaele's decision to go for food that night.

They took it in turns to keep watch for the rest of the day, and the rumble of military traffic echoing from the Cambiasca road far below informed them that Raffaele had made the right decision to wait until nightfall.

* * *

The going was slippery because of the incessant rainfall, and Giulia's wet clothes clung to her as she crept across the road. Darkness had fallen, and she stumbled and got caught in brambles. She couldn't help letting out a moan.

'Are you okay?' Raffaele asked in a whisper.

'I'm fine,' she whispered back.

'Lean on me, Piccola.'

'No need,' she said, squaring her shoulders.

She soldiered on and, before too long, she and the others had come to a house on the outskirts of the village. Light shone from the downstairs window; whoever lived there was taking no notice of the blackout regulations.

'Wait here,' Raffaele said. 'I'll go ask if they've got any spare food.'

Within minutes, he came out of the house empty-handed.

'A woman lives there on her own,' he said. 'She has nothing for us to eat. Her husband is one of Sabadini's men and she told me the Fascists have put up roadblocks everywhere. They've even been going through the woods, searching for partisans.'

Giulia glanced around in the gloom, and her gaze fell on what she hoped was a cherry orchard.

'I think those are cherry trees, look!' She pointed towards the trees. 'How about we climb up and pick some fruit?'

'Good idea,' Raffaele said. '*Brava!*'

But as soon as she'd shimmied up the trunk of the nearest tree, and felt around in the darkness for the fruit with her hands, Giulia realised the harvest had already taken place. After only managing to find about twenty cherries, she climbed back down again and handed her slim pickings to Raffaele.

Between herself and the others, they collected scarcely enough to compensate for the energy they burnt up in calories while climbing the trees.

'How about we head on down towards Intra?' Raffaele suggested. 'It's not an order, by way. If any of you don't want to take the risk, that's fine by me. You can hole up here and wait it out until I return.'

'I'll go with you, Lele,' Giulia blurted before she could even think about it. She glanced at her comrades, waiting for them to agree to come along as well. But no one did.

'Give Piccola your Sten, Lungo,' Raffaele commanded. 'I'll explain to her how to use it on the way.'

After exchanging her pistol with Lungo's semi-automatic weapon, Giulia set off with Raffaele and, as they walked, he explained that the main difference between a rifle and a submachine gun like a Sten was that, with the latter, if you squeezed the trigger and held it down, the business end carried on firing.

He showed her the movements, then added, 'It's best not to drop it when the safety catch is off.'

If she were to drop the Sten on its butt, he went on to say, it would fire a shot the moment it hit the ground. Then it would leap into the air and during the leap the weight of the breech-block would press on the mainspring, causing the gun to reload itself. As it fell again, it would fire once more, and so on. Problem was, the Sten was weighted in such a way as to nearly always fall on its butt. It wouldn't shoot straight into the air, either, but rotate, scattering bullets like a fan, or a spiral, gradually lowering the angle of fire until the magazine was finished.

'You could get shot up the backside if that happened,' he added.

'I'll be careful,' she said, placing the weapon in the lanyard around her neck.

The walk downhill under the cover of darkness would take about an hour, Raffaele said. Giulia wondered at their friends' reluctance to go with them. Perhaps they were tired? She'd had the luxury of being secured in place by Raffaele's weight last night, whereas they'd maybe only got very little sleep while they'd tried to stop themselves from slipping down the steep slope.

On the outskirts of the village of Trobaso, Raffaele suggested they take off their shoes and hang them by their laces around their necks so as not to make any noise. Giulia did as he'd suggested, then crept down the main street with him towards the church.

The burble of water gurgling in a fountain echoed across the square.

'I'm thirsty,' Raffaele said. 'Let's go have a drink.'

'Be careful. There's bound to be a sentry.' Giulia placed her hand on his arm.

His stubbornness might make him argue back, and she prayed intensely that he'd see sense. Her knees buckled in relief when the moon peeked from behind the clouds, lighting up the piazza and revealing a militiaman on duty.

'Come, Piccola. We need to move on,' Raffaele whispered.

'Where are we going?' Giulia asked as they headed out of the village.

'To my nonna's house in a hamlet above Intra.'

'Your nonna? I didn't know you had a grandmother living in this area.'

'I must have forgotten to mention it.' A smile brushed his lips. 'But first, we must cross that bridge up ahead. Take the catch off your Sten, just in case.'

Giulia's heart thudded, but she did as he'd requested. There were shadows on the *ponte*, and they approached cautiously. She heaved a sigh of relief when they turned out to be the shade of trees in the moonlight.

After reengaging the safety mechanism of her gun, she carried on walking with Raffaele and, soon, a pale band of light appeared behind the mountains, signalling the arrival of dawn.

'We're here.' Raffaele rapped his knuckles on the wooden door of a stone house at the edge of the village. 'Nonna, it's me,' he called out.

The door opened, and a kindly-looking old lady, thin grey hair scraped back in a bun, stood on the threshold.

'My dear grandson,' she said. 'You've come to visit me at last.'

She turned her gaze to Giulia. 'And who is this lovely young lady?'

'We call her Piccola, Nonna. Can we come in? We're very hungry.'

'Then it's a good thing I managed to get flour and have just baked some bread.' The old lady's eyes twinkled. 'Come inside. Eat, then rest. Afterwards, I want you to tell me everything.'

* * *

Darkness was falling the following day when, with their rucksacks stuffed with tins of sardines, loaves of bread, cans of beans and tomatoes, and cheese wrapped in grease-proof paper, Giulia and Raffaele set off for where they'd left their companions.

'Your nonna was so kind to us,' Giulia said as they made their way out of the hamlet. 'It was nice and cosy sleeping in her spare room. I'm sorry you had to make do with the sofa.'

'I was comfortable under Nonna's hand-crocheted blanket.'

'Why haven't you mentioned her before, Lele?'

'She's my mamma's mother and Ma is an only child. Nonna always came to visit us rather than us visiting her. Pa was born in Ungiasca, as you know, and we often visited his parents when they were still alive. My father's siblings have all moved to the area around Varese, where they found more opportunities for work, and he was the only one still living close enough for weekly visits.'

'I see,' Giulia said. 'Are the Bertrandis your father's cousins on his mamma's side?'

'They are.'

Raffaele seemed about to say something when the sudden

tramping sound of many footfalls came from farther down the road, causing Giulia to flinch.

Raffaele put a finger to his lips. He took her hand and led her to a thicket, where he gently pulled her into a crouching position.

Hundreds of militiamen in black shirts were marching up the *strada* and, as they marched, they sang Fascist songs. Columns of German soldiers followed behind. They weren't singing. Just marching. There must have been thousands of men. Thousands against four hundred partisans. Heat rolled in Giulia's belly. How she hated the *nazifascisti*; she'd hated them for taking Ester and her family; she'd hated them for taking her parents; and now she hated them for using unfair force against her fellow partisans.

After about half an hour, Raffaele said that the coast was clear and that he and Giulia could resume their hike. They hadn't gone far when a voice filtered through the darkness, calling out Raffaele's battle name.

Giulia froze. Her pulse raced and slipped the safety catch from her Sten. To her right, Raffaele was doing likewise.

'Lele,' the voice repeated, louder this time. 'It's Aquila.'

'Aquila!' Raffaele de-cocked his weapon and Giulia followed suit. 'Fancy meeting you here.'

'I'm on my way to Baveno,' Aquila said, falling into step alongside them.

'Why the hell would you go there?' Raffaele sounded surprised. 'It's full of Germans.'

'Precisely. I'd like to offer myself up to them in a prisoner exchange. Those bastards executed forty-three partisans by firing squad in Fondotoce.'

Giulia gave a gasp.

'Damn,' Raffaele said.

'So many of our guys have been killed.' Aquila sighed.

'Listen, Aquila.' Giulia looked him in the eye. 'Your life has more meaning now than it ever did. Don't throw it away.'

'You mustn't forget those who've survived and the new recruits who will surely come,' Raffaele added. 'You are a good commander and we all need you.'

Aquila opened and closed his mouth, clearly struggling to find the right words.

'I'm not sure—'

'Don't lose heart.' Giulia touched her hand to his arm. 'All will be well in the end.'

'You're a breath of fresh air, Piccola.' Eagle forced a smile. 'Lele is lucky to have you in his squad.'

'I think so too,' Raffaele said, and Giulia felt her cheeks flame. 'I was thinking of attaching my squad to your band, by the way,' he added. 'But only if you continue as leader.'

'Well, in that case, how can I refuse?' Aquila chuckled wryly. 'The Valdossola appears to have gone to ground, so maybe I'll resume our old name *Cesare Battisti*.'

'Any news of Giorgio?' Raffaele asked. 'We were heading to Pian Cavallone to provide backup the other day, but the enemy cut us off en route.'

'No news, I'm afraid. We won't know anything until the Naz-fascists end this *rastrellamento*.' Aquila shot Raffaele and Giulia a look. 'Where are you heading now?'

'I left the rest of my guys above Cambiasca while Piccola and I went to get food. But it's not safe there and we'll need to find a new base.'

'There's a villa near Premeno where my men and I have set up camp. Feel free to join us, if you like.'

'Sounds like a good interim plan,' Raffaele said. 'We can scout around for somewhere else once we're there.'

'Ah, Lele, always the maverick. But I'll respect your wish to be independent, of course.'

Aquila proceeded to give Raffaele and Giulia directions to the villa, then asked, 'Have you thought of a name for your squad?'

'No.' Raffaele shook his head.

'How about "Fox Cubs"?' Aquila suggested. 'Given your average age—'

'Hmmm.' Raffaele tapped his chin. 'I like it. *I Volpacchiotti* suits us well.'

Aquila smiled and said, 'I'm glad I bumped into you both. You've brightened my day. Well, I'd better let you get back to the rest of your pack.' He raised his hand. 'See you at the villa!'

After they'd taken their leave of Aquila, Giulia and Raffaele walked on in silence. Giulia smiled to herself; she'd enjoyed spending time in Raffaele's company, just the two of them. She didn't know how she would have coped with this strange, violent new life if Raffaele wasn't around. He soothed the ache in her heart from mourning Ester and worrying about her parents. What were these feelings she was developing for him? Were they deep friendship, or were they something more?

21

As soon as Raffaele and Giulia met up with the rest of the squad, they set off to join Aquila near Premeno. The enemy was still 'combing' the entire area from the Val Grande to Intragna. With all the roads blocked, Raffaele had to take to avoiding action as he and his friends trudged through woodland and across steep valleys. What would normally have taken a few hours needed two nights, with a day of sleeping rough in between. All the while, beads of sweat formed on their lips, out of fear of capture and execution by firing squad.

They arrived at the villa, footsore and weary, to find it surrounded by an enormous park, with new recruits guarding the boundary. The round-up hadn't just been a military operation; it had also taken a psychological toll. Raffaele felt sorry for the newcomers, who still had money from home in their pockets and addressed everyone as 'sir'. Escaping from being drafted into Mussolini's army, they'd joined the partisans full of optimism, only to find themselves in the middle of a *rastrellamento*, with disproportionate force used against them. Raffaele imagined that none of them had expected to be constantly hungry, terrified out of their minds, and so tired they could barely think.

A week later, the round-up was apparently over and he and his band were due to go on a march with Aquila and the rest of the *Cesare Battisti*, accompanying them as far as Esio, a small village about an hour's hike from Premeno. There, they would part company, and Raffaele, Giulia and the rest of his squad would return to their safe house near Ungiasca, to await orders.

In the meantime, Aquila planned to set up a new command at a place called La Rocca, a group of stone huts surrounded by pastureland above Scareno, which was roughly the same altitude as Pian Cavallone, but overlooking Oggebbio instead of Intra.

Raffaele was enjoying a few moments of peace and quiet, sitting on a bench gazing out at a magnificent view of the lake far below, when Paolo and Giulia came bustling up.

Giulia was still spending a lot of time in Paolo's company, which made Raffaele's stomach harden with jealousy. He should have a word with Paolo and find out what was going on. But, if he did so, he'd reveal his own vulnerability, and he didn't want to do that.

'We've just come from listening to *Radio Londra* on the short-wave,' Paolo said in a cheerful tone of voice as he lowered himself onto the bench next to Raffaele. 'The Allies took Rome three weeks ago, and now they're advancing on Florence.'

'Great news,' Raffaele said, eyeing Giulia, who'd sat herself down on the other side of Paolo.

'They've also invaded Normandy and are fighting the Germans there.' A smile spread across her lovely face. 'This could be the beginning of the end of the war.'

'It's a step in the right direction. But it will take time for them to achieve their objectives.' Raffaele couldn't help the bitterness in his tone.

'Come, guys.' Duke had approached. 'It's time for lunch, then we can sing our songs to celebrate the Allied advance. Wish I still had my accordion.'

The instrument had been left behind in their Ungiasca house, along with all their personal possessions.

'You'll be reunited with it soon,' Giulia said, linking her arm with Duke's. 'Let's go and eat, cubs.' The squad had unanimously approved their new name. 'I've heard the people of Premeno have clubbed together and have sent us some meat. We'll feast like kings, which will set us up for our long trek later.'

* * *

After it had grown dark, Raffaele and the rest of the partisans departed the villa and headed up the muleteers' path leading out of the village: seven *Volpacchiotti* with fifty Cesare Battisti *partigiani*, led by Aquila. Walking in silence, so as not to draw attention to themselves, they came across machine-gun nests and fortifications built along the wayside by the enemy. Raffaele gave a sigh. How many partisans had died since the round-up began? How complacent they'd all been beforehand...

Sudden rain fell, soaking them all, but at least it was a warm summer night and the rainwater washed away the sweat from their brows. About forty minutes after they'd left Premeno, they came upon the slate houses of Esio, clinging to the side of the mountain as if they were defying gravity. Narrow stone-paved streets led to the church square, where Raffaele saluted Aquila and confirmed he would get supplies in Miazzina to be carried up to La Rocca as soon as possible.

Another path took Raffaele and his cubs through chestnut woods and across the Intragna valley, a difficult hike that lasted most of the rest of the night.

'How are you bearing up, Piccola?' Raffaele asked as Giulia fell into step beside him.

'I'm a little tired, to be honest. I hadn't realised it would take so long.'

'We're nearly there.' He gave her an encouraging smile. 'And you're not the only one who's feeling the strain. My legs are aching.'

'Having to carry a rucksack, weapon and ammunition all this way hasn't been easy,' she said. 'But it's a lot easier than the trek you made in the snow.'

'Can't believe six months have gone by. I hope that, by this time next year, the world will be at peace.'

'That would be wonderful.' Her eyes assumed a faraway look. 'I dream about returning to Marta and finding my parents already there.'

'Hang on to that hope, Piccola. Hope is what keeps us going.'

'What is it that you hope for, Lele?' she asked.

'For life to return to normal so I can resume my studies.'

'That's what I want too,' she said.

* * *

The closer they got to the Ungiasca house, the more the skin on the back of Raffaele's neck prickled. Spent bullets crunched under his feet, and he raised his hand to signal a halt.

The front door had been smashed to smithereens.

Inside, a horrible stench greeted him. Walls plastered with excrement, cupboards, and drawers tipped open, their contents ripped into pieces. Clothes torn to shreds.

Teresa and Giulia started to retch in a corner. He hadn't realised they'd followed him into the house. Paolo, Rock and Lungo approached, and their faces turned green.

'My accordion,' Duke wailed, holding up what was left of the instrument.

'What *bastardi*,' Rock said and Lungo echoed him.

'We can't recover anything,' Paolo groaned. 'The Fascists have ruined it all.'

'Come, everyone. We'll head for Miazzina and ask the nuns at the sanatorium if they can put us up for the night. We were due to go there tomorrow, anyway, to get supplies for the *Cesare Battisti*.'

Hatred for the enemy burned through Raffaele as he led the *Volpacchiotti* back up the road. After the *nazifascisti* had attacked the partisans, planning to get rid of them, they'd probably thought they'd achieved their objective. But the disproportionate amounts of troops they'd used – soldiers must have been brought in from all over the region – made a mockery of their success. How many men had *they* lost? Many more in proportion to their numbers than the partisans, Raffaele guessed.

'Are you all right?' Giulia was matching her stride to his, which was a difficult task, given how much shorter she was.

'Thanks for asking, Piccola. This is just a minor setback. We must stay positive. We'll find a different house.'

'But what if there's another *rastrellamento*?'

'I've been thinking about that, and I believe we partisans were wrong to resist in the mountains. We should have gone down the lakeside and fought the enemy there.'

'So, you think there'll be more battles?'

'Without a doubt. Already, our bands are reforming. The enemy will round us up, and we'll reform again. And so on and so forth until the last round-up.'

'You make it sound so final.'

'At least we have the local people on our side. The Nazi-fascists aren't supported by anyone. They burn, destruct, massacre; they don't believe in life; they just believe in death.'

'We can only pray the Allies get here soon. Otherwise, there won't be any of us left.'

He had no words for her and, in the darkness, he reached for her hand. She laced her fingers through his, holding on tightly as a warm sensation spread through him, and his chest felt as if it could burst.

Dawn had crept up along the side of the mountain, exposing the opposite slope and sending a blast of wind into the red, hard leaves of the little beech tree on the overhanging rock. Two months had gone by since the *rastrellamento*, and Giulia and the cubs were living in a tiny, abandoned chalet-like dwelling with a pitched slate roof, hidden between patches of meadow and chestnut groves near Premeno. The road that led to the house was also invisible, not much more than a path in a wilderness of greenery. It was a good place to shelter and hide, and they'd given it the name of their old camp, 'Tipperary'. There was even a sign in English by the door with the words 'Home Sweet Home'.

Maybe the property had once belonged to people from England, Giulia mused as she sat on the front porch watching the sunrise and scratching the mosquito bites on her legs. If so, she hoped they wouldn't mind her and her comrades staying here. Although small, the dwelling was comfortable; there was a wood-burning stove, running water, an inside toilet, and a fire-place. Upstairs, there was only one bedroom and, by common agreement, they all slept together under the sloping ceiling, keeping the same formation they'd used in the military tent: Giulia at one end, followed by Teresa, Paolo, and the rest of the men.

Downstairs, the kitchen was separate to the living-dining room, where they spent much of their time when they weren't carrying out tasks for Aquila. He was a hard taskmaster, and kept them busy. He'd managed to procure a lorry for them, which Duke drove as they transported supplies from the outskirts of Intra to Scareno, where fatigue parties from La Rocca collected them and carried them on their backs to the mountaintop. Giulia had never been up there, but Raffaele and Paolo went to meet with Aquila in his command post on a regular basis and they'd told her they'd been impressed by how men from such diverse backgrounds could live together in apparent harmony. Maybe it was because they were all supporting the partisans' cause. When Giulia had asked Raffaele if he wasn't tempted to move the *Volpacchiotti* to Aquila's HQ, he'd said it was too steep a climb, and he'd worry about her tumbling down into the valley.

Raffaele's concern for her had made her tummy flutter, but she tried not to read too much into it. At night, when she was in that place between wakefulness and dreaming, she listened out for his breaths, distinguishing them from those of her comrades God knew how, and she couldn't help hoping he was listening out for hers too as they both dropped off to sleep.

'*Ciao,* Piccola,' Teresa said, coming out of the front door and sitting on the porch next to her. 'It's going to be hot today. How about we see if the boys want to go for a swim?'

They'd discovered their 'swimming pool', a small hydroelectric dam on the San Giovanni river, which flowed through the Intragna valley halfway between 'Tipperary' and Miazzina, and had gone there the other morning. The *ragazzi* had stripped to their underwear, and Giulia and Teresa had modestly swum in the khaki shorts and cotton blouses they'd recently received in a delivery of clothing from Verbania. Afterwards, they'd stretched out on the shore, drying themselves in the warm sun.

'I'll go see if Lele and the rest of them are up for it,' Giulia said now, getting to her feet.

* * *

The walk to the 'swimming pool' took them about three-quarters of an hour through the woods and, when they finally descended to the river valley, Giulia relished the feel of the warm sun on her bare arms. She put her towel down on the pebbly shore and surveyed the scene in front of her.

Devoid of any human activity, the reservoir was like a secret tucked away in the woods. Only the chirping of sparrows and the gushing sound of the river could be heard. The pool itself sloped from a shallow end, fed by the San Giovanni, to deeper water at the edge of the dam. Hot sunlight filtered through the trees, and Giulia couldn't wait to immerse herself in the cool depths.

'Let's strip down to our underwear, Piccola,' Teresa said from behind. 'If the *ragazzi* are doing it, so can we.'

'Good idea. We'll dry off faster after our swim.'

Giulia pulled down her shorts, unbuttoned her blouse, and waded into the pool in her underpants and bra. Raffaele, Paolo and the rest of the *Volpacchiotti* had already gone into the water and were laughing and splashing each other, and then they were all swimming and frolicking as if they didn't have a care in the world.

I do feel carefree, Giulia thought to herself. It was as if time had stood still, and they were behaving like normal young people instead of having to worry about the war.

She climbed onto Paolo's shoulders and Teresa climbed onto Duke's to have a play fight and try to push the 'rider' off her 'mount'. It didn't take too long for Teresa to win the battle; she was bigger than her, of course.

'I'm pooped,' Giulia said, leaving the others to it. Back on the pebbles where she'd left her towel, she stretched out and half-closed her eyes. The sun beat down, drying her, and the pungent, sweet, musty smells of the nearby woodland invaded her senses.

Picking at the mosquito bites on her legs, she glanced up as Raffaele approached. He spread his towel next to hers and lowered himself onto it.

'Isn't this peaceful?' she said, gazing at a dragonfly, its wings a blur of iridescent colour, as it descended to the surface of the pool.

'It certainly is, Piccola.' Raffaele cleared his throat and stared into the distance. 'I apologise for being blunt, but is there anything going on between you and Biondo that I, as your commander, should know about?'

Giulia's mouth fell open in surprise. She quickly closed it again.

'Why would you think that?'

'It's just... it's just that you're always with him.'

'No more than with anyone else.' She shook her head. 'I feel sorry for him, Lele. He's distraught about his *fidanzata* and I simply want to cheer him up.'

'Oh. Good.' A smile lit Raffaele's deep blue eyes.

'Why "good"?' She risked the question.

Raffaele reached for her hand.

'I'd like you to be my girl, Giulia. I can call you by your name when we're alone, by the way. We would need to keep our relationship secret from the Fox Clubs, though. It might affect my authority if they found out.'

Happiness floated through her, and she felt so weightless she might soar to the heavens.

'I would love to be your girl, Raffaele. Hopefully, the war will end soon and we won't need to hide our feelings from the world.'

'You have feelings for me?' He sounded incredulous.

'They kind of snuck up on me,' she said, laughing. 'At first I thought you an odious so-and-so.'

'It was because I didn't know the real Giulia.' He squeezed her fingers. 'You aren't at all what I believed you to be.'

'You mean a spoilt brat?' She kept a straight face.

'What? You didn't overhear me make that comment to my mother last September, I hope.'

'I might have done.' She giggled.

'I remember barging past you as I came through the door. I apologise, Giulia.'

'You were probably right. I mean, I've been overindulged all my life.'

'Well, you've proved yourself to be incredibly resilient. I'm so proud of you.'

'As I am of you.' She gazed at him, almost overwhelmed by the surge of feeling swelling her chest.

'There's something else I need to share with you,' he said. 'Do you recollect me telling you about how Aquila and some of his guys rode down to Intra on the tram from Premeno and "appropriated" chocolate from the Nestlé factory?'

'It was very daring of them,' she said, wondering where this was leading.

'He said that the Fascists stay in their barracks at night and that he and his men had free rein.'

'Why are you telling me this, Raffaele?' It felt so intimate to be using his real name.

'Because I thought we could do the same. Me and the guys

will go down in our lorry instead of the tram. That way, we'll come back loaded with chocolate. Not only for us, but for the people of Premeno.'

'When you said "you and the guys", I take it you also meant Luna and me.'

'No, Giulia. I want you both to stay behind.'

It was on the tip of her tongue to ask why, but she stopped herself just in time. When Raffaele gave an order, it was her duty, as a *partigiana combattente*, to obey. The old Giulia would have argued back, but not the new Giulia. She was fully Piccola now, and Piccola was a different person.

She gazed across the water, remembering swimming with Ester the summer before. So much had happened since then; it seemed years ago. Swallowing the lump of sadness in her throat, she released a deep sigh.

'What's wrong?' Raffaele asked. 'If you're mad at me for not including you on the mission, just say it.'

'I'm not mad at you, Raffaele. You must have a good reason for not wanting me and Luna to come. I was thinking about my friend, Ester, and our swims together. I still can't believe what the Nazis did to her and the rest of our Jewish guests—'

'They're pure evil, and that's why we are fighting them and their *repubblichini* puppets.' Raffaele paused as if to collect his thoughts. 'Although I don't need to give you an explanation for my decision not to include you and Luna in the raiding party, I will. Intra fills up at night with partisans from all over, and some of them clearly enjoy more than their fair share of wine. Both you and Luna are attractive young women. I would hate for you to suffer any untoward advances from any of them.'

'We can look after ourselves, Raffaele.'

'I know you can, but it might detract from the mission, and we'll need to get in and out of the factory, then make our getaway as quickly as possible. If it were a military action, I wouldn't hesitate to take you and Luna along for your shooting skills.'

'Oh,' Giulia said, not entirely sure if Raffaele's explanation held water. 'I see.' She gave him the benefit of the doubt, but she couldn't help the sudden suspicion he was worried someone might recognise her and report her to the Germans.

* * *

Later, sitting with Teresa in the living-dining room of the chalet, Giulia found herself waiting with bated breath, worrying about Raffaele and the rest of the men. They'd set off as soon as darkness had fallen and now it was well past midnight. The drive should have taken them only about half an hour or so. But they'd been gone for over three hours. Why weren't they back?

She glanced at Teresa, who was knitting a scarf for the upcoming winter, and Teresa glanced back at her.

'Don't fret, Piccola. I'm sure Lele, Biondo and the others will be back any minute now.'

As if on cue, the rumble of the lorry engine reverberated, and Giulia leapt up from her seat to rush to the door. Raffaele and the rest of the cubs were already climbing down from the vehicle.

'There you are,' Giulia said. 'We were starting to be a little concerned.'

'No need. Everything went according to plan.' Raffaele smiled. 'We have a lorry full of chocolate and powdered milk we can distribute to the villagers tomorrow.'

'What took you so long, then?' Teresa asked as they all trooped back inside the house.

'Remember I told you Aquila had mentioned there was a new band of thirty partisans, independent like us? Ex-Valdossola guys

who are based in the mountains above Cannero. They call themselves the "*Giuseppe Perotti*" in honour of an anti-Fascist general
who was executed in Turin last April.'

'We met them in Intra and they've been quite busy,' Paolo
added. 'Twenty of them mounted an attack on the Fascist
garrison in Oggebbio and took them all prisoner.'

'And that's not everything,' Raffaele added. 'Just the other
day, they surprised a German unit scouting in Val Cannobina.
After a brief fight, the enemy surrendered. The *Perotti* killed one
Nazi, took eighteen prisoner, and disarmed them before
escorting them to the Swiss border.'

'That's great news,' Giulia said, eyeing Raffaele. She could see
he was envious of the other group's success, and his next words
confirmed her suspicions.

'Next time I go up to La Rocca, I'm going to ask Aquila if we
can participate in some *Cesare Battisti* actions. I know we're independent, but we are good fighters when given the chance.'

'We are, indeed,' Giulia said, torn between her need to show
she was worthy of being included and her concern for everyone's
safety. She decided to change the subject.

'In the meantime, is there any spare chocolate for us? My
mouth is watering just thinking about it,' she said.

Raffaele chuckled and opened his rucksack to reveal several
Nestlé milk chocolate bars.

'Help yourselves, guys,' he said.

They all complied, and Giulia was soon relishing the creamy,
chocolatey sweetness coating her tongue. Life was certainly
bittersweet, she thought to herself later after going upstairs to
bed. Worry for her parents washed over her as she lay, listening
to Raffaele's breaths, but soon tiredness overcame her and she
drifted off to sleep.

PART IV

DECEMBER 1944–
FEBRUARY 1945

23

On a chilly early December morning, Giulia was up earlier than the rest of the Fox Cubs; she was sweeping the ground floor of Tipperary and thinking about everything that had happened since Raffaele and the *ragazzi* had raided the chocolate factory in Intra.

In early September, she had gone with Raffaele and the others to take part in an action to occupy the lakeside town of Cannobio. They'd joined the *Perotti* and *Cesare Battisti* brigades in attacking the Germans and Italian fascists, defeating them with minimal casualties. It was a great victory, and it gave anti-Fascist morale a massive boost.

She would never forget her frantic concern for Raffaele after he'd taken off with Aquila on a Moto Guzzi motorbike he'd commandeered. She'd been bereft, and it had brought home to her how much she'd grown to care about him.

'Where have Lele and Aquila got to?' She'd posed the question to the *Volpacchiotti* when Raffaele had been gone for nearly four hours. She and the Fox Cubs were still sitting at the table in the hotel they'd occupied. Worry had festered within her as she'd glanced at her watch. Where was he? Oh, God, what if he'd been killed?

'Come, Piccola.' Teresa broke into her thoughts. 'How about we go for a stroll through the town? It's been ages since we had the freedom to simply take a leisurely walk.'

'What a good idea.' Giulia got up from her seat, glad of the distraction.

She and Teresa left the *albergo* – which bore a heartbreakingly striking resemblance to her father's hotel in Marta – and made their way through the cobbled streets, where the population was carousing with the partisans, drinking and singing patriotic songs. Teresa linked her arm through Giulia's, and they threaded their way through the revellers, up flights of steps and along the narrow lanes leading away from the lakefront.

'Have you been here before?' Teresa asked.

'A couple of times with my parents.' Giulia sighed. 'We came by boat from Marta.'

'You must miss them a lot.'

'I think about them every day.'

'I can't imagine what you're going through.' Teresa squeezed her hand. 'It's about time this terrible war came to an end.'

'The Allies have reached Florence, haven't they? Bologna should be next, followed by Milan.'

'With luck, we'll be liberated from the *nazifascisti* by Christmas.' A smile spread across Teresa's face.

They headed back to the promenade, and Giulia gazed out across the lake. *So many memories of happier times.* And also such sorrow as she thought about Ester. She sniffed back tears and said, 'I wish Lele hadn't gone off with Aquila.'

'Don't worry about Lele, Piccola.' Teresa looked Giulia in the eye. 'He was born under a lucky star, that one. I expect he'll be back by the time we return to the hotel.'

'I hope so. Maybe we should go back and see?'

Teresa gave her a knowing look and said, 'Come along, then. Let's go and set your mind at ease.'

Giulia's stomach churned. Had Teresa guessed hers and Raffaele's secret? Would she be discreet? It would affect Raffaele's authority over the Fox Cubs, and put the squad in danger, if they found out.

Stepping into the *albergo* a short time later, Giulia felt light-headed with relief. Raffaele and Aquila were sitting at the table, glasses of wine in their hands. She wanted to reprimand Lele for worrying her so, and had to stop herself just in time.

Pretending nonchalance, she pulled out a chair and sat down.

'*Ciao*, Lele, *Ciao*, Aquila,' she said. 'How did it go?'

'They were just telling us.' Paolo smiled. 'Care to start your story again for the girls, guys?'

Giulia listened to them recount how they'd arrived at a road-block to find that the Fascists had run off when their lorry had been disabled by the partisans, and they'd pursued them with a carload of *Cesare Battisti* men.

'Our vehicle overtook us and then we heard gunshots,' Raffaele said. 'After we'd caught up with our guys, we saw that the *fascisti* had holed up in a house next to the road and were firing out of the windows.'

'It took a while to get the *bastardi* to surrender.' Aquila smirked. 'It wasn't until Lele snuck around to the back, ran into the kitchen and lobbed grenades at them that they came out with their hands up.'

Giulia had gazed at Raffaele in admiration. He was brave and fearless, without a doubt. But he could have been killed, and she could only thank God that he hadn't. She loved him, she'd realised. He'd come to mean everything to her.

The next afternoon, back at Tipperary, a loud noise had made her and the Fox Cubs look up at the sky.

'Allied fighter planes,' Raffaele shouted. 'They appear to be bombing boats on the lake.'

They subsequently found out that the Allies had sunk three Fascist ships, raising everyone's hopes that the British and Americans were on their way.

But the war was still far from over, she reflected now. After occupying Florence, the Allies had reached a stalemate with the Germans in the Apennine mountains that separated Firenze from Bologna, and had then decided to halt the campaign until next spring.

In the meantime, Giulia and the rest of the Lake Maggiore partisans had suffered one loss after another. She sighed as she remembered how, a week after Aquila had organised a local council to run Cannobio, the Germans and Fascists had reconquered the town, setting up a vile Fascist captain, Mario Nisi, as military commander.

Meanwhile, partisans in the Ossola Valley had attacked Fascist troops stationed in Domodossola and, after defeating them and driving them out, they created what they called the Ossola Partisan Republic. A month later, 5,000 *repubblichini* troops attacked and, following bitter fighting, had recaptured the entire territory. Most of the population then abandoned the Ossola Valley to take refuge in Switzerland, leaving the area almost deserted.

The heavy military defeat of the Ossola Republic and the subsequent round-up of the partisans there had put Giulia's fellow Resistance fighters in grave danger. To avoid another *rastrellamento*, the Valdossola Division and the *Perotti* brigade had crossed the border to seek asylum in Switzerland. They were followed by part of the *Valgrande*, including Giorgio and his squad – those who'd survived the attack at Pian Cavallone – and half of Aquila's formation.

Of the *Cesare Battisti*, only forty partisans had remained behind in Scareno, led by Aquila's second-in-command, and fifty others – including Giulia, Raffaele and the Fox Cubs – had dispersed throughout the villages above the lake.

Despite their defeat, Raffaele and the other partisan leaders hadn't lost heart, and Giulia was glad about that. They'd spent their time organising their bands to take raiding actions and collect weapons and food. She'd been even more glad when she'd learnt that, on 2 November, Aquila had returned to Scareno and had taken over the reins of the *Cesare Battisti* once again.

Partisan guerrilla warfare and firefights with Germans and Fascists had resumed. There'd been six clashes lately, with dead and wounded on both sides. Giulia, Raffaele and the other *Volpacchiotti* had been involved in attacking Nazi-fascist road-blocks, and she was relieved they'd neither suffered any losses nor any injuries thus far.

Their mood was dependent on weather conditions. Sunshine lifted their spirits, as did wine and tobacco. When not out following Aquila's orders, they passed the time playing poker – using bullets instead of money – and other card games. Occasionally, they went down to the village, and the locals would tell them that the Fascist Captain Mario Nisi's *Confinaria* division had been searching for partisans there. No one knew where the *Volpacchiotti* were living, though, so they weren't betrayed.

Footfalls sounded behind Giulia, and she put down her broom. It was Raffaele, she saw as she turned around, and her chest fluttered.

'*Buongiorno*,' she said.

'You're up early, Giulia.' He yawned. 'Couldn't you sleep?'

'I was feeling a little cold, but sweeping the floor has warmed me up.'

'I'll get the fire going.' He went to the log basket by the stove.

'Should have done that myself,' she said. 'Here, let me help.'

She reached for a log and her hand touched his. Raising her gaze, she caught him looking at her with such longing her breath caught.

His deep blue eyes fixed intensely on hers, making her heart pound. Without hesitation, she stepped into his arms. He kissed her softly at first, as if she might break. She closed her eyes and threaded her fingers into the thickness of his hair as their kiss deepened.

He broke off and looked deep into her eyes.

'I—' he said, then stopped speaking abruptly and took a step backwards.

Paolo and Teresa were coming down the stairs.

Giulia could feel herself blushing, and she went to the window so no one would notice. Outside, early-morning sunlight shimmered on the leaves of the pine trees. It would be a beautiful day.

'How about we go down to the village later?' she suggested, turning around. 'Unless Aquila needs us for something else.'

'Great idea,' Teresa said. 'We could have lunch in that osteria in Pollino. I've remembered that it's Duke's birthday today.'

The hamlet to the east of Premeno was rarely frequented by other partisans. Perched on a plateau overlooking the lake, it was small, with barely one hundred inhabitants, just a single shop, and an osteria run by a friendly lady called Daria. The *Volpacchiotti* liked to stop off there when making their way either down to the lake or back up again. The villagers were good people; they would share their potatoes, butter, chestnuts and wine with the squad. Sometimes, they'd invite Giulia and her friends to join them for a bowl of soup or a plate of cheese, while their children called her and the others by their battle names. Raffaele maintained that there were no spies in Pollino and everyone was trustworthy. How he knew that, Giulia had no clue, but she accepted his opinion without question. He'd added that it was because of people like the residents of Pollino that the *resistenza* would win through in the end.

Duke came down the stairs now, smiling as Giulia and the cubs gathered round to wish him a happy birthday.

'Where are we going for lunch?' he asked expectantly. It had become their tradition, if circumstances allowed, to celebrate birthdays by eating out in a place where they felt safe.

'To Daria's,' Raffaele responded. 'Hope you approve.'

'I more than approve, and I'll bring my new accordion.' Duke had obtained the instrument in Cannobio during that brief period of liberation, to replace the one desecrated during the *rastrellamento*, and Giulia was pleased that he'd done so, for his songs cheered her up during the cold, dark winter evenings when worry for her parents made it difficult for her to breathe.

The dancing began as soon as they'd finished eating, and a couple of village girls were taking it in turns to dance with the *Volpacchiotti*, who were taking it in turns to dance with Giulia and Teresa. Everyone except Raffaele, at least. Giulia glanced at him, sitting in the corner of the osteria's cosy dining room, a glass of red wine on the table in front of him. Duke was playing a cheerful tune on his accordion, a song about a girl called Gigiotta, but Giulia had just turned down a dance with Paolo so that she could find out what was ailing Raffaele, who was staring morosely at his drink, apparently lost in thought.

'Don't you feel like dancing?' she asked, pulling out a chair at the table.

'Maybe later.' His eyes met hers. 'Hope you're enjoying yourself.'

'We don't often get the chance to behave like normal young people. I mean, going out and sharing a meal with friends without worrying about who could be watching.'

'You're right. Sometimes I feel the weight of my responsibilities too much. I mean, I'm not even considered an adult yet by law. Yet I've been making decisions like a grown man for months.'

'You'll be twenty-one soon, won't you?'

'And able to vote for a democratic government in Italy next year, I expect.'

'I hope Italian women will be enfranchised then,' she said.

'Mussolini's fault for it not happening sooner. One of the many reasons I hate him.'

'Me too. But I hate him most of all for colluding with Hitler.'

'He's become the Führer's puppet. But it won't end well for him, you'll see.'

'All I can think about is the war ending. I long for peace. For the Germans to go back to Germany. For the Fascists to lay down their arms.' She released a sigh. 'I'm desperate to see my parents. It's been far too long.'

'Keep faith, Giulia. As soon as winter is over, the Allied front will move north, which will give us partisans good reason to come down from the mountains to fight for our freedom.' He sighed. 'I haven't seen my own parents since the start of last summer. They must be worried sick about me.'

Meeting his tortured gaze, Giulia slipped her hand under the table and squeezed his fingers.

'Why don't we have a dance, Raffaele? It might cheer us up,' she said. 'No one will think twice if we do so. After all, I've been dancing with the other guys.'

He led her onto the floor and the feel of their hands clasped together made her heart flutter. His breath smelt sweet from the wine he'd been drinking and she found herself savouring the scent of the air between them.

'You haven't been practising your callisthenics recently,' he said as he held her against him. 'I've missed seeing you doing handstands in the yard.'

'I didn't realise you'd watched me.' She gave a little laugh. 'To be honest, I haven't been in the mood for cartwheeling lately.'

'Promise me you won't give up. To win, we need to keep our spirits high.'

'I promise,' she said, turning her head to one side.

They were moving as one now, and every move sparked a different emotion within her: exhilaration, happiness, longing. Being held by Raffaele, she felt as if a part of her soul, that had been missing without her realising it, had finally come home. She would follow him to the end, she vowed to herself. Even if it was the last thing she ever did.

24

'Good God, it's cold,' Giulia said, coming in from guard duty. 'I hope you don't freeze while on watch, Lele.'

'I'll try not to, Piccola,' he said, using her battle name in front of the others.

He stepped outside and closed the door behind him. The glimmer of a full moon lit a polar landscape of snow. To keep warm, he made himself imagine vivid colours: reds, blues, greens, sultry tones, fields in the sunlight, grass dried by the heat, flowers buzzing with bees. But the frost burnt his fingers like fire, his skin ached with shivers that racked his body, and his feet felt like two inert stones that had to be dragged along.

'Thirty-eight degrees in the shade,' he murmured through chattering teeth. How nice, thirty-eight, thirty-nine and forty degrees in the shade, the sun in your bones, the sweat in your eyes. *What the hell am I doing here? Who the hell is going to come up to this dammed mountain tonight? I'm going inside.* He would have liked to do so, but he couldn't, of course. What would Giulia think? She'd been out here like him, without a word of complaint. All she'd said had been, 'Good God, it's cold,' with a beautiful smile curving her lips.

Stamping his feet in the frost, he thought about dancing with her on Duke's birthday – he thought about it often – and it was hard to believe that two months had gone by, that it was now the middle of February, and that he'd recently turned twenty-one. Holding Giulia in his arms, he'd prayed that he would continue to keep her safe and, thus far, he'd managed to do so. He loved her, he'd come to realise. She was brave, intelligent and adorable and, when it was the right moment, he would tell her so.

He blew out a steamy breath. It had been a while since the Fox Cubs had participated in any actions. Snow reached the level of their downstairs window-ledge and frequent snowstorms had kept it from thawing. The weather and their sedentary lives were making them lazy, but that wouldn't last forever. Raffaele stared into the distance. There would be a thaw soon enough and, once the snow had melted, their anti-Fascist activities would resume.

* * *

A week later, the temperature rose above freezing, and meltwater saturated the ground. Under a gloomy grey sky, Raffaele sent Paolo and Rock to Premeno for supplies. There was little food left in their larder; they'd been subsisting on one light meal a day for several weeks. Hopefully, the guys would return with potatoes, milk, butter, and chestnuts. Maybe even a bottle or two of wine. He sat with Giulia and the other Fox Cubs – minus Teresa, who was on sentry duty – waiting for them in the kitchen, their stomachs rumbling with hunger.

Before too long, the front door opened and Paolo and Rock came inside, overloaded rucksacks on their backs. But they weren't alone. Aquila's messenger, a young man who went by the name of Pippo, was at their heels.

Last month, the Ossola Zone Command had been set up by the Liberation Committee to take charge of all the partisans in the area, including the *Valgrande* and the *Cesare Battisti*, and Aquila had been given the title of war commissioner.

Jittering a foot against the floor, Raffaele read the note Pippo handed to him.

I need you and your squad to come to Scareno as quickly as possible.

Curious, Raffaele asked Pippo what it was all about, but the messenger had no further information.

'We'd best grab something to eat before we set off, guys,' Raffaele said. 'Or we won't have the energy for the climb.'

They made panini with the fresh bread, cheese and salami that Paolo and Rock had bought, ate them hastily, packed their haversacks, and got ready for departure.

After a long, steep hike, they arrived at the *Cesare Battisti* headquarters, where Aquila was waiting for them in an enormous chalet built on pastureland overlooking the village. He greeted Raffaele and the *Volpacchiotti* warmly, shaking everyone's hand, then went on to say that Giorgio and his squad had been attacked by the Fascist Captain Nisi's *Confinaria* brigade in the Cannobina valley. There'd been reports of deaths, and Aquila wanted Raffaele and the Fox Cubs to make haste to the reported location of the confrontation; they were the best partisans for the job, as they were used to covering long distances on foot in the shortest time. Once there, they should gather information, search for the injured and survivors, and organise an ambush of any *Confinaria* militia they found.

Raffaele, Giulia and the rest of his squad left the next morning, hiking across the mountains and through the valleys, singing patriotic songs to boost their morale. As he walked, trepidation swelled in Raffaele's throat. He had a bad feeling about their upcoming mission. In the Cannobina zone, close to the Swiss border, not everyone supported the partisans.

Walking all day, he kept Giulia close to him, her mere presence a balm to his soul. As darkness fell, the going became difficult. Coming across a *baita*, he suggested they stop for the night.

They slept on straw in the barn, all nestled together as if they were, truly, a pack of fox cubs.

* * *

The following morning, they set off again and, before too long, they'd arrived at a stone hut a few kilometres above an unfamiliar village.

'Piccola and Rock, come with me to get some supplies,' Raffaele said. 'The rest of you can wait in that *baita* until we return.'

Giulia walked beside him, with Rock close behind, after they'd taken leave of their companions. The path led them through a woodland of dormant chestnut trees and soon they'd arrived at a small hamlet with the ubiquitous parish church, a tall grey building with a separate campanile bell tower.

Opposite, a cream-coloured three-storey hotel with green shuttered windows and wrought-iron balconies glowed in the afternoon sun. The village must have been a tourist destination before the war, like so many perched above the lake. In fact, the view took Raffaele's breath away: the snow-topped mountains sloped down to the shore at least seven hundred metres below like the wings of enormous doves. A buzzard flew across his line of vision, soaring in the thermals above the deep blue waters of the lake, and he couldn't help admiring the beauty of this location.

He felt a tug at his sleeve, and smiled at Giulia.

'Could we go into that hotel and get a cup of something warm to drink?' she asked.

'Good idea. We can kill two birds with one stone and find out where to buy some food.'

Her answering smile flooded him with warmth and he had to fight the desire to sweep her up in his arms and kiss her on the lips. He restrained himself in front of Rock, though, and led them into the building.

They went through to the bar area, where a red-headed woman was standing behind the counter. Otherwise, the room was empty, which was a good thing, Raffaele thought. The fewer people knew they were in the village, the better.

He ordered barley coffees and while she was making their drinks, the woman asked about the purpose of Raffaele's and his companions' visit to her community.

'We don't get many strangers here,' she said. 'Just a patrol of around fifteen Fascists that comes up from Cannero every night to eat and drink in our restaurant.'

Raffaele's ears pricked up. The Fox Cubs could mount an ambush and take them completely by surprise.

'What time do the *repubblichini* usually arrive?' he asked.

'At around 7 p.m. They generally stay until about ten.' The woman poured their coffees. 'But you didn't tell me why you are here.'

'We've come to get supplies. Is there anywhere in the village where we can buy food?' Raffaele asked.

'The butcher in the street behind us will probably be able to let you have some meat. Is it just for the three of you?'

'There are seven of us,' Rock blurted. 'We are *partigiani* on a mission.'

'How exciting!' The woman's smile played across her lips, but her eyes had turned flinty.

An uncomfortable feeling came over Raffaele. The sooner he, Giulia and Rock were on their way, the better.

After they'd drunk their coffees, he paid the redhead and led his comrades back outside.

The butcher turned out to be most accommodating, and sold them a joint of pre-roasted lamb and some salami, which Raffaele placed in his rucksack along with the bottle of red wine and loaf of bread the man let them have for free.

Back at their camp, he and the others ate hungrily, washed themselves in a nearby mountain stream, and then settled down for a rest before they would head back to the village to ambush the Fascists.

* * *

The next morning, Raffaele blinked his eyes open, a heavy sensation of disappointment clenching his stomach. Last night, they'd waited until 2 a.m. in woodland next to the road below the hamlet, but not one Fascist had arrived. The woman in the hotel had lied to them. Too late to go and search for Giorgio's squad, they'd found another *baita* and had gone to sleep in the hayloft.

'Time to get up, sleepyheads,' he said, getting to his feet.

The Fox Cubs groaned in unison, but did as he'd commanded, coming out of the barn brushing straw off each other.

'We'll head up there.' Raffaele indicated towards a slope with yellow grass flattened by the recent snow.

They set off, and about halfway up, Raffaele's skin prickled.

He came to a sudden halt, made a slowing-down motion with his hand, and raised his binoculars. His blood froze. A massive number of armed men, dressed in grey-green *Confinaria* uniforms with wide-brimmed, domed Alpini hats, had appeared about 150 metres higher up the hill.

'Follow me, guys,' he commanded, leading Giulia and the rest of the *Volpacchiotti* back down the slope. Had they been seen? They were in open land and there were Fascists everywhere: above, below, on every pathway, it seemed.

He came to a dip in the terrain with a small stone wall in front. It would make a bolthole, for the time being, and he indicated that the Fox Cubs should lower themselves behind it. Giulia was next to him and he saw the fear in her eyes. But there was nothing he could say to comfort her. Their situation was extremely precarious. He reached for her hand and felt it tremble in his own.

'A patrol of Fascists is coming towards us,' Duke muttered a short while later from where he was positioned at the edge of the wall.

'Follow me down to the valley, guys.' Raffaele made the quick decision. 'We can come back up the other side when it gets dark.'

But the *repubblichini* had seen them and their leader called out, 'We know you have Giulia Leone with you. Hand her over or we'll shoot!'

'Never,' Raffaele shouted. He grabbed hold of Giulia's hand. That goddamned woman in the village hotel must have been an informer.

Pulling Giulia with him, Raffaele ran down the steep, barren hillside at breakneck speed, making for the stone hut where they'd spent the night. On arriving, he swerved sharply and led her to the far side, where he dropped them both to the ground.

'Where are the others?' They should have been following.

'I don't know.' Giulia shook her head.

Raffaele peered around the edge of the hut, but couldn't see any Fox Cubs. Bullets were flying everywhere. The militiamen were positioned about 200 metres away, standing against the blue of the sky, lined up like the posts of a power line. His Sten would be useless from this distance.

Without warning, he fell backwards, struck by a sudden, sharp pain in his left arm and a dull ache in his right thigh.

'You've been hit.' Giulia's eyes brimmed with concern.

He felt about in his trousers and found an uneven bullet hole, not all that deep, and withdrew his hand stained with blood.

'It's not too serious,' he said, moving his legs. 'I think I can stand.'

'What about your arm?'

Her face pale, she helped him roll up his sleeve to reveal a series of small, deep ruby-red irregular holes peppering the flesh from above his elbow to the palm of his hand.

'Shrapnel,' he said, trying to put a brave face on it.

She was no longer looking at him. Her eyes had grown huge, and she pointed towards the edge of the slope.

'Look! They're surrounding us!'

'We've got to get out of here.' His mind whirled. 'See that tree?'

She nodded, her gaze falling on an isolated chestnut.

'We'll make for it first, then head down to the valley. Ready? Go!'

But the *repubblichini* had formed a full circle just below the tree. Bullets flew and sent up flurries of leaf mould and clumps of turf.

'Get down on the ground!' Raffaele muttered.

He followed suit as Giulia complied, then blasted away at the enemy with his Sten. The nearest Fascist dived into the scrub. Another pointed his gun, and fired a shot which landed about five centimetres from Giulia's face, still pressed to the earth. Wet dirt covered her beautiful hair and Raffaele's heart bled for her.

'Run!' He grabbed her hand, and they ran as if the devil was at their heels.

They came to the edge of a gully with a stream at the bottom. A militiaman approached, unleashing a flurry from his forty-round magazine.

Raffaele rolled himself and Giulia over, then pulled them to their feet.

'See that large bramble bush? We can't leap over it, but we can skip sideways, pretend we've been wounded, and then keep tumbling down to the stream. The Fascists will probably come after us. But at least we'll have gained some time.'

They did as he'd suggested and then he said, 'This is it.' He was resigned to their fate. 'We can't head upstream and the rock face in front is like a prison wall. Descending would turn us into sitting ducks. We can only wait for the *repubblichini* to appear, then take aim and shoot until we've run out of ammunition.'

Raffaele's legs were in water up to his knees; he pointed the barrel of his weapon upwards. *Keep calm. Fire your last shots as best you can.* His pulse thumped in his throat, he was short of breath, and his chest was heaving. *Concentrate. These might be the final few minutes of your life.*

'It's too risky,' Giulia said, clearly misunderstanding his intention for them to make a last stand. 'We might kill one, two Fascists, at the most. Then the others would be more careful and their sniper bullets would get us.' She paused and indicated towards two boulders next to a plunge pool. 'If we can fit into the grotto that the water must have formed, we could maybe save ourselves.'

Raffaele turned his gaze upwards. No one had appeared yet.

'It's worth a try,' he said.

Holding his Sten in his left hand, and Giulia's hand in the other, he jumped with her into the freezing water of the pool. After diving between the rocks, they reached a cave and resurfaced in the tiny space. There was hardly any room for them to turn around, but they managed to do so and, with the water up to his belly and Giulia's chest, they found themselves forced into a hunched position under a low vault.

Awkwardly shifting his legs and arms in the cramped grotto, he lifted his weapon out of the water and pointed the barrel towards the mouth of the cave.

* * *

And so, the wait began. The bangs had waned. A few shots fired, then nothing. Minutes passed while he stared at Giulia and she stared back at him, their eyes telling of their fear and desperation.

Suddenly, the indistinct clamour of voices echoed, almost drowned out by the gushing stream. Heavy footsteps approached, and Raffaele could make out the words being spoken.

'...seen them... here... wounded. Christ... fallen into the water... can't have escaped... if we find them... they're wounded, I'm sure.'

A shadow appeared at the entrance to the grotto, barely two

metres away. Raffaele's chest tightened, and he wondered if his Sten would still fire after being in the stream.

Other shadows reflected in the pool, several of them, going to and fro before disappearing.

Raffaele's wounded arm ached and the upper part of his body felt colder than the lower part, which was immersed in the water. He longed for a cigarette and was about to suggest to Giulia that they leave the cave when the shadows returned, followed by yelling and cursing.

'...but they must be here...' Topped off with a blasphemy. '... Can't have got much further. You, look into that hole between the boulders—'

A bigger shadow was now standing right in front of the opening. Everything went pitch black.

'Can't see a thing,' a voice said.

'Shoot inside!'

The barrel of a rifle was poking into the grotto. Raffaele grabbed Giulia and shuffled them backwards until they were squeezed up against the cave wall. He kept his finger on the trigger of his Sten and prayed fervently that it would work.

'Can't reach. I should get into the water,' the Fascist said.

'Let me try! I'll shove in a grenade,' the other militiaman muttered.

A different voice came from some distance, shouting, 'Come on, guys, follow me! We'll search farther downstream.'

Silence. Had the Fascists really gone? Raffaele waited, then said, 'We should go now. It's night already and the militiamen have gone away. Brace your arms against the wall behind us and paddle with your legs. Take a deep breath first. And don't forget your Sten.'

Giulia complied, and Raffaele drew in all the air he could

before plunging underwater and feeling about with his hands and feet.

Slow seconds passed, and he'd only advanced a few centimetres. Convinced he'd reached the exit, he tried to resurface, but he banged his head on the roof of the cave. *The opening must be farther on.* His lungs felt as if they might burst at any moment.

Deft hands grabbed him and pulled him upwards. Giulia's hands, he was relieved to see. He turned his wet face to the moon and thanked God she was here with him. Putting his finger to his lips, he strained his ears. Apart from the gushing water, he couldn't detect any other sound.

Cautious as foxes, he and Giulia waded through the stream to arrive at a pebbly bank. His heavy ammo and grenade bag cut into his kidneys and were unserviceable now, so he ditched them, and Giulia did likewise with hers.

'Let's head back to Tipperary,' he said. 'Aquila is bound to hear of the attack on us and will send a messenger. Maybe that's where the rest of the *Volpacchiotti* are headed, too.'

* * *

As Raffaele and Giulia began to climb back up the slope where they'd been attacked earlier that day, snow began falling, carpeting the grass and making the going ever more difficult.

'Lean on me,' Giulia said, when Raffaele stumbled for the umpteenth time.

He complied, panting with exhaustion, but at least he could feel the blood flowing through his veins again. Except now he was burning up with fever. If Giulia hadn't been there, he'd have crumpled to the ground.

A freezing wind blew down from the mountaintop, stirring the trees in the beech wood and sending up flurries of snow.

Raffaele's and Giulia's wet clothes had frozen, and they crunched as if they'd been made of papier mâché.

Laboriously, they climbed, passing the wood and taking a route through a chestnut grove. When they reached the village where they'd gone with Rock for supplies, clouds covered the moon, and dark shadows on the sides of the unknown road made both of them startle.

Raffaele's pulse hammered in his throat as he mistook the rustle of holly trees for the whispers of enemy soldiers lying in wait and a pile of birch logs for a camouflaged VW Beetle. His wounded arm had stopped bleeding, but it had swollen to the size of a wrestler's limb and was throbbing, heavy as lead.

It was almost dawn now, and the first cocks crowed, rallying the last of Raffaele's strength. He and Giulia were leaving the village, and the road down to the lake wound precariously, plunging through frosty steep meadows and scrawny vineyards depleted of their leaves.

Without warning, a dog barked from the dark yard of a house. Raffaele could almost cry: they were bound to be discovered and handed over to the Fascists.

But no one came to investigate, so he and Giulia walked on, and eventually, they came to a cluster of stone huts.

'We can't go any further,' he said. 'We're both exhausted, cold and soaked to the skin. We'll have to risk begging for shelter. Which *baita* should we choose?'

'I can hear an alarm clock ringing from that one.' Giulia pointed in the direction of the nearest hut, which boasted a flight of stone steps leading to a wooden balcony overlooking the courtyard, with a line of washing hung out to dry.

Raffaele was grateful for Giulia's help up the stairs. He knocked twice on the oak door, and a sleepy male voice called out anxiously, 'Who's there?'

'Two partisans,' Raffaele said, 'and one of us is injured.'

The rattle of a bolt reverberated, and the door swung open to reveal a man in a vest and long johns.

Raffaele was about to introduce himself and Giulia, only everything began to spin around him. His head swam; his field of vision narrowed to a pinpoint; and he felt himself stagger to the floor.

The last thing he heard before he blacked out was the sound of Giulia pleading plaintively, 'Please, help us.' And then there was nothing.

25

With fear in his eyes, the man stepped forward and grabbed hold of Raffaele, lifting him to his feet as he regained consciousness.

'Have you been followed?' the man asked.

'We're on our own,' Giulia said.

'I'm so cold,' Raffaele groaned and staggered a little.

A withered-looking woman in a nightgown approached. With haggard features, she appeared old beyond her probable years, but was obviously the man's wife.

'You poor young people,' she said. 'Come through to the kitchen, and I'll fetch some dry clothes for you.'

Giulia thanked her and gazed around the simple room, eyeing coarsely squared wooden rafters, a double bed with brass knobs and a smaller bed where two children were sleeping, their tousled heads poking above the bedclothes, top to toe. The man was plainly a stonemason because a jacket and a hat splattered with concrete chippings were hanging from an iron rack on the wall, next to a dusty jar of holy water with olive tree twigs sticking out.

The man had dressed himself now, and he ushered Giulia and Raffaele into the kitchen. Dried broom twigs crackled in the fireplace, reviving the embers from the previous night. From the corner of her eye, Giulia saw that Raffaele had taken off his drenched clothes; he was already nearly naked and toasting his muscular body in front of the yellowish-violet flames.

She turned her back, and the woman draped a blanket around her so that she could strip off modestly.

'I'll get those clothes,' the woman said, and Giulia thanked her once again.

Shivering, she kept her back turned. She felt numb, as if this was happening to someone else, not her. The events of the past twenty-four hours seemed unreal; the situation in which she found herself seemed unreal.

'Here you are.' The woman had returned, fully dressed, and was handing her a coarse woollen skirt, socks and a thick knitted sweater. 'You can wear these until your own clothes are dry.'

The outfit was too big and scratched Giulia's skin, but it was clean and she was grateful for it. Turning around, she discerned Raffaele picking his jacket off the floor before extracting wet cigarettes from the pocket. He placed them on the hearthstone.

'My name is Giovanni,' the man said.

'And I'm Bianca.' His wife smiled.

Giulia and Raffaele gave their battle names, and Giovanni asked what had brought them to his house so early in the morning.

After hearing their story, he said, 'The Fascists are going after us civilians too, and we common people are all partisans in a way.' He went on to tell them about his financial difficulties and how he and his family were constantly hungry because food was so scarce.

Bianca rummaged in a cupboard and came towards them with a bottle of vinegar and a flaxen cloth in her hands.

'Let me disinfect your wounds, Lele,' she said.

After helping Bianca roll up Raffaele's shirt and trousers, Giulia stood by while the stonemason's wife poured vinegar onto his leg.

'The injury on your thigh is superficial,' she said. 'You've probably been struck by a sliver of stone.' She inspected his arm. 'There's something in there, but I'm not qualified to remove it. All I can do is clean and dress it.'

'*Grazie.*' Raffaele grimaced, his mouth twisting with evident pain.

Her heart going out to him, Giulia touched a hand to his good arm.

'You're so brave, Lele. It must hurt like hell.'

'It does.' He shuddered.

The sound of children's whimpers came from the bedroom, and Bianca went to calm her kids down.

Bending to the fireplace, Raffaele chose two soggy cigarettes, one of which he offered to Giovanni, who picked up a firebrand to light them both.

Giulia warmed herself by the fire while the men smoked in silence. Her mind reeled with the events of the past twenty-four hours; it had been the longest and one of the worst days of her life.

'I'm leaving to go to work now,' Giovanni said, throwing his cigarette butt into the flames. 'You two, get some rest, and I'll see you when I return.'

They waved him off, then stared at each other disconsolately. Giulia was unable to give voice to her fear for the Fox Cubs, so great was her concern, and she could see from Raffaele's tormented expression that he felt the same.

'I've made up beds for you in our storeroom,' Bianca said, coming back into the kitchen. 'They're only sacks stuffed with beech leaves, but there are blankets, so you'll be warm.'

Giulia and Raffaele thanked her, and followed her to a room off the kitchen, filled with stored apples. Two rough mattresses had been placed on the wooden floor.

'I'm about to take my *ragazzini* to school,' Bianca said. 'Try to get some sleep.'

'Would it be possible for you to find out in the village about our comrades?' Raffaele cleared his throat. 'We're hoping they managed to get away.'

'I'll do what I can.' She appeared to be fumbling for the right words. 'There's bound to be some gossip.'

'Come, Giulia,' Raffaele said after Bianca had left them to their own devices. 'Lie down and I'll cover you with the blankets.'

She did as he'd asked and turned to face him as he stretched out on the pallet next to hers.

'I'm going to pray for our friends,' she said, her eyes prickling with tears.

'Me too.' He rasped out the words.

She wanted him to wrap his arms around her so she could snuggle into his chest, but he was injured and obviously in too much pain. All she could do was thank God they'd both survived, and focus all her energy on praying for Paolo, Teresa, Duke, Rock, and Lungo. Keeping them in her thoughts, she fell into an exhausted sleep.

* * *

The squeak of the door opening made Giulia startle as she woke from a restless dream of running away from a faceless man in a black shirt. She rubbed her eyes and sat up, noticing that Raffaele was already awake.

'I've fetched my kids from school and made chicken broth for us all,' Bianca said, handing Giulia and Raffaele a bowl each.

They thanked her, then Raffaele came right out with his question.

'Did you hear anything about our friends?'

Bianca darted her gaze around the room before looking Giulia and Raffaele in the eye.

'I heard that five partisans have been killed,' she said. Then, clearly noticing the stricken looks on Giulia and Raffaele's faces, she added, 'That's what the Fascists said. They say all sorts of things. How is your arm, Lele?'

'It's throbbing.' He winced.

'Does it hurt a lot?' Giulia asked.

'Like hell,' he said, rolling up his sleeve with his good hand.

Raffaele's arm had turned into an angry-looking blue-violet sausage, and Giulia was certain it had become infected. Her throat constricted with worry.

The door squeaked open again, and Giovanni appeared. He bent to examine Raffaele's wound, his expression guarded.

'Did you hear anything about what happened yesterday?' Raffaele came right out with it.

'I heard the Fascists have left the village.'

'No, no.' Raffaele pressed him. 'I mean, did you hear anything about the partisans?'

'I heard some got killed.'

'How many?' Raffaele's voice quaked.

Silence. Then Giovanni sighed and said, 'Five.'

'But who said so?'

'People.' Giovanni sighed again.

'Did they see them?'

'They did.'

'Where?' It was Giulia's turn to enquire.

'You know where.'

Silence descended on the room. Nobody said a word. The only sound Giulia could hear was the woodworm gnawing their way into the rafters. Bianca started to weep softly, wiping her eyes with the back of her hand. Giovanni kept staring at a spot on the opposite wall.

Giulia could still see the *Volpacchiotti* in her mind's eye, alive and filled with youthful enthusiasm. She gave a sob, not knowing if she could ever imagine her friends lifeless, deprived of their vigour.

And because of me.

'Are you really sure?' Raffaele asked Giovanni.

All Giovanni could do was nod.

Bianca left the room, and cries of grief echoed from the kitchen.

'We must go,' Raffaele said, staring down at his hands.

'Where?' Giovanni asked.

'To our headquarters.' Raffaele's voice choked.

'You could stay here until tomorrow night.'

'No. No. We're going tonight. You've been kind to us, and we appreciate it, but if you show us the way to Cannero, we'll know where to proceed from there.'

'Listen,' Giovanni said. 'You can stay here as long as you like. You need more rest, and your arm is in a bad way.'

'Thanks, but we have to leave. They'll have a look at my arm at our HQ.'

'Are you sure, Lele?' Giulia asked.

He bent and whispered in her ear, 'I don't want to put these good people in any more danger. The sooner we set off, the better. The Fascists might still be looking for us.'

'Come through to the kitchen,' Giovanni said, clearly under-standing there was no point in insisting. He wiped tears from his cheeks and went to open the squeaky door.

* * *

After they'd drunk the hot milk with coffee that Bianca had prepared for them, Giulia and Raffaele changed back into their own newly dried clothes. Giovanni then said he felt he should give Giulia and Raffaele more information about the fate of their friends. Giulia's chest quivered with nerves, but she owed it to the Fox Cubs to hear the truth.

'At midday, instead of having lunch with the other stonema-sons,' Giovanni said between heart-wrenching sobs, 'I went to the cemetery to see for myself. Some villagers had carried your comrades there on ladders. They were horribly disfigured, I'm sorry to have to say. And there were hundreds of bullet wounds.'

Giovanni was unable to carry on speaking, so great was his distress, and Giulia's chest hurt so much she could barely breathe.

Raffaele had sagged back in his chair, and a strangled sound came from him.

Bianca went to hug him, crooning in a motherly fashion, 'There, there—'

And then they were all crying, even the two children, who'd slipped into the kitchen to drink hot milk.

'We should go,' Raffaele said eventually. 'It's already dark outside. We must head out now if we're to reach our base by morning.'

'I'll show you the way down to Cannero,' Giovanni said.

After hugging Bianca and the children, Giulia and Raffaele

made their way through a woodland with Giovanni, their submachine guns in their hands.

'I'll leave you here.' Giovanni pointed to the track descending to the lake. 'Come and visit when the war is over and let us know how you've got on.'

They promised to do so, and Raffaele reached into his pocket. Amid protests it wasn't necessary, he pushed a fistful of damp one thousand lira notes into Giovanni's hands.

'It's the least we can do,' he said.

* * *

'Are you okay?' Giulia asked Raffaele as they headed down the path.

'I'll be fine.' Abruptly, he stopped in his tracks and pointed.

A fox had appeared about fifty metres below them. A creature of shadows, under the moonlight its red coat had taken on a ghostly, greyish hue, which made it appear almost ethereal. Then, as silently as it had made an appearance, it disappeared into the night.

'I wonder if it's a vixen with cubs?' Giulia said.

'It's too early in the season, I think.'

'I still can't believe what happened to our *Volpacchiotti*.' The denial had formed a painful lump in her throat.

'Me neither.' Raffaele shook his head and gave a heavy sigh.

'It's my fault,' she said. 'If I hadn't been with you, the Fascists might not have come after us.'

'Listen, Giulia. You are not to blame. If the fault lies with anyone, it lies with Rock. He was indiscreet in that tavern last night. He should never have blabbed to that woman. The *repubblichini* would have come after us even if you hadn't been there, I think. They just used you as a pretext.'

But guilt ached in the back of her throat. Why couldn't the enemy forget about her? It was awful that she was still putting her friends in danger.

She and Raffaele carried on walking down the steep path, stones scattering beneath their feet. He stumbled again, and Giulia put her arm around his waist, telling him to lean on her.

'It's you who should be leaning on me,' he said. 'But thank you. My arm is hurting so much I can scarcely think.'

Eventually, they arrived at the main road skirting the *lago*. Giulia gasped as a roaring convoy of military trucks, with tiny lights on, suddenly approached. She pulled Raffaele behind a tall oleander shrub and heaved a sigh of relief as the column sped past.

At last, she and Raffaele came to the path leading to Premeno. They climbed up to the hamlet where, not so long ago, they'd danced in the osteria. All the doors to the houses were shut now, and the narrow streets were empty. Tomorrow, the village children would go to school and, when classes were over, before it got dark, they would play Fascists and partisans and would quarrel because nobody wanted to be a Fascist. The game – unlike reality – always ended with the partisans' victory and the Fascists' defeat.

'I'm in too much pain to go on, Giulia,' Raffaele said as they left Premeno behind. 'There's a spare medical kit in Tipperary, I remember. Would you be able to dress my wounds?'

'Of course. Luna gave me a few first-aid lessons a while ago.' Just saying her comrade's name brought new tears to Giulia's eyes.

'Maybe we should spend the rest of the night there. We can head up to Scareno at daybreak.'

'Good idea.' Giulia almost collapsed with relief. If she'd suggested the plan herself, she'd have encountered Raffaele's stubborn refusal to admit weakness. He was visibly exhausted, and so was she.

The little house looked just the same as when they'd left it only a few days before. Except, nothing was the same, nor would it ever be. Inside, the belongings of their dead friends were scattered about the place. But Duke would never play his accordion again; Paolo would never forage for mushrooms and chestnuts and place them in the bag he always used; Teresa would never trim her own hair and Giulia's with those scissors. Lungo would never cut that deck of cards before one of their poker games; Rock would never sling that tatty old haversack over his shoulder before going to the village for supplies.

'Are you hungry, Giulia?' Raffaele asked after he'd got a fire going in the stove.

'I am, but first let me look at your arm. We left some eggs behind the other day, so I'll make us omelettes afterwards.'

'*Grazie.*' He pulled out a chair and lowered himself onto it.

After fetching the first-aid box from the kitchen cupboard, Giulia removed the flaxen cloth Bianca had tied around his arm. The angry-looking jagged red wounds were suppurating, so she applied iodine before bandaging them up again.

'There are tweezers in the box,' she said. 'But I'm not confident enough to use them. Hopefully, you'll be able to get the pieces of shrapnel removed at headquarters.'

'Hope so,' he said. 'Thanks for looking after me.'

'You'd do the same for me, I'm sure.'

She took the first-aid box back to the cupboard and went to retrieve four eggs from the larder. Focusing on cooking, she tried not to dwell on the events of the past two days.

Raffaele had set the table, and they ate in silence, occasionally sharing a sad smile, the looks passing between them conveying their distress.

It was only when they went upstairs to bed that Giulia realised she and Raffaele would be sleeping together alone. Not that it mattered. All she wanted to do was huddle under the blankets and give way to her grief.

And it was clear, when Raffaele laid himself down next to her, that he felt the same. Heart-racking sobs rent the air. Both his and hers. They wrapped their arms around each other and cried themselves to sleep.

26

Giulia woke the next morning with Raffaele spooned around her. Chilling thoughts sent ice-cold shivers through her, and she was grateful for the warmth of his body. He was still sleeping, and she gazed at his impossibly long dark eyelashes. Tenderly, she smoothed the hair back from his forehead. His brow was cool under her fingers; the fever had broken.

'*Buongiorno*, Giulia.' He yawned and stretched. 'How are you feeling?'

'I'm still in shock,' she said.

'I feel terrible too.'

They sighed in unison.

'How is your arm?' she asked.

'Not as sore as it was yesterday.' He winced. 'But it's still painful.'

'I'll change the dressing before we set off for Scareno.'

He swung his legs from under the bedclothes and went to the window, then gave a low groan.

'It's snowing. Heavily. I doubt we'll be going anywhere today.'

She went to stand beside him. A thick white blanket had

covered the yard and the flakes were coming down so fast it was difficult to see beyond the nearest snow-blanketed fir trees.

'I hope we don't get snowed in,' she said.

'Thank God Paolo and Rock went for supplies before we left, or we'd have nothing to eat.'

Giulia's chest constricted with grief at the mention of her friends' names, and she burst into tears. Raffaele opened his arms, holding her close while she wept.

'I can't get over the cruelty of the Fascists. Their killing of the Fox Cubs was so brutal,' she sobbed, keeping to herself the guilt that threatened to overwhelm her.

'They follow brutal leaders, Giulia.' Raffaele bent and kissed the tears from her cheeks. 'Oh, God. How can my heart be breaking at the same time that it's filled with love for you? You are the most extraordinary, brave, amazing girl.'

'I love you too, Raffaele.' And she did; she loved him with every particle of her being. She loved him for becoming her port in the storm of war; she loved him for being her refuge from the turmoil of being separated from her beloved parents; and she loved him for not putting the blame on her for what had happened to the Fox Clubs.

His mouth claimed hers and he kissed her deeply. Her skin tingling, she gave herself over to him, threading her fingers into his nightshirt and clinging to him. He stroked a finger down her cheek, and she angled her face towards his palm and kissed it.

'I've been longing to tell you I love you for months, *amore*,' he said. 'Just wish it could have happened in different circumstances.'

'Me too.' A sad smile quivered on her lips. 'You saved my life up on that slope, Raffaele.'

'And you saved mine by suggesting we hide in that cave.'

She trembled as she relived the moment, and Raffaele hugged her tight.

'I learnt about grottos in a geography lesson at school,' she said.

'Thank God for that. But I'd give anything to go back in time. I would have made sure the Fox Cubs were at our heels.'

'Maybe they tried to follow us, but the Fascists were quicker than they were and shot them before they could escape.'

'Perhaps.' He lifted her chin and kissed her on the lips.

'It's so cold,' she said, shivering.

'We'd better go downstairs and get the fire going or we'll freeze.'

'I hope we've got enough wood to last until it stops snowing.'

'There's plenty in the woodshed. And we have loads of potatoes, though not much else, I'm afraid.'

Down in the icy kitchen, Giulia had to stop herself from bursting into tears again. She gazed around and said, 'It's so empty in here without the others.'

'We'll never forget them.' Raffaele went to light the stove. 'They've become martyrs and their names will live forever.'

'Do you think Aquila knows we've survived?' Giulia turned on the tap to fill a pan with water.

'I expect anti-Fascist spies will have relayed the news to him that two of us have escaped, but I doubt he knows who the two were.'

* * *

'Shall I look at your arm now, Lele?' Giulia asked after they'd finished breakfast. 'I'll disinfect it again and change the dressing.'

Together, they unravelled the bandage to reveal the angry-looking jagged red wounds.

'At least they've stopped suppurating,' Raffaele said. 'Could you try to remove the pieces of shrapnel with those tweezers?'

'I'm not sure. It'd be terribly painful and I don't want to hurt you.'

'If we don't take them out, they might penetrate further. I'll have a go at doing it myself.'

For the next hour or so, between them, they painstakingly removed all the fragments they could find. Using his right hand, and with gritted teeth, Raffaele managed to tweeze out most of them, and Giulia only took over when she could see he was getting tired. She applied iodine, then bandaged him up again.

'I need a shot of brandy after that,' he said.

'Do we have any?'

'There's some in the cupboard.'

She poured him a big glass and a small one for herself. The fruity liquid warmed the empty feeling in her stomach. She should be happy. Raffaele loved her and she loved him. But all she could think about was her dead friends and how cruelly they'd been killed. *Because of me.* Would there be no end to the horrors inflicted by this dreadful war?

The rest of the morning passed at a snail's pace. They took it in turns to go to the window to check the progress of the blizzard. But it showed little sign of abating, and Giulia feared the worst. Even if it stopped snowing, if the temperature didn't subsequently rise, they'd be stuck here until there was a thaw.

After a lunch of boiled potatoes with some of their precious olive oil, Raffaele suggested they take a nap.

'We'll need to build up our strength for the climb up to Scareno when the snow melts,' he said.

Snuggling into his chest up in the bedroom, while he soothingly stroked her back, Giulia began to relax. She wrapped her arms around him, pulled him close and raised her head. Passion uncoiled inside her as he kissed her; she threaded her fingers into his hair, and he deepened the kiss.

They came up for air and stared at each other. He gave her a questioning look, and she nodded before he moved in for another kiss, even more deep and hungry. Desire sparked between them, but she wriggled from his hold. Things were moving too quickly, and she didn't know if she was ready for where such 'things' would inevitably lead.

'You're a really good kisser,' she said, feeling the warmth of a blush.

'*Grazie.*' He drew her back into his arms, and she snuggled against his chest again. 'Try to get some sleep, *amore.* Hopefully, by the time we wake, the storm will be over.'

She woke before he did, but stayed on the mattress, watching him sleep. How was it possible to feel so much love yet, at the same time, such guilt and grief?

He blinked his eyes open, smiled and said, 'I love you with all my heart, Giulia. I've never felt this way about anyone. And I don't want us to ever be apart. Would you do me the honour of agreeing to be my wife? As soon as we get to Scareno and have had our debriefing with Aquila, I could arrange our wedding with the parish priest. If you agree, of course.'

Her mouth fell open with shock. Hurriedly, she closed it again and said, 'Of course I'll marry you. But don't you think it's a little rushed?'

'After what happened to the Fox Cubs, we need to live every moment as if it's our last, although we should also hope that it isn't, of course. There'll be other actions we'll take part in before the conflict ends. I don't want to die, but if I do, I want to die as your husband.'

Giulia glanced at Raffaele. What he'd said made sense. The

death of their friends had brought home to her how precarious life was.

'I don't want to die either,' she said. 'But if it happens, I want to experience the happiness of being your wife first.'

Sadness washed through her; she'd always imagined her parents seeing her wed. Mamma would have been excited to be helping her choose a dress. Papà would have been proud to be the father of the bride. Giulia would have asked Ester to be a bridesmaid. And Teresa too. How barbaric this war was, how senseless and cruel.

Raffaele kissed her again, and she became like liquid in his arms, dissolving into a puddle of need. Yearning spread through her, making everything tingle and her heart pound. Despite everything that made her soul weep, she was ready to take the next step.

'Make love to me, please, Raffaele,' she said.

'Are you sure?' He looked deep into her eyes.

'Now we're engaged to be married, I think we should consummate our love.'

He took her so gently, she barely felt a twinge, and then the pleasure built and built until she was calling out his name.

Afterwards, they lay in each other's arms, and she touched her fingers to his chest, enjoying the feel of it rising and falling beneath her palms.

He kissed the tip of her nose, then rose to his feet and headed to the window.

'The snowstorm has turned into rain,' he said, and she caught the relief in his words. 'We can leave for Scareno in the morning.'

* * *

Throughout the long, steep hike through woodland – where the going was difficult because of the slushy, melting snow – Giulia found herself feeling torn between the release of tension that she and Raffaele hadn't been snowed in, and regret that her time alone with him, just the two of them, was coming to an end. Last night, they'd made love until the early hours and, in the morning, they'd made love again. Giulia smiled to herself as she remembered their shared delight in each other's body; she'd never thought herself capable of giving herself to another person with such abandon.

'*Amore vero*,' Raffaele had said when she'd told him so. True love. Two words, so straightforward, yet they summed up everything she felt for him. Her heart was still so heavy, though, weighed down with so much grief and guilt about her friends and worry for her parents that she almost forgot to breathe.

She and Raffaele were approaching the enormous chalet built on pastureland above the village now, and Giulia's pulse set up an uncomfortable beat. How would Aquila react to their news?

He was waiting for them indoors; a scout had already warned him of their arrival.

After organising cups of coffee, he asked them to recount the events of the *eccidio*. The word 'massacre' had not been used carelessly by their commander, Giulia and Raffaele found out when they'd finished telling their stories.

'The Fox Cubs didn't die as combatants die in war,' Aquila said. 'They were tortured. The village doctor found 185 wounds on the five of them, both from firearms and from blunt and sharp objects.'

'Oh, my God.' Giulia felt the blood drain from her face.

'That's not all,' Aquila went on to say. 'Not only did the Fascists unload all their ammunition into them, but they also proceeded to viciously annihilate every vestige of their humanity.'

'What do you mean?' Raffaele asked.

'It seems everything they did was symbolic. They removed their shoes to signify they would never walk again. Then they disfigured them so badly they couldn't be recognised. They filled their mouths with porcupine spines to imply they would never speak again. They cut out their hearts to show there was no mercy for them. And they mutilated their genitals to symbolise they would never have heirs.'

Shaking, Giulia could almost be physically sick. Tears threatened and she took a deep breath.

'How do you know all this?' Raffaele inclined his head towards Aquila.

'There's an informer in the village who told the courier I sent to find out what had happened.' Eagle shook his head. 'Those fucking Fascists boasted loudly about what they'd done when they went to drink in a local tavern. A courageous woman who works in the town hall photographed the bodies the day after the massacre. Local nuns had cleaned them up, so that they could later be recognised by their families. When Captain Nisi learnt of this, he ordered his men to seize the film.'

'The *bastardo*,' Raffaele growled. 'I want to make him suffer for this.'

'Don't worry. It's on my list of tasks to be accomplished. As soon as a mole can give us an accurate time for Captain Nisi's scheduled car journeys on the lakeside road, I'll mount an ambush to take him down. The *Confinaria* militiamen were following his orders, and he's the one who should pay.'

'Please, include us in the action,' Raffaele said.

'Of course.' Aquila placed a hand on his shoulder. 'When the time is right.'

'Lele's injured,' Giulia said in a strained tone.

'Poof, only flesh wounds.' Raffaele shrugged. 'Piccola disinfected them and we got the shrapnel out.'

'I'll get our nurse to check you over,' Aquila said. 'Just to be sure.'

'There's something we'd like to ask you.' Raffaele took a deep breath. 'Piccola and I are engaged to be married, and we'd like our wedding to take place as soon as possible.'

A wide smile spread over Aquila's face and he clapped Raffaele on the back, then kissed Giulia on both cheeks.

'That's the best news I've heard in ages. I told you Piccola was a breath of fresh air, didn't I, Lele? I'll do everything I can to help you. It's about time we had something to celebrate. A wedding will give the brigade a huge boost. Leave it to me, guys. You'll be married before you know it.'

Raffaele wrapped his arms around Giulia and whispered, 'Remember we decided to live in the moment, my love. Hold on to that. Our friends would want us to be together, and we'll treasure their memory for the rest of our lives.'

* * *

A month later, on the morning of her wedding day, Giulia put on the blue silk dress she'd borrowed from Iris, the nurse who'd recently joined Aquila's brigade to treat injured and sick partisans. Giulia had been sharing a room with her in the chalet, and now Iris was helping her get dressed.

While Iris was at work applying makeup to her face, Giulia remembered the nurse complimenting her on her treatment of Raffaele's arm. Iris had only needed to remove a couple more fragments of shrapnel, but she'd insisted that he be kept out of any partisan actions until he'd completely healed.

The day after their arrival in Scareno, both hers and Raffaele's spirits had lifted when Giorgio arrived with the last survivors of his band of men. They'd managed to escape being rounded up, and now they swelled the ranks of a new partisan division, the '*Mario Flaim*', which had been named after a fallen hero of the *rastrellamento* last summer. The *Cesare Battisti* had also been incorporated into the new battalion, along with the *Valgrande*, and Aquila was in overall command.

'You look beautiful, Piccola,' Iris said, breaking into Giulia's reminiscing. 'Lele won't be able to take his eyes off you.'

'Thank you again for lending me this dress and letting me take up the hem. It's gorgeous.'

'You're so welcome.' Iris smiled. 'Come along. I need to get you to the church.'

They walked down the road to the village, where Giorgio was waiting to give Giulia away. Given the absence of her parents, he was acting *in loco parentis*. How Giulia wished it could have been her own father. She hoped he'd approve of her choice of husband. How could he not do so? Raffaele was the son of his trusted manager, and came from a good family.

After telling her how *bellissima* she looked, Giorgio threaded her arm through his and led her up the steps of the small ochre-coloured church.

Butterflies fluttered in Giulia's stomach while they walked down the aisle, but as soon as Giorgio placed her hand in Raffaele's, her nerves disappeared. This was where her destiny lay. With Raffaele, the man she loved.

Standing next to Aquila, who'd agreed to be his best man, Raffaele gazed at her face.

'I'm the luckiest guy in the world to be marrying you. My beautiful, brave Giulia.'

She looked at him, so handsome in his borrowed suit and tie.

He was about to become her husband; she almost pinched herself.

The ceremony passed in a blur. Soon they'd arrived at the point where they were expected to make their vows. Raffaele said his first, and then it was her turn. Her heartbeats skittered.

'I do,' she said, after the priest asked her if she wanted to take Raffaele for her lawful husband, to have and to hold from this day forward, for better, for worse, for richer, for poorer, in sickness and in health, until death parted them.

Raffaele caught her eye, pride reflected in his gaze.

'*Ti amo*,' he whispered.

'I love you too,' she said.

They exchanged the second-hand rings Aquila had helped them buy in the village, and Raffaele kissed her deeply and possessively, then walked her down the aisle and out of the church.

Myriad toasts – there was no shortage of wine in Scareno – and plenty of food in the chalet's dining room were followed by dancing. Aquila had managed to procure a gramophone, and someone put a record on.

Raffaele held Giulia close as they swayed to the music, and she basked in the love shining from his eyes. Her thoughts turned, as ever, to her parents, Ester, and the Fox Cubs. If only they could have been there...

'It's time for us to go to our room, my dearest wife,' Raffaele said, smiling warmly.

'I'm ready.' She returned his smile.

He took her hand and led her from the dining room and up the stairs. In the bedroom that had been set aside for them, he undressed her, then undressed himself.

She feasted her eyes on him. He was truly magnificent, all hard muscle, every inch of him perfect, even the scar on his leg and the pitted holes in his arm. She went to stand in front of him and stretched herself upwards, her body tingling, as he bent to kiss his way down her face to her neck.

He lifted her and carried her to the bed, and she lay back and parted her thighs.

She kept her eyes glued to his as Raffaele lowered himself, his flesh meeting her heated skin.

Later, they fell back on the bed, and her heart swelled with love as Raffaele kissed her. Whatever the future brought, she would never forget today, however bittersweet it might be for the absence of hers and Raffaele's families, and her guilt and grief for their dead friends.

'I love you, Giulia.' He took her hand and kissed her wrist.

'I love you too, Raffaele. I love you so very much.'

PART V

APRIL–OCTOBER 1945

27

A month after Giulia's nineteenth birthday, she was sitting with Raffaele on an outside bench in front of the chalet soaking up the sun. Spring had come to Lago Maggiore, bringing squalls of rain interspersed with bright rays of sunshine. Today, the weather was fine and something of the sapphire-blue sky, the soft air and the snow sparkling on the distant Alps played into the mood of euphoria felt by her and everyone else as they'd realised the Fascists' days were numbered. The Allies were on the move, at last. It was all she could think about. The enemy would soon know they could expect no mercy; the hunters would become the hunted and, when it was all over, she would no longer worry about posing a danger to her friends and could finally go and find her parents.

Taking her hand in his, Raffaele squeezed her fingers and said, 'By this time next month, the war should be over, *amore*.'

'What will we do then?' she asked.

'What would you like to do?'

'I'd like to go to Milan to get news of my parents, of course.'

'Then that's what we'll do.' He raised her hand and kissed her wrist. 'But we're jumping the gun with these plans. We should focus on the present and get rid of the Nazi-fascists first.'

'I'm excited to be going on that action tomorrow,' she said.

Finally, Aquila had set up a flying squad to ambush Captain Nisi while he was being driven from Cannero to Cannobio. And, as per their request, Raffaele and Giulia had been included in the party.

'We owe it to the Fox Cubs to seek vengeance,' Raffaele said.

* * *

The next day, Giulia found herself crouching with Giorgio on a slope above the lakeside road. She was armed with a rifle and *Il Monco* with a Mauser semi-automatic pistol. They'd been tasked with covering Raffaele and Aquila, who were hiding behind an azalea bush lower down, their Stens at the ready.

Warm sun beat down on Giulia, and the sweet scent of the flowers filled her nostrils. She glanced at her watch. That *bastardo* Nisi should be here any minute now.

The rumble of a car engine reverberated, and Giulia's pulse raced. The vehicle – a black Fiat 508C *militare* – was approaching slowly, escorted by a group of armed militiamen on foot, an easy target.

Giulia squeezed the trigger of her rifle and landed a shot on the convoy. But Giorgio muttered, 'Too early, Piccola,' and her heart sank.

Nisi's car came to an abrupt halt as his men surrounded him and opened fire.

Guns roared and bullets flew, one of which whistled past Giulia's left ear. Her shoulders tightened, and she held her breath. *What have I done?*

'Beat a hasty retreat, guys,' Aquila barked as Giorgio let rip with his Mauser, covering them while they scrambled up the slope.

'Come, Piccola,' Raffaele yelled. 'Stick close to me!'

The Fascists were following them, and Giulia's stomach churned. It would be a repeat of the slaughter of the Fox Cubs, she was sure of it. What could she do?

Without thinking twice, she put her rifle on the ground and ran down to the road, her hands raised.

'Stop shooting,' she shouted. 'It's me you want. Giulia Leone.'

28

Raffaele watched in horror as Giulia surrendered herself to Captain Nisi. Before he could do anything, the Fascists had surrounded her and were bundling her into the Fiat. Raffaele let out a growl and started to head back down to the road.

But Aquila grabbed hold of him.

'Don't even think about it,' he said. 'You'll be dead within seconds.'

'I can't abandon Piccola. She's my wife.'

'You won't be abandoning her, my friend. We'll mount a rescue operation as soon as we find out where she's been taken.'

Oh, God. My poor love. I should never have brought her on the mission, Raffaele thought. Giulia must have been the one who'd jumped the gun and fired that rifle shot; she'd been over-eager and now she'd sacrificed herself. He knew her, knew she'd acted under some misguided sense of duty. Her guilt about the Fox Cubs would have prompted her to put herself forward. How impetuous of her. He'd thought she'd grown out of her impulsiveness. The only compensation was she hadn't been killed in the process.

Fear for his beloved chilled Raffaele to the bones. What if she was put before a firing squad before he could get to her? And where was Giorgio? God forbid *Il Monco*'s luck had finally run out. Raffaele wouldn't be able to bear the death of another friend, and Giulia would be distraught. *Provided she lived.*

All the way back to Scareno, Raffaele mulled over what had happened. If Aquila hadn't stopped him, he'd have been shot trying to grab Giulia. Why hadn't she realised she was putting him in even more danger? Hot-headed as ever...

Supper was being served when Raffaele and the others arrived at the chalet. But he had no appetite. Neither did he feel like joining in the card games and sing-alongs that generally took place before bedtime.

He put on his coat and went to sit on the bench where he'd sat with Giulia. Was it only yesterday? Alone at last, he gave way to his misery. Hot tears ran down his face and he let out a keening sound, reminiscent of a wounded animal.

The sound of footfalls made him sit bolt upright and scrub at his cheeks with his hands.

A lone figure was approaching. Could it be Giulia? But she couldn't have escaped, could she? The closer the figure got, the more Raffaele discerned the stocky shape of Giorgio.

'I'm so sorry,' *Il Monco* said. 'I tried to go after Piccola, but Nisi's car sped off before I could get anywhere near it.'

'Did you see in which direction it went?' Raffaele asked.

'Yes. Towards Intra.'

'Then I'll head there. Aquila will help me rescue her,' Raffaele said.

'Count me in as well.' Giorgio clapped him on the shoulder. 'And try not to worry.'

But that was easier said than done.

29

In the back seat of the Fiat, Giulia strained against the handcuffs holding her hands behind her back. But they were too tight for her to wriggle out of. She glared at Captain Nisi. He was a burly, brown-haired man with a big nose and a toothbrush moustache, and he'd said not a word to her since getting into the car. Giulia wanted to ask him if her companions had got away, except she didn't want to give him the satisfaction of knowing how concerned she was. So she stared out of the window as the vehicle made its way along the lakeside road.

Thoughts of Raffaele filled her mind. Had he, Aquila and Giorgio escaped harm? How she prayed her sacrifice had been worthwhile.

When the car rolled to a stop in front of the Intra Hotel, Giulia thought about making a run for it, but she knew that wasn't an option. Nisi and his men had guns and would shoot her dead on the spot. She held her head high, every cell in her body quaking while the Fascists marched her to their headquarters.

Prodding her in the back with their weapons, they took her through to a reception room on the ground floor of the building.

Her pulse jumped in her throat.

A German officer was standing in front of a desk.

Obersturmführer Karl Weber.

The man was similar in appearance; he was tall and had dark blond hair and wore the same style of breeches and black leather riding boots as the hated Nazi who'd caused her such heartache in Marta.

Giulia squinted and took a second look at him. She let out a pent-up breath. Although they were similar in height and appearance, this officer was one of the *Feldgendarmerie*, not the *Waffen-SS Leibstandarte Adolf Hitler* who'd done such terrible things to Ester and her family.

'Giulia Leone, we meet at last,' the German said, his blue eyes glinting.

She pressed her lips together. Giulia, like Raffaele, Teresa and Paolo, had ditched her fake ID when they'd left Milan. A document with an address in the city would have been no use to them and they'd reverted to their battle names.

'I'm known as Piccola,' she said.

'Giulia Leone identified herself to me to save her comrades,' Captain Nisi chipped in self-importantly.

'You are the girl we've been looking for since September 1943, the Jew-lover who we found out had become an outlaw and had joined the partisans,' the *Feldgendarmerie* officer said.

'No comment.' Giulia stared at a spot on the wall.

'Take off your clothes so we can search you,' Captain Nisi barked.

'I can't. You've handcuffed me.'

He pointed to the younger of the two guards and said, 'Free her.'

The guard did as he'd asked, and Giulia removed her sweater.

'More,' the German officer snarled. 'Take everything off.'

With trembling fingers, Giulia undid her shirt and unbuttoned her trousers. The clothes fell to the carpeted floor and she stepped out of them. She pulled down her woollen socks and removed her shoes; she was only wearing her underwear now. Shivering, she wrapped her arms around herself.

'We said to take everything off,' the Nazi yelled in her ear, spit flying from his mouth.

She flinched but complied with his order, her hands shaking. Naked and embarrassed, she covered her breasts with one arm and her privates with the other.

Nisi came to stand by her side and she shot him a defiant look.

'Bend over. I need to check for hidden weapons.'

Giulia didn't move. All she could do was shiver with mortification. If she weren't outnumbered, she would have raced to the door.

'Bend over!' Nisi bellowed, pushing a hand into her back.

She did as she was bid, the guards laughing as the Fascist's searching fingers assaulted her. He parted the flesh of her privates and she cringed. *How dare he!*

'Stand up straight!' The German officer had positioned himself in front of her. 'Get dressed! The guards will take you to a prison and I will see you again later.'

Outraged, Giulia put her clothes back on. What that man had done to her made her feel unclean. The guards handcuffed her again; their gazes were fierce, but she gritted her teeth.

It was a five-minute walk from the hotel to the jail behind the old theatre building. She kept her head down, praying Raffaele would find out where she was and come to her aid as soon as possible.

The Fascists led her to an empty cell, with a chamber pot in a corner, a cot with a rough-looking blanket against one wall, and a table with a wooden chair opposite.

'Don't move,' the older of the two guards said. 'I'll take off your cuffs.'

She did as he'd ordered and rubbed at her swollen wrists.

The younger guard had planted his feet wide and was giving her looks that made her flesh crawl.

With a clang, the two men closed the cell door, locked it and left her on her own.

Giulia paced the concrete floor, biting her thumbnail and trying to be brave. She knew what happened to partisans who were caught: she would be tortured and then executed. Raffaele would be distraught. But she'd had to surrender; the alternative would have been another slaughter like that of the Fox Cubs. She was lucky the Fascists hadn't killed her outright but, if she'd died, it would have been for a good cause.

Slumped down on the cot, she curled herself into a ball, a cold feeling of dread spreading through her as she let her tears fall. Thoughts of her parents swirled through her mind. Had they been imprisoned in a cell like this one? How terrified they must have been…

In the evening, a new guard arrived with a meal of fish stew. But she couldn't eat: the food stuck in her throat and it was impossible to swallow. It occurred to her that they were probably treating her well so she would talk. She would never talk. Even if they broke every bone in her body, she would stay silent.

'Tomorrow you will be interrogated,' the guard said with a smirk. 'You must tell the truth, or else—'

Giulia lay on the cot, lonely and afraid. To stop herself from despairing, she thought about Raffaele and her parents. *Stay strong*, she told herself. *Make everyone proud of you.* She closed her eyes, waiting for sleep to claim her; she needed to rest if she were to resist what was certain to come.

* * *

Giulia woke the next morning, after a restless night spent worrying about the torture she was sure would be inflicted. Would she be strong enough to face it? She would rather die than betray Raffaele and the others.

A guard brought her bread and grain coffee for breakfast. He wished her *buongiorno*. She went to spit in in his face but stopped herself in time. She tried to sip the coffee and nibble the bread, but her stomach heaved and she hurried to the chamber pot to throw up. She spent the morning curled up under the blanket, willing herself to stay calm.

It had suddenly struck her that she'd been impetuous and rash surrendering to the Fascists. She'd thought she was sacrificing herself for Raffaele and her friends, but they might be killed if they tried to rescue her. That's if they'd even survived the Captain Nisi ambush fiasco. How foolish she had been!

At midday, the guards took her to a separate room, where they sat her on a chair. They tied her hands behind her back and shackled her feet. She squirmed and the shackles bit into her skin.

The German officer arrived; he came and stood in front of her.

'Tell us where the partisans are hiding and we'll spare your life.' He fixed her with a steely look.

'I don't know.' She held his gaze.

The slap came from nowhere, knocking her head sideways,

the sting so sharp it brought tears to her eyes. The metallic taste of blood filled her mouth.

'You Jew-loving bitch! Where is the man known as Aquila? He has been escorting *Juden* across the border into Switzerland.'

'I have no idea who or what you are talking about.' It was the first Giulia had heard about Eagle helping Jewish people, and she liked him all the more for it.

A punch landed on her stomach, stealing her breath. She clamped her teeth together to not cry out at the pain.

The SS officer twisted his hand in her hair and yanked her head back. Her scalp burnt like fire; tears of agony gushed from her eyes.

He stared at her, watching her with his pale cold eyes.

'Talk,' he snarled. 'Tell us the real names of the partisans you were with!'

'No!' she shouted. Why would the German want that information? He must want to go after their families.

Oh, God, the vile man had pulled his gun on her. Bullets flew, whizzing past her head. He was deliberately trying to frighten her by aiming wide.

'Talk!' he bellowed.

More slaps landed on her face and punches to her belly. The Nazi repeated the same questions again and again. She screwed her eyes shut to try to stem the tears. *Be brave*, she told herself.

'Speak or we will hang you by the neck until you die.'

Giulia could only shake her head.

'Untie her. Strip her naked and bend her over the desk,' the officer ordered the guards.

She heard the crack of a whip and her heart almost gave way. Sensing the German moving behind her, she braced herself.

Sharp pain sliced into her as leather hit the flesh of her shoulders, and she let out a squeal.

'Talk!'

Rage and hatred boiled inside her. She wanted to turn on the man, grab his gun and kill him. But she was shackled and, even if she weren't, he would shoot her dead before she got the chance. Giulia took a deep breath and then blew it out. The next hit came, striking like a hot knife across her back. She cried out and her feet twisted.

'Tell us what we want to know,' the officer spat out the words.

'No!' She would never give in.

Another crack of the whip. Harder this time. She shrieked at the burn.

'Ready to talk now?'

She remained silent.

The German carried on whipping her, harder and harder as he appeared to get into his stride. Giulia whimpered, and her legs felt weak and shaky. She had to be courageous and not reveal anything. Just like Signor Perego and her dear housekeeper, Maria, when they had been beaten by the Gestapo in Milan. Closing her eyes, Giulia felt the room spin around her. Her last thoughts before she fainted were of Raffaele and her parents, the people she held most dear in the world.

30

Two days after Giulia had given herself up, Raffaele and the entire *Mario Flaim* division came down from Scareno in the early hours. They positioned themselves in a field on the outskirts of Intra and waited for Aquila to give the signal to attack.

Raffaele muttered under his breath: it was taking far too long for them to get going. The plan was to occupy the town and then spring Giulia from wherever she was being held. Raffaele had been worrying about her so much he'd barely slept and had needed to force down every meal. He should never have taken her on the mission to ambush Captain Nisi. But he'd thought she'd be safer with him than up in the chalet.

He gazed at the sky: a beautiful sunrise was painting the clouds in hues of pink and orange. Could Giulia see it? Where was she? How was she? Raffaele sighed. In the quiet of daybreak, every sound and movement had become amplified: there were muffled curses as someone dislodged a stone, or a *partigiano* knocked his weapon against his ankle.

Minutes passed until, at last, Aquila gave the battle-cry, '*Partigiani all'assalto!*'

Everyone started yelling. They ran across the field and fanned out when they reached the first houses. Squads of six and eight branched off along the side streets, while Raffaele's detachment raced with Aquila's down the main road to the town centre.

Raffaele's breath came in quick bursts as he fired his Sten and dodged forward, one doorway at a time. Progress was painfully slow and exhausting. The sun rose higher and sweat poured from his body. All he could think about was Giulia, how much he loved her, how he couldn't live without her, how he would reprimand her for risking her life.

As Raffaele and his comrades approached the rectangle-shaped Piazza Cavour, enemy fire intensified, coming from the German HQ in a three-storey building up ahead, pinning down the partisans and slowing their advance. Was Giulia in there? Or had the Fascists taken her somewhere else? Raffaele prayed ardently that she was safe from harm.

Aquila called a council of war. The *partigiani* needed to intensify their assault. It would mean casualties, but they had to defeat the Germans.

The battle wore on, hot and intense, but the courage and determination of the partisans remained high, even as the enemy showed little sign of surrendering. Raffaele felt proud of his comrades: they were a valiant group of fighters, for sure.

'There's nothing to be done but mount a blockade,' Aquila said when the longest day had turned into night. 'We can fight on in the morning.'

After he and the others had eaten the panini they'd packed in their rucksacks, Raffaele sat on the pavement under a portico and leant against the wall. If Giulia had been with him, he'd have tucked her into his side and her face, usually animated with expression, would have softened as she drifted off to sleep, radiating a peacefulness that would have calmed his nerves. A secret smile would have flickered across her slightly parted lips, as if she were dreaming of happier times. The way the moonlight would have caught the curve of her cheekbones, highlighting the subtle shadows beneath her closed eyes, would have taken his breath, and an overwhelming sense of protectiveness would have filled him as he'd have watched her chest rise and fall. The image was so vivid in his mind he almost found it difficult to believe she wasn't snuggling up to him right now.

How was she coping? He hoped to God she wasn't being tortured. A sick feeling came over him as he thought about what the Fascists had done to the Fox Cubs. The sooner he got to Giulia the better...

31

Giulia woke to the sounds of cannon fire. Had the Allies arrived at last? She prayed that would be so but, when the guard brought her breakfast, he said, 'The partisans are under fire from a German mortar in Piazza Cavour. They came down from the mountains yesterday.'

Oh, dear Lord. Giulia felt a pang of dread. If Raffaele had survived the ambush and was with them, she hoped he hadn't been hurt. Or worse, killed.

The day before, she'd been woken by dawn light coming through the barred window. She'd found herself fully dressed and had winced as she'd remembering being stripped naked and beaten by the despicable Nazi officer. All day long, she'd waited to be taken to him. How blithely she'd said she wanted to be married to Raffaele, she'd recalled. She'd wanted to enjoy the happiness of being his wife sooner rather than later in case she died. Would she be executed by the Nazi-fascists? She'd have preferred to have died in battle...

Long hours had passed. A new guard came on duty; he brought food on a tray, but she had no appetite, and could only drink water. When would the German officer send for her? Giulia had found herself wishing it would happen soon; she'd wanted to get it over and done with. Being in limbo had been excruciating.

But that was yesterday, and today she was spending the longest morning of her life listening to the sounds of the battle until finally, in the afternoon, an eerie silence pervaded. The German officer still hadn't sent for her; he'd probably been too busy fighting the partisans.

Dread filled Giulia as she waited for the summons. The cruel man had beaten her senseless, literally. Her entire body ached and there were vivid purple bruises everywhere. What more would he do to her before delivering the final blow? She paced her cell, her limbs shaking, while she hoped against hope that Raffaele was all right and that he'd come for her soon.

The window was too high up for Giulia to look out; she could only see the sky. When the afternoon had lengthened into evening, the guard who brought her food told her that the partisans' action had been unsuccessful. Her eyes filled with tears and she contemplated trying to break out of the jail. But her impulsiveness had got her into trouble too many times. The moment had finally come for her to stop behaving rashly and act like a sensible adult. Even if she could escape, she probably wouldn't get very far before being killed.

The following day, the guard brought her breakfast, then left Giulia to her own devices once more. Myriad thoughts whirled through her mind. Where was Raffaele? Was he safe? Mamma and Papà must have been thinking those same thoughts about her when they'd been held in the Milan prison. Would the Nazi officer decide not to execute her but send her to a labour camp instead? If so, Giulia hoped it would be the same one as her parents.

Her skin prickled; someone was coming. Footsteps tramped and keys jangled in the lock of her door. Could it be Raffaele?

But the militiamen who'd escorted her to the jail burst into her cell and Giulia's heart sank.

'We have orders to take you to Captain Nisi,' the older Fascist said.

'Why?' she asked.

'You'll find out soon enough.' The man handcuffed her hands behind her back.

Giulia's stomach roiled. Fascist torture was even worse than that meted out by the Germans. She thought about what Nisi had ordered his men to do to the Fox Cubs, and a sour taste filled her mouth.

32

Two days after he and the rest of the partisan division's failed attempt to occupy Intra, back in the field on the outskirts of the town, Raffaele roused himself from a restless sleep. When the Germans had started firing on them with a mortar, Aquila had given the order to retreat. Raffaele had been champing at the bit ever since: he couldn't bear it that Giulia still hadn't been rescued; he couldn't bear thinking about what she must be suffering; he couldn't bear being without her.

But at least he had lived to fight another day. According to intelligence sources, some of his comrades hadn't been so lucky: several had been killed in the battle and others captured and then executed by the enemy.

Playing the waiting game in a soggy meadow wasn't Raffaele's idea of fun. It was boring, cold and uncomfortable. If Giulia had been with him, they would have snuggled together under their blankets and told each other stories of happier times. Her relationship with her parents was as strong as the one he had with his own ma and pa. He missed them so much, but not as much as he was missing Giulia.

Raffaele rolled up his blanket and put it in his rucksack. He was about to make his way over to the food tent when Aquila bounded up to him.

'I've just been listening to my radio. Bologna has been liberated by the partisans, and the Allies have crossed the Po river.' Eagle smiled broadly. 'The Germans are retreating northwards to escape being rounded up. A scout has just arrived with the news that the *SS-Feldgendarmerie* have left Intra.'

The cowards, Raffaele thought.

'What about the Fascists?' He heard the hope in his tone.

'They've abandoned their bunkers and have withdrawn to the Intra Hotel on the lakeside.' Aquila's eyes narrowed. 'Time for us to go and get them—'

'Erm, any idea where they're holding Giulia?'

'Our mole in Fascist HQ sent a message earlier that she's being kept in the town jail.' Eagle clapped Raffaele on the back. 'How about you and I head there while Giorgio and the rest of the division start dealing with the *fascisti*? It shouldn't take us long, and we can meet up with them as soon as we've sprung Giulia from the prison.'

Raffaele's heart thudded: finally, he would liberate his beloved.

* * *

After a quick breakfast to refuel, Raffaele and his comrades broke camp and marched into Intra with their cartridge belts slung around their necks and weapons at the ready. Aquila sent Giorgio and the rest of the men to the Intra Hotel, as planned, while he and Raffaele made their way to the prison behind the theatre.

The two-storey white building was set back from the road,

and a heavy wooden door barred the entrance. Raffaele tried it, but it was locked. *Damn!*

'Nothing for it but to blow the lock off,' Aquila said, taking a stick of dynamite from his haversack.

Raffaele waited on the other side of the street while Eagle lit the fuse. Within seconds a massive explosion lifted the door from its hinges. Raffaele and Aquila raced inside, their Stens cocked.

But there was no one to be seen.

Keeping their guns raised, they searched the front offices then went down to the basement cells.

The entire place was empty.

Cazzo! Raffaele sagged against a wall, disappointment heavy in his chest.

'Come,' Aquila said. 'Giulia must have been taken to the hotel by the Fascists.'

Raffaele and his commander hastened in the direction of the waterfront. But the closer they got to the lake, the more they were surrounded by jubilant locals.

'The Fascists have gone,' a woman said to them. 'They left during the night by boat.'

Raffaele felt sick. Had they taken Giulia with them?

He and Aquila elbowed their way through the throng. Masses of people had burst onto the streets, and were crowding around them and the other partisans, hugging them, lifting them on their shoulders, clapping, cheering, crying, laughing, and shouting.

Eventually, Raffaele and Eagle arrived at the Intra Hotel and went inside. Giorgio met them in the lobby and said, 'The *Confinaria* are still in Cannero, and I found out that Piccola is with them.'

'What'll we do now?' Raffaele asked Aquila.

'You and Giorgio gather a squad and meet me at the railway

bridge. I'll organise a lorry and we'll head there as soon as possible.'

* * *

In Cannero, a gush of warmth greeted Raffaele as he climbed off one of the two lorries Aquila had commandeered. Raffaele wiped sweat from his brow: the climate in the small lakeside town was more Mediterranean than sub-alpine, thanks to its sheltered position and sunny exposure.

But, yet again, disappointment was constricting his throat: the wooden front door to the Fascist headquarters was open, and it didn't take long for him and the others to realise that the building was empty.

A middle-aged man approached and said, 'They've retreated to Cannobio.'

'They're like scared chickens running away from a fox,' Aquila muttered.

'We are the foxes,' Raffaele said. 'And it's time to avenge our cubs.' *And rescue Giulia.*

Soon, they'd arrive in Cannobio, where they found the Fascist barracks surrounded by locals, who were hurling stones and rocks at the two-storey structure.

After Aquila had sent Giorgio to warn the civilians and suggest they move to a position of safety, he barked orders to Raffaele and the rest of the squad to lob their grenades through the open ground-floor windows.

A series of loud, rubble-inducing blasts ensued, and then a white tablecloth trembled from an upstairs window and Raffaele's heart trembled along with it. Was Giulia inside and, if so, was she okay?

33

Her chest fluttered as Giulia paced the concrete floor of a basement cell. The echo of explosions was ringing in her ears. What could be causing them? Was it the partisans? She took a deep breath and slowed her steps, praying that she would see Raffaele burst through the door any minute now.

When she'd been brought here yesterday, instead of being handed over to Nisi, she'd been delivered to an elderly sergeant, who'd informed her that half of his brigade, including its captain, had escaped over the frontier into Switzerland.

'Please, let me go,' Giulia had begged. The militia's Fascist pig of a leader had run away like a deserter. It was he who'd wanted her imprisoned. Surely his minions had no good reason to keep her.

'We know you were with the *Cesare Battisti*. Our spies also confirmed your presence with the *Mario Flaim*,' the sergeant had said. 'The Allies will soon be here. They've crossed the Po and the partisans have occupied Milan. Our German friends are on the retreat and have abandoned us.'

'Then release me,' Giulia said.

'We haven't decided what to do with you, but you won't be released.' The sergeant had frowned.

Giulia's heart had leapt at the news of the Allied advance, partisans' success and the German withdrawal. Things seemed to be moving quickly. Dare she hope that the war was nearly over? Her spirits had soared at the notion she might be reunited with her parents very soon. Maybe Poland had already been liberated and Mamma and Papà were on their way home? She hoped against hope Raffaele would arrive sooner rather than later. *Provided he'd survived.*

The sergeant had organised for her to be escorted downstairs, where she was provided with a basin of water, soap and a towel, as well as food and a warm blanket. She'd spent the night tossing and turning on an uncomfortable cot in the filthy cell and now she was waiting with bated breath for what she hoped would happen next.

She kept her ears pricked, and the sound of running footsteps set her pulse racing.

'Giulia!' Raffaele's voice came through the door. 'Where are you?'

'Here,' she called out, tears of happiness welling up. 'Thank God.'

With a rattle of a keychain, he unlocked the door, and she fell into his arms.

He hugged and kissed her and she hugged and kissed him back, giddy with relief and joy.

'Did they hurt you, *amore*?' Raffaele stood back and looked her up and down.

'The Nazi officer whipped me.' Her voice caught on a tremor. 'But I didn't reveal anything.'

'My poor, brave darling.' Raffaele held her gently. 'I hope you aren't in any pain.'

'Just a bit bruised,' she said. 'Nothing worse than what my family's housekeeper and Papà's deputy experienced.'

'I apologise for taking so long to get to you.' Raffaele led Giulia towards the staircase. 'I wanted to come straight away, but the Germans forced us to retreat.'

'I hope you are all safe, my love,' she said.

'Some of our guys were killed, and others were captured and executed.' He glanced at her. 'I was terrified you'd suffered the same fate and have spent the worst week of my life worrying myself sick about you.'

'I'm sorry I jumped the gun and then gave myself up, Raffaele. I've been riddled with guilt about it, after all you've done to protect me. It was a spur-of-the-moment thing. When Nisi's men started going after you and Aquila, I truly believed you would suffer the same fate as the Fox Cubs.'

'You were as impetuous as ever, *amore*.' Raffaele frowned. 'I hope you'll never do anything like that ever again.'

'I've learnt my lesson,' Giulia said. 'It could have gone so badly wrong for me. I realised I'd had a lucky escape and decided not to try to escape from the prison.'

'Well, I'm glad you've finally come to your senses.' Raffaele smiled at her. 'Come, let's go find Aquila.'

Giulia heaved a sigh of relief: she'd been worried Raffaele might have been cross. If the boot had been on the other foot, she would have been furious with him for risking his life so unthinkingly.

Eagle was upstairs, and she heard him telling Giorgio to take charge of escorting the Fascist prisoners onto lorries.

'Oh, dear Lord,' Giulia said, pointing to a stack of weapons on a table. 'Those are the Fox Cubs' guns. I'd recognise them anywhere.'

'Me too.' Raffaele was eyeing Paolo's Sten. 'Those godforsaken *bastardi fascisti*.'

A jacket had been slung over the back of a chair, and Aquila went to fish in its pockets. He pulled out a roll of undeveloped film.

'Look what I've found,' he said. 'It could be the photos taken of the *Volpacchiotti*, which would be enough evidence to bring Nisi to trial for his crimes—'

'Better than nothing, I suppose.' Raffaele sighed.

An image came into Giulia's mind of the burly, brown-haired man with the big nose and toothbrush moustache, and she prayed the evil captain would get his just deserts.

'Come,' Aquila said. 'I've ordered that the militiamen be detained in the local elementary school. One of the lorries will return to pick us up. You and Piccola can interrogate the *fascisti* there, Lele.'

They went back downstairs, and Giulia silently slipped her hand into Raffaele's. He turned to gaze at her and she caught his pain-filled expression; their shared frustration tore her apart.

At the *scuola*, they found the prisoners bizarrely sitting on the children's small benches in the assembly hall. Giulia and Raffaele went up onto the stage and stood behind a lectern.

'Which of you attacked a group of seven partisans last February and massacred five of them?' Raffaele's voice rang out. 'I know it was some of you because we found our friends' weapons on the second floor of your barracks.'

Silence. Giulia and Raffaele stared down at the faces of the Fascists, who stared back up at them, feigning innocence.

'Shame on you,' Giulia said, bitterness coating her tongue. 'You haven't even got the courage to own up to the horror you inflicted. That wasn't war... it was carnage.'

'Piccola, there's nothing more to be done here.' She felt Raffaele tug at her sleeve. 'Aquila has organised a group to guard the prisoners and is heading back to Intra. He wants us to go with him.'

* * *

The lake looks beautiful today, and the mountains are like the spires of enormous cathedrals rising into the sky, Giulia thought as she stood beside Raffaele on the ferry pier in Intra, waving Aquila, Giorgio and most of the other partisans off. They were about to cross by boat to Laveno, from where they would head to Varese for the chance to harass the retreating Germans.

'Are you sorry not to be going with them, Raffaele?' she asked, squinting her eyes in the April sunshine. He'd been reticent all the way back from Cannobio.

'Not at all. It's time I went home, *amore*. I'd like to tell my family we're married.'

Sudden nerves assailed her. How would Raffaele's parents react? It might come as a shock to learn of their wedding.

'Will they be okay about it?'

'Ma took to you straight away, remember? They will love you, *amore*.' He lifted her hand and kissed her wrist.

'Can't we go to Milan first? I need to find out what's happened to Mamma and Papà. Maybe Signor Perego will have learnt something.' She couldn't help feeling resentful. Raffaele knew that his family had been safe throughout the conflict, whereas she'd been fraught with worry.

'It would be too dangerous, Giulia. The war hasn't ended yet and the Germans are still occupying Italy.'

'We could follow the same route we followed last time.' She gave Raffaele a rebellious look. 'We got away with it then—'

'If you don't mind, I'd rather not tempt fate a second time, my love. Please, be patient. Hopefully, we'll have good news soon.'

Good news. How wonderful that would be. Giulia held on to that hope as she cycled with Raffaele to Baveno on the bikes they'd borrowed. She wouldn't press her point about leaving for Milan straight away. The old her would have done so, but she was no longer the impetuous girl she used to be. Hadn't she decided to be sensible? Sensible Giulia would bide her time. *All good things come to those who wait.* She remembered the quote from her English studies. Hard as it was to do so, she would try to be patient.

34

As soon as Giulia and Raffaele stepped through the front door, his entire family gathered around to hug and kiss them and, once they'd gone through to the kitchen, Raffaele broke the news of their marriage.

'I'm so happy for the two of you,' Ludovica, his mother, said, fetching a bottle of Nebbiolo from the cupboard. 'Congratulations.'

She poured the wine for all except the youngest children, and they clinked glasses.

Myriad questions followed and, with the Fascists and Germans gone, Giulia and Raffaele felt safe about sharing some of what they'd been going through for the past eighteen months.

'I wish you could have been at our wedding,' Giulia added. 'But it would have been too risky. Maybe, when the war is officially over, we can have a celebration at the hotel with my parents—'

'I wouldn't be surprised if the war in Italy is over by this time next week.' Raffaele smiled.

'I hope so,' his father said, putting down his glass of wine.

'But how will you support your bride, son? I'm sorry to bring this up, but you need to be practical.'

'I plan on finishing my work placement in Verbania. Once I'm qualified, I'll get a job in Milan. Giulia wants to go to university there.'

She was on the point of saying that Raffaele wouldn't need to support her, that her father was sure to carry on paying for her education, but she kept her thoughts to herself. Instead, she said, 'Up in the mountains, I learnt to sew quite well. Maybe I could get work in a clothing factory.'

'Let's discuss all this later.' Ludovica took Giulia's hand. 'Now is not the time. Now we must celebrate Raffaele's return and welcome you into the family. We've been extremely worried about you both. My mother gave us an update about you, but that was months ago.'

'How is Nonna?' Raffaele asked.

'Fit as ever. She'll live until she's well over a hundred, mark my words.' Ludovica chuckled.

* * *

'We heard about what happened to Paolo and Teresa Demichelis,' Raffaele's father said later, when his younger children had left the table. 'Their parents went to claim their bodies, but the damned Fascists had already buried them in a mass grave.'

'We'd like to visit their mother and father this afternoon, before we head for Marta.' Raffaele sighed. 'There's information we'd like to give them about the perpetrator—'

'You plan to go to Marta so soon?' Ludovica sat back in her chair.

'There's no room for us to sleep here, Ma. We'll be back tomorrow, don't worry.'

'I've tried to look after the hotel, Giulia,' Signor Ferrero said. 'But I'm afraid I've struggled, single-handed. It was impossible to hire any staff.'

'Thank you for all you've done.' She smiled. 'My parents will be very grateful when they return.'

'You must be looking forward to seeing them, my dear.' He glanced away from her, and Giulia felt a sudden chill in the atmosphere. Was there something he wasn't telling her? She searched his face as he turned to look at her, and felt reassured when he smiled.

'It was Giulia who arranged for your salary to be reinstated,' Raffaele chipped in, his eyes gleaming with pride.

'You went to Milan?' Signor Ferrero sounded surprised.

'On a secret mission,' Giulia said. 'Raffaele will tell you all about it later, I'm sure.'

'I'm extremely proud of you both.' A smile spread over Ludovica's face.

'As am I,' Raffaele's father said. 'I suppose you'll want to be setting off now, but I'll see you at the hotel in the morning.'

* * *

The Demichelises lived on the outskirts of town, in an apartment block at the end of a narrow street without a pavement. The buildings were tall, blocking out the sunlight and giving an oppressive feel to the scene.

A fair-headed lady poked her head out of the window after Raffaele had pressed the doorbell at the entrance.

'Raffaele!' she called down. 'I'll send my husband to open the door for you.'

Signor Demichelis, a thin man with greying hair, showed them a place to stow their bicycles and led them upstairs to where his wife was waiting on the landing.

Raffaele introduced Giulia as his bride, and Signora Demichelis ushered them into a simply furnished living room with wooden sideboards lining the walls. Embroidered white linen drapes dressed the windows, and there were plain woven rugs on the terracotta-tiled floor.

'Would you like a coffee?' the signora asked, indicating they should sit on the sofa while her husband pulled up a chair opposite.

Giulia and Raffaele thanked her but declined, saying they didn't want to disturb her and Signor Demichelis, and that they'd come to offer their condolences and give them some important information.

'I understand you were with our son and daughter before they were killed,' Signor Demichelis said in a flat tone of voice.

Giulia's heart filled with sadness as she listened to Raffaele recount the terrible events of that horrific day. She would always feel sorry that she and Raffaele had been separated from the Fox Cubs after the Fascists had said they knew she was with them.

'Paolo and Teresa died as heroes, and their names will forever be remembered in the annals of the Resistance,' he added.

'We were denied funerals for them,' Signora Demichelis said with tears in her eyes. 'There's not a day goes by when I don't think about them in that mass grave.'

'We'll rebury them in Baveno as soon as the war is over, my dear,' her husband said.

'There's something I'd like to tell you.' Raffaele leant forwards. 'A roll of film has come to light. We believe there could be photos of Paolo, Teresa and our three other friends' bodies. They were horribly tortured, I'm sorry to have to say.'

'So we've heard.' Signor Demichelis rasped out the words.

'The pictures might prove a crime was committed. Our commander has them, and he thinks they could be used as evidence against Captain Nisi.'

'Then he'll pay for his actions?' The hope in Signora Demichelis's question wrenched Giulia's heart.

'We can only have faith that it will be so,' Raffaele said. 'But he has fled to Switzerland, from what we've heard.'

'If there's any justice in this world, he'll be brought to trial.' Giulia spoke through the tightness in her throat as she held back her tears.

'We can only pray.' Signor Demichelis heaved a sigh.

'Thank you for coming to see us, and congratulations on your marriage, by the way,' Signora Demichelis said. 'Are you sure you wouldn't like a coffee?'

'*Grazie*, Signora.' Raffaele thanked her. 'You're very kind, but we'll leave you in peace now—'

'Teresa and Paolo's younger brothers and sisters have gone for a walk down to the lakeside,' she said. 'They'll be sorry to have missed you.'

'Please, say *ciao* to them from us.' Raffaele got to his feet and reached for Giulia's hand.

Her fingers trembled in his, and he squeezed them reassuringly. There were no words to express how sad they were both feeling so, as they went to retrieve their bikes, they said nothing.

* * *

Cycling from Baveno to Marta, Giulia remembered that fateful occasion when she and Ester had cycled to Stresa the day the

Germans had arrived. Nothing much appeared to have changed on the lakeside road: the beautiful villas were still intact, although their gardens looked a little unkempt.

Before too long, they'd arrived at the tree-shaded Marta square. Wheeling her bike through the gates of the hotel, Giulia noticed that grass had grown through much of the gravel and the outside paint was peeling.

A sudden shower of rain sent her and Raffaele running to the kitchen entrance, where they left their bicycles propped against the wall. She took the key Signor Ferrero had given her and opened the door.

A musty smell permeated the air as she stepped across the threshold and she went to open a window.

'Come,' she said, taking Raffaele's hand. 'Let's go upstairs to my room.'

Dust covered the surfaces of the furniture in the suite, and she remembered how rude she'd been to the maid for not dusting properly. Raffaele had been right to think of her as a spoilt brat...

Her thoughts turned to that fateful night when she'd tried to escape with her parents and Jewish friends. Tears wet her cheeks and Raffaele drew her against him, rocking her gently, saying how courageous she was and how much he loved her.

But her teeth had started chattering; she was shivering violently and feeling dizzy.

'I need to lie down,' she said.

He lifted her in his strong arms and carried her to the bed, where he laid her down and stretched out beside her, warming her with his body.

'Take deep breaths and release them slowly.' He rubbed her shoulders. 'Try to relax.'

Closing her eyes, she focused on breathing and, before too

long, the shakes had eased. Feeling his lips brush her forehead, she melted into his embrace and breathed in his scent.

'You're so beautiful, so caring and so wonderful, Giulia.' Raffaele lifted her hand and kissed her wrist. 'I love you so much, *amore mio*.'

'I love you too.' She kissed him on the lips. 'Whatever happens in the future, we'll always be together, won't we?'

'Of that there can be no doubt,' he said.

35

A month later, while dusting the ground floor of the hotel, Giulia was thinking about her life since she'd returned to Marta. Four days after she and Raffaele had left Intra, they'd learnt that Mussolini had been captured and then executed by partisans near Lake Como. She would have preferred he'd have been brought to trial for his crimes, but at least the world had been rid of a hated tyrant. Then, in early May, news came through that Hitler had died from a self-inflicted gunshot wound. Perhaps it was a fitting end to him, and Giulia hoped history would never repeat itself, and there'd never be another leader who duped his people into following him blindly down a path of evil.

In the meantime, peace had been declared and, not long afterwards, Aquila came to visit. He told them he and the rest of the partisans had been involved in 'escorting' columns of retreating German troops across the border, after which he and his men had been required to hand their weapons over to the Allies and to stand down.

'What are your plans now?' Raffaele had asked.

Aquila then revealed he'd fallen in love with Vittoria, the

daughter of the chairman of the Liberation Committee in Verbania. After Aquila finished his studies in Turin, he planned to return to Intra for their wedding.

'So you've not seen the last of me yet,' he'd added. 'Once we're married, Vittoria and I will live by the lake.'

Since then, Giulia and Raffaele had settled into a routine, of sorts. They cycled to Baveno every morning and returned to the hotel after lunch, where they spent the rest of the day carrying out general maintenance work with Signor Ferrero.

Each time she looked at the *lago*, Giulia thought of Ester. She kept to herself the fact that she doubted she'd ever swim in its waters again. Last week, Raffaele had gone out on a boat with one of his fisherman friends, but she'd declined the invitation to join them for fear of showing disrespect by sailing over her Jewish friends' watery grave.

The squeak of the door alerted Giulia to Raffaele approaching; he'd gone out to do some gardening. Tomorrow they would set off for Milan by train. *At last.* Nerves bubbled in Giulia's chest. Yesterday, Signor Perego had cabled that he had information for her about her parents. She alternated between excitement and apprehension. Why hadn't he come right out and told her that Mamma and Papà were coming home?

* * *

The journey to Milan from Fondotoce took twice as long as usual as there were troop movements taking priority on the line. When she alighted from the railway carriage in the late afternoon, Giulia linked arms with Raffaele as they headed for the exit. She gazed up at the gigantic glass and metal arched roof covering the platforms. Despite the structure having taken several direct hits in the Allied bombing raids, Giulia felt relieved that the building, with its blend of Art Deco and Nouveau styles, and a grand, imposing façade boasting numerous sculptures was still mostly intact.

They took a taxi to Via Pietro Verri and, because of several deviations, their driver drove them past the ancient moat that surrounded the medieval Sforza castle. Giulia remembered viewing, years ago, one of the ceilings frescoed by Leonardo da Vinci and, glancing at the round towers damaged in an Allied bombing raid, she hoped that da Vinci's work had survived. She wound down the window to take a better look.

'Look, Raffaele!' Three enormous ebony ravens were soaring from the bomb holes in the fortress's central tower. Their slow, powerful wingbeats lifted them above the wounded spires, giving Giulia an unsettling feeling of being watched. Ravens were considered to be harbingers of misfortune, apparently. Were these a bad omen? Apprehension gripped her chest.

Raffaele held her hand and said, '*Coraggio, amore.*' His encouragement soothed her; she was being silly. Superstition had never bothered her in the past; she shouldn't give in to it now.

'We've arrived,' their driver said, rolling his vehicle to a stop in front of Giulia's father's shop.

She pasted on a smile to hide her nervousness while Raffaele paid the man and, breathing in a deep breath, she steeled herself to hear what Signor Perego had to say.

He was waiting for them behind the counter and immediately asked his assistant to look after things while he took Giulia and Raffaele through to his office.

Giulia introduced her father's deputy to Raffaele, and Signor Perego offered them refreshments after they'd sat on chairs in front of his desk.

'*Grazie*,' Giulia said. 'Maybe later. Please, what is the news about my parents?'

'I'm sorry, Giulia.' Her father's deputy leant towards her. 'But they didn't make it, I'm afraid.'

'What... what do you mean they didn't make it?' She shook her head in confusion. 'What's happened to them?'

'Let me start again,' Signor Perego said in a woeful tone of voice. 'Your parents were taken to a place called Auschwitz in Poland. The camp was liberated by the Soviets last January. They were shocked at what they found.'

'Oh, dear Lord.' Giulia gripped Raffaele's hand and held on to it as if it were a lifeline.

'The SS men who ran the camp had fled, taking fifty-eight thousand prisoners with them as slaves. They'd left seven thousand inmates behind,' Signor Perego added. 'The poor prisoners evidently looked like human skeletons because the Nazis had been trying to work them to death. The inmates said that the buildings the Nazis blew up before leaving Auschwitz were gas chambers used to poison people, and a crematorium to burn their bodies. Hundreds of thousands of individuals died there.'

'But... but how do you know my parents didn't survive?' The question trembled on Giulia's lips.

'The Americans have published lists of survivors who are waiting in displaced persons camps in Austria and Germany.' Giulia's father's assistant gave her a sorrowful look. 'There is no record of your parents anywhere.'

Signor Perego's words pierced Giulia like a shard of ice, numbing her. The terrible truth was too awful to comprehend. She knew the Nazis had behaved like monsters – what they'd done to Ester and the other Jewish people on Lake Maggiore was proof of their bestiality – but what her father's deputy had just told her far exceeded even that heinous crime.

'Is there any chance my mamma and papà somehow escaped?' she asked, clutching at the straw of hope.

'We'd have been told by now, Giulia.'

She felt empty, as if the well of her emotions had run dry. *How can this be happening?*

'Raffaele and I have arranged to stay in my family's apartment tonight,' she said, the numbness in her soul reflected in her curt words.

'Maria knows about your parents.' Signor Perego was already ushering Giulia and Raffaele to the door. 'Once you've had time to assimilate things, we'll need to make arrangements for everything to be transferred to your name.'

Giulia gasped. Her father's deputy's words brought home to her, once and for all, the finality of her parents' passing. But it was all too much. She couldn't cope with it at the moment.

'We're returning to Marta tomorrow,' she said. 'I'll be in touch.'

Outside, on the pavement, Giulia felt her legs wobble, and she leant into Raffaele's side.

'I've got you, *amore*,' he said, putting his arm around her. 'You're being very brave. I'm so sorry.'

'It's too awful, I just can't talk about it now.'

'Understandably so. Remember, I'm here for you. I love you so much and can't bear for you to be suffering so.'

'I'm almost tempted to head straight back to Lago Maggiore, but Maria is expecting us and I don't want to let her down.'

'Are you sure you're all right to be walking? I can hail a taxi if you'd prefer—'

'No. I want to walk. It might help clear my mind.'

His strong arms comforted her somewhat and she was glad of his support while they made their way to Corso del Littorio. The streetlights came on, and Giulia blinked in the brightness of the lamps. They made the scars on Milan's ruined buildings appear even more livid. Her own scars ached dreadfully now, threatening to dissipate the numbness that had invaded her soul.

'We're here,' she said as they arrived at the door to the apartment building. She took the key from her handbag and inserted it.

Inside, she led Raffaele to a birdcage elevator, and they rode up to the sixth floor.

Another key opened the door onto a wide hallway. Maria, the woman who'd been a part of Giulia's life since early childhood, came towards them, and Giulia ran to the housekeeper, who'd opened her arms. The emptiness within her filled with emotion, and she wept hot tears of grief into Maria's comforting bosom.

36

Time passed, and summer came to the lake, which shimmered in the sunshine like a giant liquid mirror, the surrounding mountains reflected on the surface of the crystal-clear water like a mirage. Giulia still couldn't take a refreshing dip, though. She sat on the jetty and watched others swim, glad that Raffaele also refrained from doing so out of respect for those whose bodies had been dumped so brutally in its waters. Instead, she and he often went to visit Giovanni and his wife, Bianca, the kind couple who'd helped them after the massacre of the Fox Cubs. It was cooler up on the mountainside than down by the lake, and they'd take what food they could spare as well as candies for the children.

When autumn arrived, sprinkling the trees and meadows with gold, Giulia resumed her studies, her father-in-law having found her a tutor, and Raffaele picked up where he'd left off at his work placement in Verbania. All the while, sorrow for her parents ate into her. They filled her thoughts every waking hour of every day and, at night, nightmares of them dying in a gas chamber made her wake up screaming. Raffaele would comfort her as best he could, and she would pretend to be comforted. But the grief never left her. Little everyday things reminded her of them. A song they loved would play on the radio. A beautiful sunny day would remind her of sitting on the portico between them. Mamma's scent still lingered in her wardrobe and pain would engulf Giulia anew.

More than once, she thought she saw her father. One time, she was strolling through the gardens and there was Papà, sitting under a tree reading a book. She ran to greet him, happiness bubbling through her and not even asking herself how or why he was there. But the closer she got, the more his image became distorted and she realised it was a shadow playing tricks on her imagination.

Another time, she was convinced she could see him in the dining room, walking past the table where he always sat with Mamma. Again, it was a shadow distorting reality, this one cast by curtains swaying in the breeze.

She'd almost grown used to the apparitions: they were a symptom of her grief, Raffaele had said. Her parents were gone. She'd never see their beloved faces again. Never hear their soothing voices. Never touch their warm hands. The heartache was so bad she had to keep finding places where she could be alone, so Raffaele wouldn't hear the raw sobs rip from her breast. He did his best, and thanks to him she wasn't alone in the world. But a future without Mamma and Papà, even though she had a new family with the Ferreros, was a future without parental love. Nothing could compensate for the loss and, although she tried to put a brave face on it, she felt utterly bereft.

* * *

On a chilly late October morning, Signor Ferrero's day off, Giulia was sewing the lining onto a curtain, thinking about her father and how surprised he would have been to see what she was doing.

Without warning, she heard his well-known voice. Was it another figment of her imagination? This was the first time an apparition had spoken, though.

He seemed to be calling out for her and, although she couldn't see him – the door between the hotel lounge and lobby was closed – it was definitely Papà's voice.

I must be going crazy.

'Giulia!' the voice repeated.

The door crashed open.

Her heart raced and she leapt to her feet.

Papà was coming towards her. It really was him. She hadn't been imagining things. Nor had she gone mad. He seemed to have shrunk inside his skin and his previously brown hair had gone completely grey, but it was definitely him.

He set down the suitcase he was carrying and opened his arms.

She ran into them, weeping tears of happiness.

'Where have you been?' She hugged him. 'I thought you and Mamma were dead.'

It was then that she noticed her mother wasn't with him. Where was she? Worry caught in the back of Giulia's throat.

'Your mother has passed away, my dear, I'm so terribly sorry.'

'Oh, no!' She let out a cry. 'What happened?'

'It's a long story, sweetheart. We'd best sit.'

They sat on the sofa, hands clasped as if they never wanted to let each other go.

'How did you know you'd find me here?' Giulia asked.

'I went through Milan, on the chance you were there. Signor

Perego told me you were married to Raffaele Ferrero. To say I was surprised was an understatement. But he said Raffaele has been a good husband to you.'

'We love each other very much.' Giulia looked her father in the eye. 'Why didn't you contact me from Milan?'

'I thought about it, but felt I needed to tell you about your mother in person.' He released a deep sigh.

A river of sorrow flowed through Giulia as she asked, 'How did poor Mamma die?' The question sounded surreal to her ears. Her vibrant mother had always been so full of life.

'I didn't find out until well after the camp was liberated. When we arrived at Auschwitz, your mother and I were separated and I had no further news of her.' Papà's eyes darkened with pain. 'After the Russians freed us last January, I searched for her, but she was nowhere to be found. I wanted to make my way home as quickly as possible, to see you. But that wasn't easy.'

'Why was that, Papà?' Giulia gave his fingers a squeeze.

'Like many of the other inmates, I was so weakened by starvation I couldn't make the trip straight away. Also, large parts of Europe, including Italy, were still occupied by Germany.'

'It must have been terrible for you. How did you find out Mamma had died?'

'In early March, I was given Polish travel documents and, with a group of fellow inmates, ended up in Katowice, housed in an old army barracks with around 400 other displaced people from all over Europe.' A deep frown creased Giulia's father's forehead. 'There, I met a Jewish lady I knew from before the war, who was a fellow prisoner, and she told me your mamma had died in the bed next to hers, almost certainly of typhus.'

Giulia burst into tears; she couldn't help herself. Reaching into her pocket for a handkerchief, she sobbed as if her heart would break.

Her father put his arms around her, and they wept hot tears of grief together until they literally had no tears left.

'Why did it take so long for you to get home?' Giulia asked as she dried her eyes.

'I was still in Katowice when the war in Europe ended and it wasn't until mid-June, four months after I'd arrived there, that I was put on a goods train with hundreds of other Italians.' Papà's shoulders slumped. 'The train was supposed to take us to Odessa to board a ship, but they made us all get off in Žmerynka.'

'Where's that?' Giulia tried to picture a map of Europe in her mind's eye.

'It's a railway hub about 350 kilometres north of the Black Sea. We waited three frustrating days camped in the station and when we were put on another train – our numbers had grown to 1,400 Italians from all over the place, I was told – we had no idea of our destination.'

'That must have been so hard for you, Papà.' She couldn't imagine what he'd been going through.

'Indeed. As we started heading northwards, we understood we were no longer being taken to Odessa and a ship home to Italy, but into the heart of the Soviet Union.' Papà's mouth pulled to one side in a grimace. 'They deposited us in a camp near a village about one hundred kilometres south of Minsk, and there we stayed for three months, until mid-September.'

'Good Lord,' Giulia said, aghast. 'What an ordeal for you.' Her poor father must have been so frustrated.

'At least we were quite well fed. It was boring, though, and all I could do was long to see you again, my dear,' he said in a weary tone of voice.

'But it took you more than a month to get home, Papà. Why was that?' She still couldn't fathom what had happened.

'The single-line tracks were in a terrible state and we couldn't go faster than fifty kilometres per hour.'

'It must have seemed interminable.' *Poor Papà...*

'We were all impatient and spent the days alternating between sleeping and chatting to each other, feeling relieved to be heading south until, from the position of the sun, we realised we were being taken north again, then west through Romania and into Hungary.'

'Oh, my goodness. How exhausting!' Giulia gasped.

'It was. We made frequent stops because of poor weather and the need to take on water and food. When we stopped in Vienna, I got no pleasure seeing the defeated Austrians. They, too, had suffered.'

Trust Papà to be so magnanimous. If it had been her, she'd probably have felt the opposite.

'The train then took us to a transit camp in a place called St Valentin, which was run by the Americans,' her father said, sudden laughter breaking through his lips. 'They made us take a bath and disinfected us with something called DDT.'

'That must have been strange.' Giulia tilted her head. 'Did you proceed to Italy from there?'

'No. You can imagine our surprise when we arrived in Munich. What a circuitous route our train driver took, most likely because of troop movements and the state of the infrastructure.'

'Were you able to get off the train in Germany?' she asked, her stomach giving a twist. If it had been her, she'd have been torn between curiosity and disgust.

'Yes. I was shocked at the piles of rubble everywhere. Passing the inhabitants in their ruined streets, I wondered if any of them had been aware of what had been happening in the extermination camps.'

Giulia remembered her shock when hearing about the gas chambers from Signor Perego, and there had also been reports in the press about the atrocities. Believing her parents to have been murdered in Auschwitz, she'd felt both powerless and horrified at the same time.

'Would you like to tell me about it, Papà?' Maybe him talking about it would help him deal with what he'd experienced.

'No, my dearest. Not now. Perhaps never. I want to try to put it all behind me.'

'I can understand that,' Giulia said, brushing a kiss to his cheek. To be honest, she felt relieved he preferred to keep the details from her. She didn't want to burst into tears again. 'How long were you in Munich?' she asked.

'Only two days, thankfully. Finally, we set off for Italy and, a couple of days ago, we arrived in Verona.' He sighed. 'On Italian soil at last, the entire trainload of people dispersed, and I managed to make my way to the home of a business associate who lent me the money to buy a ticket to Milan.'

'Signor Perego must have been very surprised to see you.' Giulia was glad she'd put off him transferring her father's assets to her name: she hadn't been able to face it yet.

'He was astonished. And I was overjoyed when he told me you'd survived.' Her father's eyes turned sorrowful. 'He also mentioned the horrific fate of our Jewish guests. I had no idea. I thought they'd been deported and was worried they'd been murdered in one of the camps.'

'What the Nazis did to them was awful.' Giulia gave a sigh.

'Has anyone informed the police about what happened?'

'Not as far as I know.' She shook her head.

'Then I'll do so. And I'll contact the newspapers as well. Obersturmführer Karl Weber gave the order, I'm sure, and he should definitely be arrested for his crimes. There have been so many Hitlerite atrocities. It will take time for all the perpetrators to be tried, but I'm sure they will be, in the end.'

'I hope so.' Giulia's heart ached as she thought about her mother. Would the Nazis responsible for murdering millions of people ever be brought to justice?

She told her father about the Fox Cubs, and how Paolo's parents were going to report the Fascist captain for ordering their slaughter.

'I'm sorry to hear that, my dear.' Giulia's father reached for her hand. 'Signor Perego told me you'd been fighting with Raffaele up in the mountains. I expect you have quite a story to recount—'

'I do indeed, but I prefer to wait until Raffaele gets back and we'll tell you together.'

'You've grown up so much, daughter. I have to admit that when Signor Perego told me about your marriage, I had grave doubts. But now I'm not so worried.'

'I still plan to finish my education. And go to the university in Milan.'

'What about Raffaele?'

'He'll find a job in the city as soon as he's qualified. We don't want to be a burden on you.'

'Spoken like a true grown-up. I'm so proud of you, Giulia,' her father said, hugging her. 'Now, if you don't mind, I'm feeling extremely tired and would like to go up to my room for a rest.'

* * *

Giulia made up a bed for her father in one of the double bedrooms. She offered to swap with the suite where she and Raffaele were staying, but Papà wouldn't hear of it. Alternating between happiness that her father was home and deep sorrow that her mother hadn't made it, Giulia went to the kitchen to prepare dinner. Shame it was Raffaele's father's day off – he was a much better cook than her – but she'd become competent enough to make lasagne, and there was enough minced beef in the fridge to prepare a ragout.

She was stirring bechamel sauce on the stove when the door to the kitchen swung open and Raffaele came into the room.

'That smells good,' he said, kissing her on the cheek. 'How was your day, *amore*?'

'You're not going to believe this, but my father is alive.' She heard the happiness in her voice. 'He turned up this afternoon.'

Raffaele swept her into his arms and whirled her around, almost dancing her across the floor.

'That's wonderful, *amore*.' He kissed her on the lips, then set her down. 'Please, tell me everything.'

They sat at the kitchen table and, with tears in her eyes, she told Raffaele about how her poor mother had lost her life. He held her close, soothing her while she wept.

'What an incredible story,' he said, after she'd recounted her father's long journey home. 'I can't wait to see him again, although I'm a little nervous.'

'Why are you nervous?' She glanced at him.

'He's my dad's boss and I've married his daughter. He'll probably give me a grilling.'

Which is exactly what Papà did after supper. The meal had gone well and he'd complimented Giulia on her newly developed culinary skills. Conversation had revolved around stories of hers and Raffaele's partisan activities, her time in prison and how Raffaele had freed her. Papà recounted tales of his journey home, while plainly avoiding talking about the horrors of Auschwitz.

They went through to the lounge for coffee and liqueurs once they'd finished eating and Raffaele helped Giulia clear the dishes.

Giulia sat on the sofa with Raffaele, and her father positioned himself in the armchair opposite.

'So,' Papà said. 'You are married.'

'You know that.' Giulia wondered where this was leading.

Raffaele took her hand, then cleared his throat.

'I love your daughter, Signor Leone. With all my heart.'

'As I love Raffaele,' Giulia said. 'I hope you'll give us your blessing.'

Her father huffed.

'A bit late for that as you're already married.' His steely gaze swept over Raffaele. 'But the fact that you kept Giulia safe from the Germans and then helped break her out of a Fascist prison goes in your favour, young man.'

'Raffaele is so brave, Papà. And he was such a good partisan leader, always putting his squad first.'

'I'm sure he can speak for himself, Giulia.'

'Your daughter was the bravest of all, Signor Leone.' Raffaele leant forward. 'Her resilience impressed me and everyone else.'

'And now you speak for her. What a pair you are!' Papà's eyes twinkled. 'Giulia told me you'd like to move to Milan while she studies at the university. You are both welcome to stay at my apartment. It's more than big enough, and Signor Perego assures me it has been spared bomb damage.'

'We went there,' Giulia said. 'After we were told that you'd died in the camp.'

'I'm sorry you suffered, sweetheart,' her father said. 'It was total chaos there after our liberation, and my name must have been left off that all-important list.'

'Raffaele helped me with my grief.' Giulia shuffled closer to him on the sofa. 'Will you give us your blessing now, Papà?'

'With pleasure.' A wide smile spread across his face. 'I wish you every happiness, both of you. I'll never get over losing your mother, Giulia, but being with the two of you is already helping restore my faith in humanity, a little bit.'

* * *

'That went a lot better than I'd expected,' Raffaele said to Giulia after they'd gone up to their suite that night and had sat on chairs by the balcony window overlooking the lake. 'When your father gave us his blessing, I nearly fell off the sofa.'

'He's realised I'm mature enough to be married, that I'm not a spoilt brat.'

'Will I ever live that down?' Raffaele chuckled. 'The way you coped up in the mountains and even more so now on the lake has proved me completely wrong. But you know that already, don't you?'

Thankfully, Raffaele hadn't referred to how rash she used to be. It had been a while since she'd been so hot-headed and she vowed to try to avoid being impetuous ever again.

'I'm just happy your dad is still working for my father,' she said. 'Papà needs him now more than ever. What he went through on that gruelling journey home, on top of his suffering at Auschwitz, has taken a lot out of him.'

'I can understand why he doesn't want to talk about his experiences in the camp. It must have been hell.'

'Poor Papà. What happened to him has affected his outlook on life, and I fear it will take him time to come to terms with things.'

Raffaele lifted Giulia onto his lap, kissed her on the forehead, then tucked a strand of hair behind her ear.

'I think the war has changed a lot of things, *amore*. Our children will grow up in a different world.'

'How many shall we have?' She giggled.

'That's entirely up to you. As many as you like—'

'A girl for you and a boy for me would be nice,' she said. 'We'll see what the future brings.'

'We can only give thanks that we have a future. So many don't.'

Giulia thought about Paolo, Teresa, and the other Fox Cubs. Often, she and Raffaele would take flowers to the graves where they'd been reburied. And she'd started throwing bouquets into the lake for Ester and Ester's family recently as well. If only she could do the same for Mamma, but she'd been cremated by the Nazis and her ashes dispersed. Giulia released a sigh.

Raffaele hugged her tight, and she rested her head on his shoulder.

'Thank you,' she said.

'For what?' He stroked her cheek.

'For... loving me. I couldn't have faced all this heartache without you.'

'Ditto, *amore*. Together we can face whatever challenges life throws at us.' He kissed her. 'You and me against the world, eh? With a force like you behind me, how can we not succeed?'

She smiled and gazed out the window at the silent lake shimmering under the moonlight. A gentle breeze stirred the trees by the shore, and they seemed to be whispering that all would be well, the bad times were past, and she and Raffaele could look forward to a future filled with love.

EPILOGUE

5 JULY 1968

The waters of the lake were a gentle caress as Giulia swam towards the shore. She thought about that night, so long ago, when the trees had whispered their message of hope. The years had gone by and they had, indeed, been filled with love. It was the only thing that could mend hearts broken by war, and it had been Giulia's guiding light. She'd kept her loved ones at the centre of her world, and had been rewarded by so much love in return.

Soon after his homecoming and, having entrusted the hotel to Giulia's father-in-law, Papà went to live in their apartment in Milan. But he came back to the lake each weekend and, when Giulia started university and Raffaele found a job in the city, they both went to stay with him, although they hopped on a train to Fondotoce every Friday evening to spend Saturdays and Sundays in Marta.

After Giulia graduated, she applied for and got a teaching job in Verbania. Not long afterwards, Raffaele obtained a transfer to the factory where he'd done his work placement. He was the general manager now and, together, they'd bought a two-storey house overlooking the lake, not far from where Aquila now lived with his wife and three children. There'd been no question of Giulia and Raffaele remaining in Milan. 'I'm from Lake Maggiore,' Giulia had said. 'It's where my heart is and always will be.'

In the meantime, once Raffaele's siblings had grown up, his mother had come to live with his father at the hotel. She was a formidable housekeeper and helped run the place like clock-work, delegating strenuous tasks to younger staff once she and her husband reached their late sixties. Giulia's in-laws planned to retire in a few years' time, and Giulia's father would sell the hotel then, given that neither she nor Raffaele had any interest in taking over.

Giulia sighed to herself as she thought about Teresa and Paolo. Two years after they'd been killed, following their parents' statements and those of the villagers where the Fox Cubs had been slaughtered, a case against Captain Nisi was heard in the extraordinary Assize Court of Novara. He was tried and sentenced to death in absentia. That despicable man had disap-peared off the face of the earth. A sour taste coated Giulia's tongue whenever she thought about him, and she hoped he'd get his just deserts in this life or the next.

Thankfully, such had not been the situation with Karl Weber. Papà and other hotel owners had filed a complaint against him, for it wasn't only in Marta where he'd ordered the execution of Jews. The former obersturmführer was arrested in November 1966, along with two further ex-SS officers, after it had been proven that they'd given the orders for the killings, and not central command. It had been a long, slow process of gathering evidence, but he and his cronies had eventually been brought to trial in Milan at the end of last January, nearly twenty-three years after their heinous crimes and, yesterday, they'd been sentenced to life imprisonment. To say Giulia had been overjoyed at the announcement would be putting it mildly. Ester and her family had received justice at last.

Treading water, Giulia thought about when she'd finally been able to face swimming in the lake. It had been when her first child, the daughter whom she and Raffaele had named Ester, had started to learn to swim. Little Ester had pleaded with Giulia to go into the water with her and Giulia couldn't refuse. As she took that first step, it had seemed as if her old friend was giving her permission to do so. Every time Giulia swam in the lake, she felt close to her, and enjoyed memories of the happy times they'd spent together.

She gazed towards the pebbly beach in front of the hotel. There was Raffaele, sitting on a deckchair beside Papà, who still commuted to and from Milan every week. He was in his early seventies now and still going strong; he maintained that work gave him energy, as well as his grandchildren.

Said grandchildren had spotted Giulia and were waving at her. She waved back at her three daughters and one son: the baby of the family, Paolo, who was seven years old. Giulia and Raffaele had waited until she'd taught high school English for a few years before having children, and then they had them in quick succession. Ester was fourteen, Teresa, eleven, and Irma, nine. All four kids waded into the water to meet her, instigating a splashing contest which nobody won. Raffaele approached with a beach ball and soon they were throwing it from one to the other, declaring anyone who dropped it to be out of the game.

Giulia did a handstand on the shingle; she'd kept up with her callisthenics over the years. Sitting on Raffaele's recently vacated deckchair, she gazed at her adored father and smiled.

'Happy?' he asked, smiling back at her.

'So happy,' she said. 'Today has been a perfect day.'

* * *

MORE FROM SIOBHAN DAIKO

The next sweeping, epic wartime story from Siobhan Daiko is available to order now here:

https://mybook.to/SiobhanDaiko11

AUTHOR'S NOTE

I was inspired to write a story set on Lago Maggiore when I was researching the Jews under Mussolini for my novel, *The Girl from Venice*, and read about the atrocities committed by the Nazis on the lake soon after the armistice.

Years beforehand, I'd spent a wonderful summer in the area, when my parents rented a house in one of those charming villages overlooking the *lago*. I swam in its crystal-clear waters and absorbed the magical atmosphere of the place, making memories which have stayed with me ever since. I didn't know then about the horrific events during World War II, and it was only later, when I started my research, that I found out.

I've set part of my book in the fictional town of Marta, loosely based on Meina, where a hotel hosted Jewish refugees from Thessaloniki who were killed by the Nazis in September 1943. Karl Weber is a fictional character derived from the Waffen-SS oberstumführer Hans Krueger, who was sentenced to life imprisonment on 4 July 1968 for ordering the execution of the Jews.

After I'd watched the movie *Hotel Meina*, stemming from the events that inspired my story, I decided to research the partisans who'd appeared briefly in the film. The more I read about them, the more my heart broke. They were so brave, young, and patriotic, if a little hot-headed, and many gave their lives for the cause.

Raffaele is inspired by a real *partigiano*, Nino Chiovini, battle name Peppo. Many of the events lived through by my *partigiani* feature in Chiovini's diary and books.

Aquila is also based on a real partisan, the charismatic Armando Calzavara, battle name Arca, who led the *Cesare Battisti* battalion, and to whom Nino Chiovini often refers in his writing.

Names of real people have been changed, with the exception of Captain Mario Nisi, who orchestrated the slaughter of Chiovini's squad near the village of Trarego in February 1945.

I have read the following books for inspiration and information:

Istituto Lorenzo Cobianchi, Associazione Casa della Resistenza Verbania, *Memoria di Trarego*

Marco Nozza, *Hotel Meina*

Nino Chiovini, *Fuori Legge???*

Nino Chiovini, *La Volpe*

Nino Chiovini, *Piccola storia partigiana della banda di Pian Cavallone*

ACKNOWLEDGEMENTS

I continue to be hugely grateful for all the support I receive from the entire team at Boldwood Books.

A big thank you to my wonderful editor Emily Yau, whose editorial comments and suggestions have made this a better book, I'm sure.

Also, I'd like to thank Cecily Blench for her expert copy editing and Jennifer Davies for proofreading the manuscript.

I'm grateful to the bloggers who've been such staunch supporters of my work in recent years. Thank you for taking the time to read my books and review them.

Last, but not least, I'd like to thank my husband, Victor, for his love and encouragement, for supporting me throughout the writing process and for helping me on research trips.

ABOUT THE AUTHOR

Siobhan Daiko writes powerful and sweeping historical fiction set in Italy and in the Far East during the second World War, with strong women at its heart. She now lives near Venice, having been a teacher in Wales for many years.

Download your exclusive bonus content from Siobhan Daiko here:

Visit Siobhan's website: www.siobhandaiko.org

Follow Siobhan on social media here:

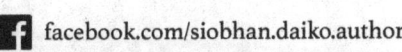

facebook.com/siobhan.daiko.author

x.com/siobhandaiko

instagram.com/siobhandaiko_books

ALSO BY SIOBHAN DAIKO

The Girl from Venice

The Girl from Portofino

The Girl from Bologna

The Tuscan Orphan

Daughters of Tuscany

Daughter of War

Daughter of Hong Kong

The Girl from Sicily

Lady of Venice

The Girl from Lake Maggiore

Letters from
the past

Discover page-turning
historical novels from
your favourite authors
and be transported
back in time

Join our book club
Facebook group

https://bit.ly/SixpenceGroup

Sign up to our
newsletter

https://bit.ly/LettersFrom
PastNews

Boldwood